Angela was about to bare her very soul.

'I need so desperately for you to believe me...'

Jesse watched her, unable to say anything. His heart was beating hard. He knew that she was asking for something immense—at least to her. It was somehow a thousand times more intimate than if they had tumbled together onto that sofa and made love.

'You asked me to trust you,' she went on, her voice shaking again. 'And now you know why it can't come easily to me. But I'm trying. I'm giving this to you, Jesse. I'm asking you to believe in me. Help me. Stand by me. Please...'

Dear Reader,

Once again, we've got an irresistible month of reading coming your way! Let's start with a brilliant story of love and danger, *Compromising Positions* by Beverly Bird, where Jesse Hadley and Angela Byerly have been framed for the murder of a prominent socialite. As they work to clear their names, their passion ignites...

Suzanne Brockmann has created three tough, combat-hardened Navy heroes in TALL, DARK AND DANGEROUS, a brand new mini-series that starts this month with *Prince Joe*. You'll love getting to know devilishly attractive Joe Catalanotto as he impersonates a European prince with the help of Veronica St. John. *Forever Blue*, the next TALL, DARK AND DANGEROUS, is available in November.

THE GUINESS FAMILY continues with *The Quiet One*, the third novel in this five book series by Alicia Scott, and *Days Gone By* comes from Sally Tyler Hayes; it's an emotional second-chance story with an adorable six-year-old as well.

Enjoy!

The Editors

Compromising Positions

BEVERLY BIRD

First published in Great Britain 1997
Silhouette Books, Eton House, 18-24 Paradise Road,
Richmond, Surrey TW9 1SR

© Beverly Bird 1997

ISBN 0 373 07777 7

18-9710

Printed and bound in Great Britain
by Mackays of Chatham PLC, Chatham

BEVERLY BIRD

has lived in several places in the United States, but she is currently back where her roots began on an island in New Jersey. Her time is devoted to her family and her writing. She is the author of numerous romances, both contemporary and historical. Beverly loves to hear from readers. You can write to her at P.O. Box 350, Brigantine, NJ 08203, U.S.A.

Other novels by Beverly Bird

Silhouette Sensation®

The Marrying Kind

Silhouette Desire®

The Best Reasons
Fool's Gold
All the Marbles
To Love a Stranger

For my doctor friend, Gwyn A. Nethaway,
blond curls and all.

Chapter 1

She shot into his office like a stray bullet. Jesse Hadley looked up from his desk, surprised, and a sudden, vivid memory hit him out of nowhere.

He'd been seven, maybe eight. It had been one of those autumn weekends his family spent at the country house in Lords Valley, everyone dressed in perfectly creased attire, pretending to be relaxed. There'd been a sparrow sitting on the back porch rail, and because he was a boy, because it was there, he'd made an impulsive grab for it.

He'd caught it.

For an incredible, amazed moment, he had only stared at it. He'd felt its heartbeat explode against his palm. It was one of those things that should never have happened and that he would never forget. He realized that something about this woman reminded him of that sparrow.

It wasn't in his voice.

"Can I help you?" he asked in a mild tone.

She crossed her arms over her chest and seemed to hug herself, as though she was cold. Or scared. Like a bird that blinked and somehow ended up in a kid's palm.

Actually, Angela Byerly was mostly stunned.

She'd always thought Jesse Hadley to be devilishly attractive—from his pictures in the papers, from the distant, wary glimpses she'd gotten of him over the months. In court, he was king of the jungle. He moved with dangerous, confident grace, with a sort of tense laziness, like a cat. He was powerful, and he knew it. He was unconscionably wealthy; and he didn't apologize for it. He was arrogant, and he would take without asking. It was in his eyes.

Still, she hadn't anticipated the sheer impact of this man up close.

She didn't know how to handle it. He wasn't just good-looking; he was drop-dead gorgeous, and there was not a doubt in her mind that he knew it. He had black hair, and his eyes were green, a very deep green that reminded her of emeralds. And they were expressive, shadowing in one moment, then clearing sharply in the next, even as his face revealed nothing. He had dimples, which theoretically should have made him look cherubic, cute, even gentle. But his face was too chiseled for that, and the end result was that he looked aristocratic and uncompromising and hard.

Aristocratic or not, he'd made a big mistake.

"How dare you?" she finally whispered. She was so angry, she didn't trust her voice.

Jesse dropped his pen, steepled his fingers and leaned back in his chair. He was a man well schooled in hiding his reactions. "You *do* have the right office?" he asked.

Color bloomed high on her cheeks, a delicious, almost dewy, pink. That was when he realized that however frightened and nervous she might be, she was also beautiful. She whipped around, giving him her back. She had a lot of hair. Blond, long, falling well below her shoulders, it was a mass of curls and ringlets. Caught at the moment by a leather thong at her nape, it was too loosely gathered to be called a ponytail.

Jesse's eyes coasted downward. She wore a white lab coat that stopped at midthigh, right above the hem of a vivid floral dress. The dress captured every hue in the rainbow. It was tight, and very short.

She had incredible legs.

He had just reached the startling turquoise pumps on her feet when she jerked about to face him again.

"Okay," she said with great control. "My problem here is your lack of consideration. Of *cooperation*."

She advanced on his desk, still hugging herself. He noticed that her hands were fisted now, and a piece of paper was crumpled in her left one. He'd thought that her eyes were brown, but when she stepped into a shaft of light from the window, he realized that they weren't, not really. At this angle, they looked more golden.

The sight of her was fascinating, and he continued to stare without realizing it. The crisp white lab coat over the attention-demanding dress, the mass of long blond curls gathered at her neck, those shoes in a color he had never seen on a woman's feet before...all in all, he was intrigued.

"Who are you and what's that?' He motioned to the paper.

Her eyes slid away form him. Skittishly. "I'm Dr. Byerly. Angela Byerly. The chief medical examiner."

Jesse felt surprise hit him in a one-two punch. "Odd that we haven't met before this."

She shrugged one shoulder with unstudied grace. She wouldn't quite look at him, he realized. "Not really. Philadelphia is a big city."

"Not that big."

"I work. I go home."

"Apparently."

"What's that supposed to mean?'' Her eyes finally came back to him, a deep, turbulent brown now. And they were defensive.

This was unbelievable, Jesse thought.

He knew *of* her, of course. He had heard all the rumors—that she was thirty-six years old and had never been married. That she was one of those incredibly brainy types. That she had a medical degree and a law degree, and that she had earned them almost concurrently, give or take a few years. Which told him that the vast bulk of her twenties had been eaten up by her studies. She'd come to Philadelphia by way of Quantico, Virginia. She'd worked for the FBI in some kind of specialized capacity, but at the moment he couldn't remember what. He *did* remember that the city had had to offer the moon and the stars to get her.

Why hadn't he ever wondered about her before? He answered himself almost immediately. Because brainy, studious types had never really been a source of curiosity for him.

"It wasn't intended as a personal affront," he said slowly.

"Our offices work together in the natural course of upholding the law. It just seems strange that I've never run into you before."

"I've never been this angry with you before now," she snapped, and it seemed to him that the retort had more or less slipped out before she could harness it. It also sounded as though *not* running into him had been a deliberate choice.

"You've always sent memos," he reminded her, fishing. "E-mail. That sort of thing."

"And they've always accomplished the job, haven't they?"

He sat back and hooked his hands behind his head. "Nine months," he mused aloud. "You were hired nine months ago."

"Not quite eight, actually," she corrected, biting down on the words.

He shrugged. "Okay. So for eight months—give or take a week or two—I've gotten a flood of memos, but no personal appearance until now."

"Was I supposed to present myself and genuflect or something?"

His mouth quirked. "The latter wouldn't have been necessary, but the first might have been a nice touch."

"We've spoken on the phone," she argued. Then she scowled. "Why are you making such a big deal of this?"

Jesse wondered. "Nature of the beast, I guess. It's ingrained habit to question what I don't understand. And I'm curious. You never testify, either. You always send Ed Thackery to court."

"Or Brigid Cross," she corrected stiffly. "They're both better at that sort of thing than I am."

He wondered about that, too. "Ed thought he was going to get your job eight months ago."

She only shrugged. "What's your point, Mr. Hadley?"

"My point is, I've never *seen* you."

"Why *would* you?" she demanded, exasperated.

Why indeed? Philadelphia *was* a big city, he conceded. It had a volatile, almost overwhelming crime rate. She worked at it from an evidentiary angle, at crime scenes in the dead of night, or under fluorescent lighting in the bowels of a building down the street. He, on the other hand, was the district attorney, a public face, the man the citizens had elected to put their bad guys away.

"Well," he said finally, then realized that he had absolutely no idea what to say next.

"Let me explain something to you," she said tightly. "I'm the youngest chief M.E. this city has ever had. I'm also the first *woman* to ever hold the post. You mentioned Ed Thackery yourself—and he's not the only one waiting for me to fall flat on my face. There are a lot of people out there outraged by my salary, my perks, people who vocally wonder whom I slept with to get all that. Well, I didn't. I've *earned* everything I've gotten. And I'm not going to screw up. With or without your help, with or without your efforts to undermine me, I'm here to stay."

Jesse felt surprise hit him again. She looked just as taken aback by the torrent of words that had escaped her, boiling up from somewhere deep like a volcanic eruption. He guessed that it didn't happen often.

"*Undermine* you?" he repeated incredulously. "Why the hell would I do that? I never laid eyes on you until five minutes ago, and I don't give a damn what they pay you."

She thrust the paper at him, the one he had noticed earlier.

He kept one wary eye on her as he took it and smoothed it out on his desk. He glanced down at it quickly. It was a release form. Actually, it was a copy of a release form. He scanned it.

"Apparently the remains of one Lacie Shokonnet were released to her next of kin," he observed. "Her parents. So?"

"So you signed it."

He glanced down again. Something dull and painful moved in his chest. It was his name. It looked like his writing. But he hadn't signed it.

He had never seen the thing before in his life.

Something warned him to keep that to himself for the time being. Maybe it was the Hadley in him, the from-the-cradle training to be perfect, above reproach. Or maybe it was ego. If there was an unsightly crack in his office, he instinctively did not want this woman to see it.

"I wasn't finished with her," Dr. Byerly said when he didn't answer.

"No?" he answered vaguely.

"You could have at least checked with me first."

"Hmmm."

"The mother claims she went to get her out of her crib yesterday, and the child was dead. Sudden infant death syndrome. But she was fifteen months old, and SIDS rarely befalls children over one year. So I called the Division of Family Services and checked our old records. I found out that she had an older sister who apparently died of the same thing. SIDS also occurs infrequently among siblings. And DFS says they've received seven calls over the years stating that the kids have turned up at the baby-sitter's and at the welfare agency with bruises, and the parents always seem to have an explanation. It all stinks.''

Another long speech, Jesse thought. And she was still agitated.

"Something's wrong here," she went on. "If those little girls died of SIDS, then I'm the Queen of England."

"No tiara," he muttered. She didn't even crack a smile.

"I noticed what could have been blunt force trauma," she continued, "to her seventh cervical vertebra—"

"English," he snapped, losing his sense of humor, as well. "Give it to me in English."

"Right here." Angela Byerly pointed to the back of her neck.

"Blunt force trauma," he repeated. "And that indicates... what?"

"She was hit with something. If it affected her spinal cord, that in turn could have caused brain swelling. I wasn't done with her yet," she repeated, then she began to pace again. "Too damned many deaths are blamed on this quirky thing—"

"SIDS," he clarified.

"Yes." She flashed golden brown eyes at him.

He wondered if she was a natural blonde. He'd never met a woman with such fair hair and such dark, depthless eyes. He had to drag his mind back to what she was saying.

"I really think we need to be more attuned to the possibility that some of these so-called SIDS cases might stem from abuse or other causes."

She was an idealist, he realized, a woman wishing hard for a perfect world. "I won't argue that."

"SIDS could so easily become a convenient catchall for parents losing their tempers, what with all the press it's gotten lately. We have to keep an eye on the situation."

"I agree."

"God help us, in many cases, it's a bona fide tragedy. But—"

"Dr. Byerly, what do you want from me here?" he interrupted. She let her breath out and stopped pacing. For a moment, she looked confused. "Some admission of culpability," she said finally. "You screwed up big time, Counselor."

Jesse stiffened.

"She only came in yesterday morning!" she rushed on. "The cops who caught the call had her sent to my office because SIDS is still considered an unexplained death. I did a preliminary on her—X rays and whatnot—and found the neck injury. I went to pull her out this afternoon to do the rest of the autopsy, and she was gone because *you'd* released her without even consulting me!"

Jesse fought off his own need to pace. That would reveal far too much agitation.

But, oh, he was agitated. He *hadn't* released Lacie Shokonnet.

"I'll look into it," he said shortly.

"It's too late for that." Dr. Angela Byerly threw her hands up in a volatile gesture. "We've lost this one, Counselor, thank you so much. Harry and Melissa Shokonnet are going to walk. I just wanted to make damned sure you knew how I felt about it."

"Calm down," he snapped, and this time there was something dangerous in his face. "I said I'll look into it."

She turned away from him in disgust.

"Who took the body?" he demanded.

She stopped with one pretty, fine-boned hand on the door. For the life of him, he couldn't picture those hands doing what he knew they did for a living.

"Coral-Beachem Funeral Home," she answered. "They cremated her twenty-five minutes before I was able to track her down. At her parents' request. Convenient."

Jesse swore. "The older sibling? Any possibility we can exhume her?"

"No. Same thing. She was cremated."

His stomach rolled a little at the images that brought to mind. Jesse rarely visited crime scenes personally. He had never set foot in the morgue. For all his outward confidence, he was cowed by death, blood and bodies.

"I'll be in touch," he managed, but doubted if she heard him. She was already gone, slamming the door hard behind her.

Jesse tried hard over the next several hours to put the woman out of his mind. Even if it had proved possible, the thing with the Shokonnet baby lingered just below the surface like a dull, persistent toothache.

It didn't improve his mood any when Caro was not at the airport.

Jesse looked around the empty gateway at Philadelphia International, then he crossed to a busier one on the opposite side of the concourse. He spoke with the woman at the desk there. No message awaited him. She suggested that he go back downstairs to ticketing and check there.

He didn't bother.

He left the terminal, heading back to the parking garage with quick, aggravated strides. He'd wasted an hour and a half on this wild-goose chase, and that was the least of it. Caro had been coming into town for his sister's wedding on Saturday. Jesse made it a point never to show up alone at any affair that any member of his family might be attending, his sister excluded.

He knew even before he got home and played back his voice mail what had happened. Caro had, of course, changed her plans.

As it turned out, she had headed off to Milan with some international race car driver. Her behavior was not a new phenomenon. The women he chose to associate with craved excitement. They started out believing that that excitement could be tapped from the vast Hadley fortune. Invariably, after a few months, they found out that whether he needed to or not, Jesse Hadley worked for a living. And he liked it.

Still, Caro had lasted a little longer than most, and she was a moderately disappointing loss. "Damn it," he muttered aloud.

His mother would spend Saturday throwing at him every available, homely socialite she could get her hands on. And his father would hound his every step, wanting to talk about his mayoral candidacy. His sister often chided him for the way he dodged parental bullets, and he did not deny her insight. He showed up at the Hadley estate whenever a social occasion demanded it. He arrived early, so it could be said that he was also paying a family visit. And he always brought a date. The elder Hadleys were nothing if not socially proper. They wouldn't corner him and harangue him in polite company.

A politician needs a wife. You're far too old to be running about this way. It's paramount to your image that you settle down.

No, don't pursue that homeless issue. Let them kill each other over turf wars. They don't vote. You have far more important issues to address if you're going to run for mayor.

Mayor, he reflected. Proof that they managed to catch him alone now and again. He would not be seeing out his next term as D.A. He would be reluctantly running for top dog.

He was a Hadley.

Jesse shrugged out of his suit coat and tossed it over the banister. He loosened his tie and went into the parlor. His favorite Waterford snifter was sitting on the right end of a polished sideboard beside a matching decanter. Wood was laid in the fireplace, more for its aesthetic value than for practicality since it was nearly June. Two Queen Anne chairs bracketed the hearth, and an antique fire screen sat behind the right one. There was a Cézanne above the mantel.

It was Jesse's favorite room, though not necessarily to relax and recline in—he rarely had time for that. He came here to let the elegance and beauty of it seep into his pores. It was neat, orderly and sane. As his life had been, for the most part, prior to about five o'clock this afternoon when an irate, not-very-orderly blonde had blasted into his office wearing too-bright flowers and horrendous shoes.

He pored some cognac into the snifter, took a mouthful and let it settle on his tongue as he headed upstairs deep in thought. Only two people in the city of Philadelphia had the power to release a body involved in a criminal investigation. The cops couldn't do it. The mayor couldn't do it. The governor couldn't do it. Hell, the *Supreme Court* couldn't do it. Only the chief M.E. could authorize such a release when she was satisfied with the results. Or the district attorney could do it.

Angela Byerly hadn't signed that form. And he hadn't, either. His stomach squeezed with the beginnings of real pain. He took another sip of brandy anyway.

The release had been signed Jesse *M.* Hadley.

In print, in the typed closing of all his letters and official documents—hell, even in the press—he used the initial. And someone had signed the release that way. The catch was, *he* never used the *M* in his actual signature.

He filled the whirlpool bath and considered the possibilities. It could be that the Shokonnets had a friend inside the coroner's or the D.A.'s office. God help him, that sort of thing had happened before, most notably in a case involving his own secretary and Tessa, his sister. But it didn't quite feel right. Christian Benami— the man who had planted Jesse's secretary in his office earlier this year—had been wealthy and powerful. Jesse hadn't gotten the impression that that was the case with the Shokonnets. There were few people in Philadelphia—in the *country*—who were as wealthy and as powerful as the Hadleys. Jesse knew every one of them who even came close.

What made a lot more sense was that someone was out to discredit him. As the D.A., he was an elected official. This was an election year. He would have to run again for district attorney—and win—so that he could leapfrog over to City Hall. The mayoral election wasn't for another eighteen months, and his chances would be optimum if he were running from another elected position.

He was a shoo-in for the D.A. spot. The Republicans hadn't even officially announced their candidate yet, but none of the names that had been mentioned were particularly credible. It would take a lot more than a premature release from the morgue for any of them to gain ground on him.

That left Angela Byerly. As she had pointed out, there were a good many people waiting, if not eager, to see her fall. But then, why not forge *her* name?

Half an hour later, after a short spell in the bath, he returned downstairs to his study. He went back to work.

"Eric," he dictated to Eric Zollner, one of his investigators, "I need you to look into a couple named Harry and Melissa Shokonnet, and particularly their two children. One died of apparent SIDS—" he paused, thinking "—on Tuesday night, I believe. The older sibling died of SIDS, as well, but I don't have a date on that one." Jesse scowled. "We know that Family Services has received numerous calls regarding them. Check all the area hospitals to see if the kids were ever brought in for emergency treatment, and do a background check on the parents. See what you can get without a court order. I don't want to alert anyone yet that I'm looking into this."

None of his subordinates would dare question his desire for secrecy on this, he thought. He was the D.A., and he was a Hadley.

He pulled the tape out of the tiny recorder, labelled it, then dropped it into his open briefcase. He inserted another. "Jeanette, I need you to pull the personnel records on everyone in the M.E.'s office—anyone in that building, as a matter of fact, all the way down to the janitors." He hesitated again, then clicked off, replacing that tape, as well.

The last one he dictated to his secretary, Libby Dwyer. "I need your desk log for...say the past four weeks. I need to know of everyone who was in and out of my office during that time." Not a likely route to the culprit, he considered. No one had seen his correspondence, or they would have known about the *M.* But someone *had* gotten their hands on one of those forms, either from his office or Angela Byerly's.

He finally sat back in his chair, folding his hands behind his head. He decided that he would personally look into the doctor's background.

She didn't seem to like him much. Or, at least, she was unduly wary of him. He felt insulted, indignant and...well, alarmed. Because he couldn't quite get that sparrow out of his mind.

He wasn't willing to dredge up the end of that memory, but he was alone now and it crept up on him. He had, of course, opened his hand again immediately after he'd caught it. Once he'd recovered from his split second of shock, he'd instinctively let the bird fly. But it hadn't. It had rolled out of his hand and fallen to the porch with a horrible little thud, dead as a doornail.

His mother had been typically appalled and wouldn't even discuss what had happened. But his nanny had said that it had a heart attack. Jesse had walked away from the experience learning something much more profound than mere biological science. He had *felt* that heart going wild before it had broken. And he knew then that capturing something that was meant to fly could kill it.

He would never, ever have hurt that sparrow. But, of course, the sparrow hadn't known it. The sparrow wouldn't have believed it.

He thought again of Angela Byerly's legs and her multihued flowers. He wondered why she thought he might hurt her. He was still wondering about it hours later when he should have been dwelling on the traitorous, polished, undemanding Caro—whom he had not once ever glimpsed in turquoise shoes.

Chapter 2

By Saturday afternoon, Angela's impulsive visit to Jesse Hadley's office still made her heart squirm. She had been out of her mind.

No, she hadn't. She'd been angry, just as she had told him. And that was *another* mistake she'd made—admitting that her temper was the only thing in the world that could have goaded her into walking the two blocks between their offices and confronting him face-to-face.

For nothing. Nothing had come of the meeting.

Well, what had she expected? That he would admit he'd been wrong? And just as she had told him, there was nothing he could do about any of it anyway. Not now.

Confronting him had been a stupid waste of time, and she was almost angrier with herself than she'd been with him. She was also a practical woman. Since it was over and done with, and there was no taking it back, she would have to put the whole scene out of her mind.

Unfortunately, that was going to be easier said than done because John Gunner and Jesse's sister, Tessa Hadley-Bryant, were getting married this afternoon.

Angela hated weddings. She much preferred funerals. Not that she considered herself a morbid person, she thought, digging into a dresser drawer for a pair of hose. She celebrated life with her every breath—intentionally and doggedly balancing the ugliness of her job with brightness and clarity and hope. She understood death and worked with it in clinical terms, sorting through it to find clues no one else would understand. And she wore flowers and outrageous colors so that it wouldn't permeate her world.

Funerals and christenings, at least, were life events that deserved somber observation. Weddings were just the celebration of a passing stage. She might have enjoyed them for that alone, but people always tried to make more of them.

She would go to this one because she sincerely hoped that it was a life event that would be joyous and permanent. She had been wary of John Gunner's bride at first. Like her brother, Tessa Hadley-Bryant was upper-crust Philadelphia society down to her bones. But there was no denying that she loved John Gunner.

So Angela would go to their wedding. In fact, she pretty much *had* to go. They were sending a car for her to minimize the chances of her weaseling out. John knew her well.

He ought to, she reflected. They'd more or less grown up together before she'd gone to college, to law school and medical school, before she'd escaped this city with all its tortured memories, only to come back when it had hailed her as a prize acquisition and paid her accordingly.

Ego. Pride. Those were the reasons she had come back in spite of everything that had happened here. The money they paid her was just part and parcel of that. She'd come back for the same reason she dressed the way she did. Out of a refusal to bow her head in shame, to hide her light under a bushel. To balance the ugliness with something that pleased her.

"We really ought to be going, ma'am." The deep male voice drifted up to her from the foyer downstairs. It was the limo driver. A *limo,* for God's sake! Tessa had insisted. At least she would enter their lair in style.

John had told her that she didn't have to stay. Even a quick appearance would make him happy. He'd told her that it was time to bury the past. How could she explain, even to him, that there was still an irrational fear lurking inside beneath the bright colors and the pride?

She finally found a pair of hose and sat down on the bed to

pull them on. They were white. She moved to her closet. Red, she decided. She would wear red. It was glaring, arrogant, *there*. It would counterbalance the quakes she felt inside. Unfortunately, everything red in her closet was too casual for a wedding. She began pushing through the hangers, glancing back over her shoulder at the digital clock on her nightstand.

So far, so good. She was going to be at least half an hour late.

She finally found a red linen dress that she thought would do the trick. It was plain, sleeveless, with a mock turtle neckline. It would go with the white hose if she wore pumps to match, and…yes, there it was, at the very top of her closet, a white hat with a wide brim and a huge, fake red carnation. But she didn't own a pair of red pumps.

She rushed through her makeup and took the towel off her head, running her fingers through her damp blond curls. She would open the limo windows, she determined. By the time they got to Independence National Historical Park, her hair would be passably dry. The wedding would be held at Christ Church there.

She grabbed the hat and ran downstairs. The limo driver was waiting just inside her front door.

"Your shoes, ma'am," he said stoically.

"We're going to have to swing up Broad Street on our way."

Angela went to the front door, peering out to see how far away the limo was parked. She figured she could probably make it without ruining her hose.

She sprinted out the front door and slid smoothly into the back seat. She pulled her left foot up onto her lap and nodded in satisfaction. No runs.

"Ma'am," the driver said as he settled himself behind the wheel.

"Angela," she corrected absently. "Ma'am makes me sound like a sixty-year-old dowager." It made her sound like one of *them*—one of the Hadleys and Glowans and Prices who made up Philadelphia's elite.

"It's four-forty…Angela." She knew exactly what time it was. "We'll be late if you want me to detour all the way over to Broad Street."

Even later, she thought. It was what she was counting on. "Well, it's either that or I show up barefoot," she returned placidly.

The man put the car in gear and drove.

The shoe shop Angela had noticed last week was still open. She gave the driver a fifty-dollar bill and pointed at the display window. "See that pair of pumps right there in the far corner? The red ones. I need them in a size seven."

"You want me to purchase these for you, ma'am?"

"*Angela.* And you'd better do it fast if you don't want to be late for the wedding."

He got out of the car.

With any luck, Angela thought, she would sneak in for the tail end of the ceremony, make a perfunctory appearance at the reception—just long enough that she wouldn't be letting John down. Then she would leave, without encountering either of the men she had hoped to avoid. If she kept her time at this shindig to a minimum, it ought to be possible.

Jesse Hadley was bad enough, and it was a sure bet that he would be at his sister's wedding. One short week ago, he would have looked right through her, never even realizing who she was. She had pretty much ruined any chance of that happening now. Still, it wasn't Jesse she dreaded encountering.

Her palms were beginning to sweat. She looked around for a napkin or tissue.

She wondered if Wendell Glowan would remember her. Probably not.

Charles Price III would. And he traveled in Hadley circles. Of course, John wouldn't have insisted she come if there was any chance Charlie might turn up. She couldn't believe he'd do that to her.

"Sooner or later, you're going to have to trust someone," she whispered aloud. And John Gunner was as safe a bet as anyone.

Angela leaned closer to the window and combed her fingers through her hair as the driver came back. Her stomach was rolling now.

Vows were exchanged. Tessa beamed. Gunner looked a little bemused.

Jesse turned to follow them up the aisle, and he felt a little dazed himself as he scanned the mismatched bunch who had gathered in the church. The left pews were filled with classic hats, sleek hairdos, somber suits and gloves—the Hadley side. Of the immediate family, only Jesse's father had not gone into politics. He was the senior partner of Hadley, Glowan and Russ, the foremost law firm in Philadelphia. Jesse's mother was a Glowan. Her sister had married a Russ.

Wendell Glowan, his uncle, was a superior court judge who had just been nominated to the U.S. Supreme Court. Various cousins sat in the U.S. Senate and in Congress, and at least one of them was probably going to run for the presidency in a few more years. Jesse's grandfather, Marshall Hadley, had once been the governor of Pennsylvania. He'd passed away years ago, but Diantha, his widow, was very much in attendance today and holding court in one of the front pews.

If the Gunners were impressed, it didn't show.

The pews on the right were awash with splashes of color. It all reminded him of the dress Angela Byerly had worn on Thursday. He was having a surprisingly hard time getting the woman out of his mind. He found himself remembering jarring flashes of her at odd moments—those turquoise shoes, all that hair. Eyes that changed color.

She was the only other human being who was even marginally aware of the significance of that release form. He supposed that was as good a reason as any to dwell on her from time to time, but he wasn't pleased that it was her physical appearance that came most readily to mind.

The Gunner clan called out happily to each other from the back pews to the front now that the ceremony was over. A little boy attempted to climb over one of the seats and he fell, smacking his head against the back of the next one.

Jesse winced for him. More voices rose, in alarm this time, as the boy began wailing. No one on the Hadley side even deigned to look that way.

Jesse swore beneath his breath and stopped to pick up the boy himself. The kid kept howling.

"He's probably got one of those concussion things!" someone cried.

"Get Dr. Angie!" someone else shouted.

Jesse's heart slammed against his chest. His head snapped up hard and quickly enough that he felt a spasm in his neck. "Angie who?"

They could have been speaking of anyone, but against all reason he knew they weren't. And he was right.

He spotted her standing at the back of the church. The word *hiding* came immediately to mind. It could just as easily be said that because she had arrived late, she had hovered there in the back to avoid disrupting the ceremony. But her spine seemed to be pressed against the wall in the brief second before she began pushing her way through the crowd.

She wore a dress that beat the floral one hands down. It was just as short, but this one was a vibrant red. Having noticed that, Jesse had more or less intended that his gaze should stop right there, but his eyes wandered down her legs again, down, down, until they finally found a pair of bright red shoes this time.

"Good God," he murmured.

"Give him to me."

"What?" He looked up at her face again. Her hair was loose today, a riot of spun gold spilling over her shoulders. It was incredible. And just as amazingly, his fingers itched to bury themselves in it, to take handfuls of it and tilt her head back to see her yield.

This woman would not yield easily.

Nor was she even his type, he mused, feeling dazed. On the one occasion he'd encountered her, she'd left him feeling disoriented, confused—as if a Mack truck had broadsided him.

"The *child*," she clarified tightly. "Please. Give me the child."

Jesse thrust the boy at her. He realized that she again seemed reluctant to meet his eyes.

She ran her fingers—fingers that routinely touched and probed the dead for their secrets—expertly over the child's scalp. No matter what they did for a living, he had the absurd impression that her fine-boned, elegant hands belonged on the Hadley side of the church, while the rest of her...

He was absolutely clueless as to where the rest of her might belong.

"No dents," she observed finally. Then she shifted the boy's weight so that he was straddling her hips, facing her. She locked her hands together under his bottom and smiled.

She hadn't smiled in his office at all. With all that yellow-white hair spilling over her shoulders, she reminded him of the sun rising—radiant, brilliant, illuminating.

"Feel sick to your stomach?" she asked the boy. He shook his head. "Okay, tilt your head back a little there. Let me see up your nose."

"My *nose?*" He'd recovered enough to giggle.

Angela Byerly cocked her head to the side. "You're fine. Nothing up there but—" She broke off suddenly. "Never mind. We're hobnobbing among the elite here. We'd best keep that to ourselves." There was a strong bite to her last words until she turned to the boy's mother. "I think he's fine. Just keep an eye on him. If you notice any bruising around his eyes or behind his ears, find me and let me know."

The woman nodded solemnly.

"Are you going to the reception?" the man beside her asked. He shot a wide-eyed look over to the Hadley side of the church.

Jesse followed his gaze, unable to fathom it. He felt the beginnings of a headache.

"For a little while," Angela answered. "Then I'll be at home. One way or another, you'll be able to find me."

She handed the boy over to his mother and turned away. Jesse reached out an unconscious hand to stop her, then he let it fall to his side. What in the world would he say to her? It wasn't the time or place to talk about the business of the Shokonnet release—and he hadn't learned anything new yet in any event. He let her go and moved silently after her.

Angela felt him behind her.

She didn't want to be so aware of him—God *knew* she didn't want to. Jesse Hadley was the kind of man who could chew her up and spit her out without so much as a burp afterward, and she had far bigger worries right now. She needed to keep her eyes open for Wendell Glowan, for Charlie Price. Yet every nerve tingled with the sense of him behind her.

Angela hurried out, trying to lengthen the space between them. She paused only as long as she had to, hugging John warmly and Tessa a little more reservedly.

Nearly a hundred people were trying to push through the outer doors, an impossibility. Jesse Hadley moved through them, his hard arm brushing against her shoulder as he passed her. Angela pulled back sharply as he touched her, but he didn't seem to notice.

He made his way to the massive carved doors and threw them open so that everyone could spill out.

Angela spilled out with the rest of them and took a deep breath of the warm, humid air. "Half an hour at the reception," she murmured, "and I'm out of there."

Six limousines were lined up at the curb. Beyond them was a scattering of Cadillacs, Mercedes, Lincolns and, notably, one Rolls-Royce. She wondered which was Wendell Glowan's car. She wondered if any of them belonged to Charlie Price.

She hadn't notice Charlie in the church. The judge was another matter. He'd been in the second pew on the left. She glanced around and couldn't see him outside.

She made her way to the limousine that had brought her. Her gaze went past the elegant, pricey cars. Other automobiles were crouched like poor relations behind them. There were Jeeps and sedans, sport-utility vehicles and a plethora of Philadelphia Police Department cruisers. Angela felt her mouth try to curl into a smile in spite of her nerves. The reception would be at Tessa's parents' estate. It was a safe guess that the Hadleys had never had the likes of the P.P.D. in their parlor before.

Jesse stepped around her and opened the rear limo door. Angela jumped. She hadn't realized that he had caught up with her.

"What are you doing?" she demanded.

"This is the car you were going to, right?"

She looked quickly at the driver. *Damn.* "Yes. He brought me. Tessa..." She trailed off.

His green eyes sharpened. Like a cat that had just scented prey, she imagined.

"You're a friend of Tessa's?" Why hadn't his sister mentioned it? He'd thought she was here in a more-or-less official capacity.

Angela shook her head. "No. I mean, by association, I guess. I'm a friend of John's."

Why hadn't Gunner ever mentioned it?

Probably, he figured, because Gunner's world had once been full of beautiful, unorthodox women just like this one. Gunner would not consider Angela Byerly an oddity at all.

"Get in," he said too shortly, and he thought he heard her gasp. But when he glanced at her again, her face looked like stone. Alabaster, except for two streaks of hectic color high on her cheeks.

"No, thank you."

"This is my car," he said inanely.

Her heart stuttered. Tessa had sent her brother's car for her? *Damn it,* she cursed silently.

"Fine," she responded. "Ride in it. Excuse me."

"How will you get to the reception?"

"I'll hitch a ride with someone."

"That's ridiculous." What was it about him that she seemed to find so offensive? He was insulted all over again.

Angela shook her head helplessly. Then she expelled her breath and turned back, sliding into the car. Making a big deal of it, she decided, would only make things worse. That was the other thing she had learned about his kind. The faster you ran from them, the more they were compelled to follow.

Jesse sat across from her, and the limo began rolling. "Champagne?" he asked finally.

She kept her gaze doggedly on the window and the passing streets, then glanced around deliberately to see that he had already poured for her. "Certainly." She took the flute from him, exercising great care not to touch his hand.

Her eyes went back to the window. Jesse felt another strong spurt of irritation that she was ignoring him—as though he was above being ignored, he chided himself dryly. Though, of course, he was—at least as far as the city politics and a handful of models and actresses and heiresses were concerned. But this idealistic doctor with great legs and too much hair was simply shutting him out.

She settled a little deeper into the plush leather and crossed the legs in question. Jesse cleared his throat. "Nice shoes," he said at last.

Her eyes flicked back to him. Suspiciously. "Do you like them?"

"They're different."

Good enough, she thought. That was what she strived for. "Thank you."

"Can I ask you something?"

Her gaze flashed to him again. "What?"

Actually, too many questions crowded onto his tongue to be counted. *What the hell have I ever done to you? Why were your friends glowering at the Hadley side of the church?*

"Why do you do it? What you do for a living." He looked at her hands again and tried to imagine them cutting, weighing, examining. Something in his gut rolled over queasily and he wished he hadn't.

"Someone has to."

"But why a woman with legs like miles of heaven?"

Angela lost her breath for a moment. She didn't want to feel the pleasure that scooted through her, warm and ticklish. She took a deep swig of champagne and coughed a little.

"That's Cristal Rosé," Jesse said carefully. "Louis Roederer. A hundred and ninety dollars a bottle."

"So?"

"So it might be worth savoring."

"Some other time." She gulped again and tried hard not to let him see her shiver with the goodness of it. It was not something she would ever have spent money on herself, but it delighted her—cold and crisp, it made swallowing a sensual experience.

"Your job?" Jesse pressed, because what she was doing with the champagne made him uncomfortable.

Her eyes darted to him. "Oh. I got my medical degree in forensic medicine," she said finally. "With a minor in pathology."

He nodded. He was self-contained, she thought, and oh, so polite. It made her stomach flutter with nerves. She'd learned the hard way that manners often went no deeper than the surface.

"Pathology means the causes and nature of disease," she went on, her throat tight.

"I know that."

Yes, of course he would. He was very educated in his own right. "Basic bodily malfunction," she finished. "When something goes wrong, I like to know why." She looked out the window again. *Please, just let him shut up.*

She couldn't have said why she was babbling responses as if someone was holding a gun to her head. She was usually far, far more cautious than this.

Maybe it was his eyes. She allowed herself one more quick glance at them. At the moment, they were curious and as piercing as a hawk's, as though he could see the answers inside her head if he only stared hard enough.

"It seems morbid," he pointed out levelly.

"I balance it."

"With wild dresses?"

How could he know? "What's wrong with the way I dress?" she demanded.

"Nothing." *Everything.* "It just sort of...demands attention."

He wasn't prepared for her reaction. Color flooded her face this time. If she had been angry when she had barged into his office on Thursday, now she was livid.

What the hell did I say? he wondered.

"Keeping your attention in line is *your* problem, Counselor."

Suddenly, he was angry, as well. "And what's yours?"

"My what?"

"Your problem!"

"I don't have one. Or at least I didn't until you released Lacie Shokonnet's body."

"How the hell did we get back to that?" His voice rose. He saw her flinch.

"It's the only common ground we've got," she said coldly.

He realized belatedly that the limo had stopped. They had reached his parents' estate. His head was pounding now.

Jesse got out of the car first. He refrained from giving her a hand, though all his breeding rebelled. Actually, it felt damned good to leave her high and dry and march inside by himself. Under any other circumstances, he might have grinned. He didn't get many opportunities to act so petty. But this woman had a chip on her shoulder the size of the Hope Diamond.

Angela got out of the car more slowly, plunking her hat on her head. She was still shaken. *Sort of demands attention.* Something in her stomach curled inward upon itself. *Like uncle, like nephew.* She wanted to cry, but there was no private place to do it. The limo was already moving off behind her.

Damn them. Damn them all. Of all the women in the city, why had John Gunner chosen to marry a *Hadley?*

She took a deep breath, calming herself. Half an hour, she promised herself. She made her way toward the house.

Jesse looked back at her from the door at the last moment, without meaning to. His breath left him on a rush and his irritation gave way once more to confusion. He stared at her.

She walked toward the house looking for all the world like a woman who expected to meet her Maker within. And she wore the most incredible, garish hat he had ever seen in his life.

Chapter 3

Huge white columns rose on either side of the front door. Angela slipped between them and into the foyer, feeling a little like Cinderella, but not at all looking forward to the ball.

She followed voices—and Jesse Hadley's broad shoulders—to the back of the house. There she found an immense veranda that ran the whole width of the mansion. Many of the guests had already moved down onto an emerald green lawn.

Angela remained where she was. The food was here. It would give her something to do with her hands.

She nibbled on a rumaki and carefully checked out the crowd. She spotted Wendell Glowan at one of the tables sprinkled with designed nonchalance around the lawn. He was grinning widely, talking loudly, and his face was already flushed. She wondered how much he'd had to drink, then decided that she didn't want to know. She didn't trust herself with such knowledge. She didn't want to know *anything* about the judge that might give her the high and lofty idea that she might be able to destroy him.

Her...a Byerly. Fat chance.

Charlie Price was nowhere to be seen.

She looked toward the polished dance floor that had been constructed on the lawn. It didn't take the Gunners—or any of John's friends—very long to make themselves at home. They swarmed and mingled, and a few were already gyrating to the beat of the band. The police department was well represented. Give *them* a little of that bubbly, Angela thought, and it ought to turn out to be quite a party. The cops she knew were famous for letting their hair down emphatically whenever they were given half a chance.

John stopped beside her. She felt a rush of real pleasure.

"How are you holding up?" he asked.

"I'm here," she replied simply. And that said it all.

Gunner grinned.

"How did you avoid inviting Price?" she asked suddenly.

His grin went crooked. "By insisting that we had to do this this weekend. He's out of town."

Relief flooded her, and gratitude. "Thanks."

"I'd sure as hell rather see you at my wedding than him. Listen, I've got to find Tessa."

"John." She stopped him as he stepped away.

"What?"

"Congratulations again."

The grin came back. "Yeah. Thanks. Maybe you'll even catch the bouquet."

She managed to keep smiling at him as fear rattled briefly inside her. "Not if I can help it."

When he was gone, she turned away to study the buffet table again. The shrimp looked interesting. There were little chilies tucked inside them and some sort of dipping sauce. Excellent, she thought, popping one into her mouth. She chewed, then wrapped six of them, along with six of the rumaki, into a napkin, opened her purse and dropped the bundle inside. The kids from the neighborhood—especially the girls—would never forgive her if she didn't bring something back from the other side of the tracks.

"Sending it to Somalia?" Jesse asked from behind her.

Angela spun around, her hair swirling. She hadn't seen him coming this time, either. She'd relaxed once she'd known for sure that Charlie Price wasn't going to pop up. She'd trusted John to keep him away—had made herself trust him—but knowing for sure was a relief.

It took her a moment to squelch any visible reaction. She was damned if she was going to let this man get to her. Half an hour, she promised herself again.

"Do you know how many people you could feed with this?" she countered idly.

"One hundred fifty, if the caterer's bill is to be believed."

"It would feed three hundred if they were used to having nothing."

"We already donate heavily to several charities."

"Oh, I'm sure you do." She finally looked at him. "Why are you doing this to me?" she asked bluntly.

He didn't pretend to misunderstand, though he was discomfited. No social niceties and casual flirtations here. She certainly said what was on her mind.

"I don't know," he admitted.

"I don't want to talk with you."

He almost smiled. "I can tell."

"So why are you pushing it? Why can't you just leave me alone?"

The words rolled off his tongue as blatantly as hers seemed to, startling even him. The woman had an extremely odd effect on him. "You intrigue me," he answered.

She took a quick, almost infinitesimal step backward. If he hadn't been watching her, he would have missed it. "So get *un*-intrigued," she snapped.

"Trust me. I'm trying." He hesitated. "Dance with me."

She took another step back. "No!"

"Why not?"

"I don't *like* you!"

"For God's sake, you don't even *know* me!" He was vaguely aware of people watching them now. He could barely believe he had shouted. With grim effort, he lowered his voice. "Look, I need a favor."

"Ask one of your constituents." She resumed eating. With enough chewing, she hoped, conversation would be impossible.

"You *are* one of my constituents," he observed. "In a manner of speaking."

"No. I didn't vote for you."

"Why not?" He'd won the last election by a landslide.

"You're a Hadley."

Surprise shimmied through him all over again, though it probably shouldn't have. Was her antagonism as simple as that? What had the Hadleys ever done to her?

"That always worked in my favor," he said carefully.

"Not in everyone's opinion."

"So tell me about yours."

"I think you give as much thought to staying on top as to doing your job well." She began to inch away from him.

"Wait a minute."

He caught her elbow. It was pure instinct. He only wanted to stop her. But she looked at him with such indignation—and yes, there was panic again—just as there had been the first time he met her—that he felt foolish and quickly dropped his hand.

"So do you," he said awkwardly.

"I beg your pardon?"

"You give as much thought to staying on top as to doing your job. You said as much in my office."

His mother was bearing down on them from across the lawn. He caught sight of her out of the corner of his eye. She had Lisette Markham Chauncy by one skinny elbow. The woman was thirty-nine and a spinster. She looked easily ten or more years older than her age, and she was so excruciatingly shy that it was painful to talk to her. The highest-priced salon in the world couldn't do anything with her limp hair. It was streaked with blond this month, but its natural dishwater color still showed through in odd places. She wore a shapeless silk dress in a drab color.

"Damn it," he muttered, then caught Angela's arm again and swung her into his own. Her hat fell back onto the veranda, the carnation bobbling merrily.

"What do you think you're doing?" she cried.

"Dancing with you."

She managed to pull back just far enough to smack a hand against his chest. "And I said no!" Her voice sounded shrill.

"For God's sake, I'm not going to hurt you!" And impossibly, he thought of that damned sparrow again. Quickly, almost unconsciously, he relaxed his hold on her. She seemed to tremble for a moment. She didn't wrench away. She didn't move at all.

Angela knew he wouldn't hurt her. Of course he wouldn't—at least not here, not now. "We're on the porch," she tried saying in a more reasonable tone. "The dance floor's on the lawn."

"So we'll dance in that direction. Watch your step. The stairs are right behind you." He guided her down the five short steps to the lawn.

He was out of his mind, she concluded. She liked that in a person.

The more he insisted on badgering her, the more that insidious little observation crept into her head. She *could* like him. If she let herself. He was not what she had expected him to be. He wasn't rigid. He wasn't cold. He was, however, extremely high-handed.

He was staring over her left shoulder. And he looked...alarmed.

"What?" she demanded, craning her neck around to see, as well. A tall, thin, well-dressed woman was heading toward them. She had another plainer-looking woman by the elbow. Suddenly, the older woman stopped short, and the younger one took a few more steps before being wrenched backward by her grip. The younger one looked disappointed, the older one annoyed. "Who are they?" Angela asked.

"The one on the right is my mother. Isobel Glowan Hadley."

Angela looked up into his face again. She was tall. Jesse was taller by a good many inches. "You're afraid of her," she declared slowly.

"Too strong a word. I avoid her. You would too, if she were yours."

Angela wanted to laugh, but wouldn't let herself. "Why?"

"She wants me to marry that woman," he answered aggrievedly.

"You can't be serious."

"I am."

Astounded, she realized that he was telling her the truth. And she knew, all over again, that the Hadleys inhabited a whole different world from the one she knew.

"Just tell her no."

"Obviously, you've never met my mother." Jesse gave a quick, harassed glance down into her face before his gaze went back over her shoulder again. Angela followed his glance and saw the women retreating. She felt Jesse exhale slowly.

And that was when she became aware of just how tightly he was holding her.

His left hand—wide and strong—held her right one. Their fingers were laced together. His hands were not what she would have imagined, either. They were not soft and smooth, his nails weren't buffed. They weren't really white-collar hands. Faint calluses covered the little pads of skin at the base of his fingers. Incredibly, almost absently, he ran his thumb over her knuckle. His touch was rough and warm.

She felt a shuddering kind of feeling deep within her, and she was frightened by it, astounded and appalled.

His right hand was at the small of her back, holding her close to him. Their thighs were flush together. She could feel his heart-beat.

"We're...not...dancing," she managed to protest.

He looked surprised. "Oh. Sorry." He began moving again.

She struggled mightily for something to say. She knew she had to pull away from him, but she couldn't seem to find the strength. Her legs were hollow.

"Why does she want you to marry that woman?" she asked finally.

"Because that woman is a Chauncy. Lisette Markham to be exact."

"So?"

Something happened to his mouth that might have been a smile. A pained one. "So her daddy is loaded."

"So is yours. So are you."

"Precisely."

No false modesty there, she noted. But she had already known that about him.

"Hadley marriages are not made in heaven, Doctor. They're made at the bank."

"Your sister's wasn't."

"No, that's true. Tessa can certainly dig her heels in when she chooses to. She's the exception to the rule." He looked down at the woman in his arms again. "Thank you for dancing with me."

Those simple words shook Angela all over again, more than she cared to admit. A Hadley thanking a Byerly. Well, well. She didn't want to believe that he might be different. It was just manners again. But his eyes looked so candid, so sincere.

"Think you can keep this up for about another three hours?" he went on, grinning now.

"I'm not staying for three hours," she blurted.

He'd fix that. "Too bad. You've been helpful."

"You want *me* to run interference for you?" she asked incredulously.

"In addition to the Chauncy woman, there are about six other unmarried heiresses running loose around here." Then, of course, there would be the inevitable press of his father, his uncle, his cousins, all wanting to talk politics.

Angela looked around again and could almost spot the heiresses. For the most part, they were watching Jesse, fairly drooling.

She surprised herself with a quick bubble of laughter. "I guess you're a catch."

"They think so."

"Do you?" she asked, genuinely curious.

One of his brows went up, but he didn't give her a quick, pat answer. She liked that, too.

"I think," he said slowly, "that I'd be damned impossible to live with."

"Why?"

"I work a lot. I'm rarely home. And when I am, I like the quiet."

"And?"

"Isn't that enough?"

"It wouldn't deter them."

Jesse laughed aloud. "No, I guess it wouldn't." Then he fell quiet again. "I'm a loner," he said finally. "I like my freedom and my solitude. It would bother me to give that up. And there's not much else in my life that I truly enjoy."

Angela felt surprise whisper through her. "You don't like your job?"

"I love my job. I don't want to be mayor."

He heard his words and was stunned. Could she be trusted with such information? God knew she seemed capable of anything. It wasn't like him to be so careless with his words. What the hell did this woman do to him?

"So don't run in the election," she said quietly.

"I have to."

In one succinct, unladylike word, she told him what she thought of that.

He looked down at her, shocked, then he laughed hard. She felt the strength of the sound in his chest, much too flush against hers.

"It's not that easy," he said, his expression serious again.

"Why?"

He didn't elaborate, couldn't say more.

"So you'll run, and you'll probably win, and you'll hate it."

"Hate's too strong a word. It's all relative."

"We should all have such problems."

"It's not a problem. It's a nuisance. Sort of like my mother dragging all these unmarried women out of the woodwork."

"A mayor ought to be married," she mused. She was goading him and realized that she was enjoying it. *Playing with fire,* came the sudden thought. Still, she kept on. "Family image and all that, right?"

He gave her an appraising look. "Now you're catching on."

"So why didn't you bring a date? That might have held your mother in abeyance."

"I tried."

"Where is she?"

"Milan."

Jesse found that he was much less annoyed with Caro's change of heart now than he had been two days ago. What was it about this woman that diverted him so? On the surface, she very nearly appalled him. She was prickly. Marginally rude, or at least shamelessly blunt with her opinions. She was quite possibly smarter than he was. His ego told him that he could have gotten two monster degrees almost simultaneously if he had wanted to, but honesty made him admit to himself that he wasn't really sure.

She was outrageous. He thought of the hors d'oeuvres she had taken, and those shoes, and the hat that still lay on the porch. People were stepping carefully over and around it with little sidelong glances, as though it might jump up and grab their ankles.

He sure as hell couldn't take her among the polite company he was accustomed to, at least not without keeping one worried eye on her. His mother would take one look at her and keel over. In fact, Isobel had already done pretty much that.

Interesting thought there, he decided, then pushed it away. Not even to goad Isobel could he see himself squiring this woman around the city. In three short days, she'd already left visible cracks in his smooth, polished world.

Yet he was acutely aware of the heat of her skin beneath his right palm, through the thin fabric of her dress. He slid his hand downward, ever so slightly, and she was warmer and softer still.

"Is your hair real?" he heard himself ask, and for the first time in his life he almost blushed.

"I beg your pardon?" She had heard him. She was simply too astounded to answer.

"Never mind."

"Of course it's *real!* Would I *buy* this stuff?"

"What do you mean?" he asked, mesmerized.

She jerked her hand free of his and attempted to run her fingers through her curls. It was a tough job. "It takes me the better part of an hour to get a comb through it."

He'd thought she'd achieved that look on purpose. "Oh," he managed to respond. "Actually, I was talking about the color."

She never had the opportunity to answer that one.

"Jesse," a deep voice rumbled from behind him, "whenever you can tear yourself away from your lovely companion, I'd like a word with you."

Jesse knew the voice. He didn't turn around to acknowledge it because he was too amazed by what happened to Angela Byerly's face. The blood seemed to literally be siphoned from her complexion.

"I've got to go," she choked. In the next instant, she jerked free from his arms and ran. She was gone before he could react.

"Jesse—" his uncle began again.

"Later," he snapped. He turned away and hurried after her.

"Maybe she'll leave a slipper," Wendell called out, laughing.

It doesn't matter. I know where to find her. If I want to. Still, his uncle's reference to Cinderella made him feel oddly light-headed. He hastened into the house, then jogged down the central hallway. People stared after him, openmouthed. She was doing it to him again, making him react in ways he'd never reacted before.

He didn't slow down.

By the time he reached the front porch, the limo—*his* limo— was moving down the wide, curving drive. He had no doubt that she was inside it.

"*Damn* it." He braced a hand against one of the white columns to watch it go. He felt let down, empty.

Then he heard movement behind him. Her jerked around angrily, expecting to find his uncle. *Damn that mayoral election.* And what the hell was it about the men in his family that they thought they could interrupt anything, at any time, when there was business to be discussed?

He found his new brother-in-law instead. Gunner tugged at his bow tie, finally pulling it free and stuffing it into his pocket. "I would not," Gunner said slowly, "have gotten all dressed up in this monkey suit for any other woman but my new wife."

"No," Jesse agreed absently. "You look uncomfortable." He glanced back at the limo just in time to see its brakes flash as it turned onto the street.

Gunner's eyes, too, followed the car. "What happened?"

"I was about to ask you. She said you two were friends."

Gunner only shrugged.

"She doesn't like me," Jesse heard himself say after a moment.

"It's not you," Gunner replied. "She's a little wary of men in general. What did your uncle say to her?"

"My *uncle?* Nothing. Why?"

Gunner didn't answer.

"What the hell is going on here?" Jesse growled. He was getting tired of the feeling of being in the dark.

"Your esteemed uncle screwed her over at one point in time," Gunner said finally. "Beyond that, I can't tell you any more. It's not my place."

"Screwed her over?" Jesse repeated incredulously. "Wendell?"

"It's not my place," Gunner repeated, then grinned. It wasn't entirely a pleasant look. "How's that for learning my Hadley-ese?"

"She can't ever have appeared before him," Jesse said shortly.

Gunner shrugged.

"Hell, it's *impossible!* She's the chief M.E., for God's sake! They wouldn't have pulled her away from Quantico if she had a record! *Quantico* wouldn't have had her!" He couldn't have said why he was so upset with the possibility.

He looked down the driveway again. It was unlittered. Not a glass slipper in sight.

Jesse turned away with a mild oath and went back into the house. He was halfway down the central hall before he noticed a single curly yellow hair clinging to his lapel. He ducked into the study, held it over the wastebasket there, then he reconsidered and slipped it into his tuxedo pocket.

Wendell Glowan had looked right at her. No, Angela thought wildly, no. He had looked *through* her, just as he had then.

In the future, Miss Byerly, you might want to be more circumspect in your behavior. Now, as then, her pulse thundered with the injustice of it. She'd had *witnesses.* People who could have told the court exactly what had happened, if they'd had the chance.

Some of them would have. Others had bowed out at the last moment, leaving her attorney scrambling. It had happened just around the time evidence had started disappearing.

She slid down more deeply into the plush seat of the limo. She kicked her new shoes off and curled her legs beneath her. The driver glanced back at her pale face in the mirror, but said nothing.

Glowan had dismissed her case. He'd thrown everything Charles Price III had done to her right out of court. The jury had never heard a word of what the remaining witnesses might have said. *She* had been the one to come out of that courtroom feeling dirty, guilty, raw.

The dismissal hadn't stopped Charlie. That hadn't been the end of it. He'd come back often enough, simply because there wasn't a thing she could do to stop him. She was a Byerly, and he was a Price, and an even more powerful Glowan had protected him.

He'd kept right on taunting her until John Gunner had finally stopped him.

She huddled into the rich leather that Hadley money had paid for and beat away the fear once more. John was right—the whole fiasco was in the past. She should be able to let go of it. But she had known that entering the Hadley lair today would be just like hearing Charlie's echoing, mocking laughter all over again. *You're no different today. A law degree as hard-earned as any of ours? Doesn't matter. A medical degree to boot? No, no, you're still that kid from South Philly. You're helpless, defenseless, powerless, no matter what they pay you now, and don't you ever forget it.*

Yes, she thought, feeling nauseous, that was it exactly. Because she *was*—she was just the same inside. And the Hadleys and the Glowans and the Prices of the world knew it.

Deep down inside, she was still that shy, skinny girl who had stood in front of The Honorable Wendell Glowan fifteen years ago, waiting for justice to be meted out. Waiting for the consolation of knowing that the guilty would be punished and the righteous would be soothed by it.

She'd been wrong.

The guilty were not punished when they had money, when they could buy witnesses and judges and pay to have evidence disappear. The righteous were only as mighty as their family ties. She'd learned that painful truth that day, and through many thereafter, and she had spent every one of her days since fighting it on her own terms.

She would not apologize for her looks. She would never cower beneath sackcloth. She would stand proud, and she would never, *ever,* allow one of those people into her world again.

She had stepped into their world today because she'd thought everything would be under her control. She had gone to John and Tessa's wedding, and she had pretended, for sweet, short moments in Jesse Hadley's arms, that pride and strength were enough. But now, as then, Wendell Glowan had looked right through her.

No, nothing had really changed. She laughed a little wildly, a little giddily.

The limo stopped in front of her row house. She scrambled from it without a backward glance and rushed inside, barely making it to the bathroom before she was ill.

Chapter 4

It took Angela the better part of a week to put the whole wedding fiasco behind her. She was angry at herself for running out, even as she knew she'd been incapable of doing anything else.

The Shokonnet case was a lost cause, but there were others that needed her attention. They kept her occupied, and by the following weekend, she felt like her old self. If there were vulnerabilities inside, if there were fears, then she buried them deeply enough that none of her colleagues knew they were there.

She did not encounter Jesse Hadley again. She made sure of it. Unfortunately, not seeing him did not mean that he was off her mind. So on Sunday morning, she jogged.

It always helped. The physical punishment, the thud of each of her steps on Philadelphia's concrete, tended to clear her head. She tuned everything out but the quivering strain of her muscles, focused on the labored burn of her breath. She pushed herself harder than was comfortable, and it was purging.

She headed west across Oregon Avenue toward the Italian Market, a significantly long run. Halfway there, she finally forgot—again—those few special moments in Jesse's arms. She forgot that, for a while, he had seemed to genuinely enjoy her company.

She forgot everything but Wendell Glowan's intrusion, because that was all that counted.

She ran on, and she thought about Jesse's eyes.

If he was high-handed and as purely arrogant as he seemed, how could he possibly have eyes like that? Then again, maybe they weren't as startling and as deep as she remembered. Maybe they *hadn't* backed up his every word with honest emotion. She'd been rattled at that wedding from start to finish. It was hard to tell, she decided, just how much of what she thought she'd seen had been real. It was impossible to say how much was simply a product of her imagination.

She reached the Italian Market and put him firmly out of her mind. Again.

She bought flowers and half a dozen perfect peppers. She found the deli vendor she liked best and got some excellent Genoa salami. She swigged a cup of coffee at a corner market and headed home.

She was just getting breathless when she reached her stoop. She snagged the newspaper as she bounded up the steps and thrust her key in the lock. Her phone was ringing. She hard it pealing even before she stepped into the foyer.

She hurried into the kitchen to grab it, opening the newspaper as she went, her purchases tucked under her arm. She scanned the headlines as she dropped everything on the breakfast bar and grabbed the phone. "Hello?"

"Jesse Hadley."

Something hot, then cold, scooted through her blood. It was a simple, unapologetic announcement of his identity. Not "good morning," no "hello to you, too." She thought he would have used the same tone if he had said, "This is God calling."

She put the paper down. She tucked the phone against her shoulder to bend over, her hands on her thighs, trying to get her breath. Her muscles were spent and twitching.

"What do you want?" she demanded.

There was a pause. "Did I interrupt something?"

Yes. My sanity. Every boring, mundane aspect of my life I've worked so hard to achieve and that I cherish. "No."

"You're breathing hard."

She decided to let him wonder about that. It was probably best all the way around if he didn't think she was available, if he thought that maybe he'd caught her in the midst of hot, lurid passion. The idea was so ludicrous, she gave a strangled laugh.

Not that she was his type anyway. Every time she'd seen his picture in the paper, he was with a starlet or a model, someone stunningly beautiful and—Angela had always thought privately—with drugged-out eyes.

"Are you angry?" he went on after a moment.

"More like resigned. I can't seem to get rid of you."

He hesitated, then ignored that. "You haven't seen the paper," he said, and it wasn't a question.

Angela straightened slowly. She looked over at it. "Why?" she asked warily.

"Check front and center."

It would have to be at the bottom half of front and centre, she concluded. She'd only looked at the top. She picked up the newspaper again and her breath snagged.

Negligence Charged In M.E.'s Office

She moved around to the other side of the breakfast bar and sat hard. "That's not true!" But as she said the words, they echoed in her head with a familiar ring. *Not true, I didn't. Not true.* She had said those same words fifteen years ago in a courtroom, too, and it hadn't done any good then, either.

Panic began to build inside her, old and habitual and not entirely reasonable.

"Negligence?" she retorted. "Who? With *what?* Nobody's charged me with anything!"

"They have now." His voice was flat. "Unofficially and only through the media, of course."

"What did I *do?*" she demanded tensely. She was too careful for anything to have gone wrong.

"Nothing."

Suddenly she was angry. "Hold on."

She slammed the receiver down on the breakfast bar. She hoped the cracking sound hurt his ear. She spread the newspaper flat and read fast and furiously.

It was the Shokonnet baby.

The report said that the case had fallen apart because she'd dropped the ball, had let the body go too soon. Specifically, a Detective Carlton O'Donnell was saying so. Her heart started hammering hard. She took a careful moment to stick a cup of water in the microwave and get control of herself, then she picked up the phone again.

"I didn't release that body," she said with exquisite calm and care. "*You* did. And who's Carlton O'Donnell? I've never heard of him!" Her voice started rising in spite of all her efforts.

"My point exactly," Jesse said. "Calm down."

She realized that he said that to her a lot. "Calm *down?*" she shouted, just to be contrary. "Someone's accusing me of something I had no part in!"

"I know. I have a copy of that release form, if you'll remember."

"With *your* signature on the bottom of it!"

"I had nothing to do with this," he said in that flat, cool tone that she was beginning to loathe. She'd much preferred his laughter when he was dancing with her.

Don't think about that.

"Angela," he said, and his voice changed, softening.

Something happened inside her, something ticklish like the time when he had admired her legs. He had never called her by her first name before.

She knew she had to correct him, but she couldn't find her voice. "What?" she demanded instead, her voice thin as a wire.

"I didn't sign that release form."

"Of course you did."

"No. I didn't." There was something unequivocal in his tone now. "I never use the initial *M,* and my name was signed with an *M.* Look at your own copy."

As though that alone made it true, she thought wildly. As though no one would dare doubt his word. They probably wouldn't.

"I don't have my copy here," she returned. "So just tell me what you're saying."

"Someone forged my signature."

"That's convenient," she snapped, wanting to believe him, unable to. "Why didn't you tell me this before? You let me blast you that day and you didn't say a word!"

He didn't answer. He didn't have to. She knew the reason. He was a Hadley. He wouldn't trust anyone with anything that could affect his position, his reputation. It occurred to her that that almost made it seem as if they had something in common. But why was he confiding in her now?

"On Thursday, I thought somebody was setting me up for a fall," he explained. "I would say, based on this article, that it's not me they're after."

"Then why are you getting involved?"

"Because I *am* involved."

That she could accept. He would cover his own backside. Nobody had forged *her* signature.

"I've already been in touch with the newspaper," Jesse went on. "The reporter claims that the leak came from O'Donnell himself. He allegedly told the reporter that he was upset because you'd released the body prior to any and all evidence being obtained, and now we can't possibly prosecute. Ergo—negligence."

"Who *is* this O'Donnell?"

"A new guy, just transferred from CAP to Homicide."

Crimes Against Persons. Okay. "How'd he get involved?" she persisted.

"He didn't," Jesse said flatly. "I've talked to him, too. He says he never spoke to the paper."

"So...who?" Her heart was beating hard again. "Who called the paper trying to make me look bad?"

"Someone who knows that O'Donnell caught the case." Jesse stated the obvious with reasonable patience. "Someone pretending to be him. Carper—the reporter—said the interview was done over the telephone. Nothing unusual in that, but he claims not to have taped it. I also have to wonder why he didn't interview you for your side of the story."

"Well, he didn't," she stated flatly.

She was in trouble, Angela thought sickly. And then she was furious.

She had done everything by the book for eight months! She had done a damned fine job! And now somebody, somewhere, was making up things to hang on her. Who? *Why?*

"The paper's going to print a retraction in tomorrow's edition," Jesse responded.

"What are they supposed to retract?" she snapped. "The Shokonnet baby *was* cremated."

"But no negligence has been charged."

"Oh, God," she said again. Jesse was silent. "Did you tell this Carper guy that it was *your* signature that was forged?"

"Of course not."

"You—"

His voice cracked back over the phone line, angry now. "We'd look like fools, damn it. I won't have the public knowing about this. I won't add fuel to the fire. I won't give the *Inquirer* another juicy tidbit to print."

"Spoken like a true politician," she mocked.

"What do you want from me, Angela? I *am* a politician." This time there was nothing gentle about his voice when he used her name.

"And this is an election year."

"Get off your high horse, damn it! You've got as much at stake here as I do."

She could feel his anger throbbing over the phone line. And then she realized that it didn't particularly frighten her, not in the way a simple glance at his uncle's face had frightened her. And that made her head swim all over again. It amazed her and alarmed her.

She did not want to trust him. She *couldn't.*

"So you want to sweep this dirt under the carpet?" she accused.

"Publicly? Yes. Privately, no. I'm working on it."

"Why?"

"What do you mean, *why?* Because I want to find out who the hell is doing this! It's my job."

"It's *my* problem." Her beeper sounded. It was probably her office, calling about this mess, but the timing was perfect. "I've got to go."

"Then call me back. We're not finished with this." He barked his phone number at her before she was ready for it. She didn't write it down.

"Good*bye,* Counselor. I'll deal with this myself." She hung up the phone hard.

After a long moment, she carefully got up to take her cup out of the microwave. She made her coffee. Her hands were shaking.

She sipped, then raked her fingers through her disheveled hair. Jesse had gotten the paper to print a retraction. She had a little bit of time to try to find out who would want to accuse her of something she hadn't done, and why. And she would do it on her own terms.

My God, she realized, even John Gunner was gone this time, off to Australia on his honeymoon. She was really on her own.

Her first hour at work on Monday revealed that no one in her office had spoken to a reporter named Carper. At least, she didn't think they had. She knew that she could expect the guilty party to lie, but there were no sliding glances, no telltale signs when she called a meeting of all her staff. Even Ed Thackery seemed perplexed by her questions, and of all her deputies, he was the one she would most suspect of trying to undermine her to get her job.

She didn't hear from Jesse again until the following Sunday morning. He called her at home again.

"Hear anything?" he asked. This time he didn't even identify himself.

She realized with a sinking heart that he didn't have to. She knew his voice now. And as soon as she heard it, her pulse rioted with far too many emotions for comfort. Alarm, certainly. Wariness and expectation. But the worst was pleasure.

It made her voice sharp. "About what?" she snapped, deliberately vague.

"Shokonnet. O'Donnell. Carper. Negligence." His voice was businesslike and abrupt. He might have been working his way through a list of to-do things on his desk, ticking them off.

"Nothing, Counselor," she said shortly. "Besides, I told you— it's not your problem."

"Like hell it's not," he argued.

Her beeper went off. She had never heard anything so sweet in her life. "I've got to go."

"Do you do that on purpose?"

"What?"

"Make that thing sound off whenever I'm talking to you."

"There's a thought." She disconnected before he could answer. She collected herself, made sure her breathing was even, then she dialed her office.

He got to her, she realized. He really got to her.

"Medical examiner's office," a thin male voice answered. Ed Thackery. Well, wasn't this her day? She wondered why he was handling phones. She wondered where the dispatcher was. Another Sunday zoo, she thought. Everything happened on weekends when people were partying, drinking and driving, fighting with their spouses and friends. The hospital ERs got them on Saturday night and passed them on to her office on Sunday morning.

"It's Dr. Byerly," she answered. "What's going on?"

There was a deliberate pause. She'd come under fire for using the professional title among her own colleagues. But she'd known that she was going to have a hard enough time garnering respect—being a thirty-six-year-old female—without making it easy for anyone by allowing them to chat with her on a first-name basis. Ed didn't like it. He never had.

"Well, *Doc*, we've got a hot one on our hands," he answered finally. "Figured you might want to handle it yourself."

No, Angela thought with a sigh, if it's that hot, he doesn't want to touch it for fear of something going wrong and besmirching his own reputation. For one dismal, horrible moment, she tried to remember what it had been like, long ago, to trust people.

"It's Lisette Chauncy," Ed went on.

The name rang a bell. "Who is she?"

"Macademy Steel? Railroads?" Ed's voice was almost but not quite sneering as he refreshed her memory. "Daughter of Gwen and Abe Chauncy? He's the big daddy patron saint of the Pennsylvania Academy of Fine Arts."

The floor seemed to shift beneath Angela's feet. "Oh, my God." The woman at the wedding two weeks ago, she remembered. The woman she and Jesse had been laughing about....

Angela shot a hand out, bracing herself against the breakfast bar. The M.E.'s office performed maybe eight thousand autopsies a year. But not once, not yet, had she been forced to look down into the still and lifeless face of someone she had known or met while they were alive.

"How?" she asked, her voice faint.

"I don't know the details. The Homicide guys are on their way up there now. They're waiting for one of us to come do our thing."

"Call them back and tell them I'm on my way."

"Better you than me, Chief. Big Daddy Chauncy is screaming for justice."

Angela didn't doubt it. And being who he was, he *would* get it.

She wrote down the address and went to get her bag.

Jesse was as angry as he could remember being in a good, long while. And that in itself amazed him—the slow, hot burn of temper in the pit of his stomach. Irritation he was familiar with—he felt that often. But at no time in recent memory had anyone ever dared to make him truly angry.

Trust this woman to do the job.

He'd extended a helping hand, and she had slapped it. Dr. Angela Byerly had a major attitude problem, he decided. He didn't know what bone she thought she had to pick with his uncle, but it was paranoid and prejudiced of her to hold it against him. The hell of it was, Wendell didn't know what bone she had to pick, either. Jesse had asked him about it. Wendell didn't remember ever having laid eyes on Angela Byerly before in his life.

Which should have been enough, Jesse figured, for him to put the crazy doctor out of his mind. It was possible she was unstable. He looked again at the unbelievable hat sitting beside him on his desk. He'd rescued it from the veranda when she'd fled without it. No stable woman he knew would ever wear such a thing.

It really was the most atrocious piece of feminine attire he had ever seen in his life. And he could still see it on her, her blond curls tumbling beneath it.

"Damn it," he said aloud.

Granted, he had phoned her on a reasonably flimsy pretext. The Shokonnet case was getting colder and colder as the weeks went by. Homicide had put the file aside. There was really nothing either he or Angela could do now but tighten security and make sure that such a thing didn't happen again. It had, no doubt, been nothing more than a prank by someone disgruntled over her hiring. The days since then had been quiet.

Still, it continued to bother him. Someone had gone to a lot of trouble to disparage one or both of them, swiping a blank release form, then contacting the press.

His phone suddenly rang again, startling him, breaking into his thoughts. He reached to answer it, smiling to himself. A point in her favor. It hadn't taken her long to come to her senses and call back.

"Jesse Hadley," he answered.

"It's Roger Kennery."

Jesse blinked, feeling disappointment swell inside him. And that was new and unwelcome, too.

"Roger," he said carefully. "What's up?"

The man was the captain of the homicide unit of the P.P.D. He was someone else Jesse rarely encountered in person. He spoke to Kennery on the phone when a case demanded it, but they rarely met face-to-face.

In the same moment, Jesse registered that Kennery's purpose couldn't be good if the man was calling him at home on a Sunday morning.

"Something's happened up in Chestnut Hill," the captain answered. "I thought you might want to be notified on this one right out of the starting gate. In fact, given that your sister is out of town on her honeymoon, I'm on my way up there personally. I'm calling from my car phone."

Jesse considered what he didn't say. This was obviously one of those cases that Kennery unabashedly threw his sister's way because of her family connections. Tessa might be a Hadley, but to their parents' great chagrin, she was also a damned fine homicide detective. Her husband was the maverick of the Homicide Unit, but he was one of the best the P.P.D. had to offer. They'd been partners before they got married, when protocol demanded that they be reassigned.

"Money involved?" Jesse guessed. "Political clout?"

"Chauncy clout," Kennery clarified.

Jesse stared at the wall, not assimilating the captain's reply. "I beg your pardon?"

"Lisette Markham Chauncy," Kennery repeated. "Her maid found her at nine-fifteen this morning when she didn't come down for breakfast."

The room seemed to tilt.

"She's *dead? Lisette?*" Jesse shot to his feet only to sit down again hard. He had the absurd notion that at least now he knew why Angela's beeper had been sounding off while he'd been speaking to her. "Dead?" he repeated.

And then an unpleasant sensation swept over him. A cold, clammy feeling of guilt. He had talked so disparagingly of the woman the last time he had seen her.

"Murdered?" he asked, his voice strangled. What a stupid question, he thought immediately. Of course it was murder, or Kennery wouldn't be calling him.

Lisette? Mousy, harmless, husband-hunting Lisette?

"Like I said, I'm on my way there now," Kennery replied. "Thought you'd want to know."

"Thanks. I'll...uh, I'll meet you there." Jesse hung up.

He was shaken enough that he didn't think about Angela again until he pulled into Lisette Chauncy's driveway. The dark green coroner's van that always gave him the willies was already parked there. Jesse got out of his Mercedes, feeling vaguely ashamed.

In spite of the shocking circumstances, he was actually looking forward to seeing her again.

Chapter 5

Angela was having a hard time maintaining her emotional equilibrium on this one. It wasn't just that she had glimpsed the victim—however briefly—striding across a lawn only two weeks before. It was more that something about this whole crime scene was so profoundly sad. She suspected that Lisette Chauncy was enjoying a great deal more attention now than she had ever had when she was alive.

The detectives along with the lab and forensics staff worked in the woman's bedroom without any of the off-color and grim jokes that usually accompanied their procedures. No one wanted to make a mistake here, she observed. There would be no oversights on this one.

Angela schooled her own expression into professional curiosity as she watched, but everything inside her was cringing. She had been out running again before Jesse, then Ed, had called. She kept her hands deep in the pockets of her sweatpants so no one would notice if they trembled.

She thought she was putting on a pretty good show of cool practicality until Jesse Hadley walked into the room.

Her breath left her. Her pulse slammed. What was he doing here? He *never* showed up at crime scenes.

Then again, this victim was a Chauncy, and a personal friend to boot.

"Doctor," Jesse said, stopping beside her. Just as though they had not argued on the phone just an hour or so earlier.

She dragged air in and managed to give him little more than a curt nod. Inside, she scrambled to regain her composure.

She wouldn't look at him, but it didn't matter. He smelled good, and he was close enough that she couldn't avoid realizing it. This was crazy, she thought helplessly. She was at a *murder* scene. She was upset and striving mightily not to show it. And all she could think of in that moment was that he smelled like something dark and strong and mystifying. Something tantalizing that actually made her want to lean closer and breathe it in.

She couldn't quite put her finger on the scent and knew that even if he told her the name of it, she probably wouldn't recognize it. It would be something expensive and exclusive.

She felt him staring at her and swallowed carefully.

Jesse was thinking that she was the most improbable-looking chief medical examiner he had ever encountered. He had no doubt that if anyone here didn't know who she was, they would ask her to leave the room. No colorful, short dresses this time—they had been hard enough to accept, especially in light of her position. This morning, her hair was caught up at the crown of her head with some stretchy, elastic, purple thing. From that point downward, it spilled wildly to her shoulders. She wore no makeup. She had on gray sweatpants that clung loosely to her bottom and thighs, running shoes with no socks—glimpses of skin peeked out at her ankles—and a loose T-shirt that had been cut off at the waist. The front of it was emblazoned with some artwork depicting a Grateful Dead concert.

She looked innocent and fresh-faced and naive. Only her expression belied the image. Her jaw was clamped tightly enough to hurt *him.*

"Well?" he asked finally. He didn't want to know and had to ask. "Where's Lisette?"

"She's already in my van."

Thank God. He didn't think he could have endured encountering her body. He drove his hands into his jeans pockets in case they might reveal his agitation.

"Did you talk to her parents?" Angela asked after an awkward moment. From downstairs, she could hear the aggrieved shouts of Abe Chauncy and the steady, heart-wrenching sobs of Gwen, the woman's mother.

"Certainly."

"And?"

"They want blood, and they want it yesterday."

"Of course." She hesitated. "Captain Kennery thinks it was someone she knew. I'd have to agree with him."

Jesse's heart skipped. "You've got to be kidding."

Her pretty face hardened again. "Meaning that the people she knew don't kill each other? *Any*one can be incited to murder under the right circumstances, Counselor."

He was quiet for a moment, acknowledging that without words. "So what happened exactly?" he asked.

Angela took a careful breath. "She was found sitting—propped up, actually—in bed. She was wearing a lavender silk negligee. Her mother swears Lisette never owned anything even remotely like it, but it's always been my experience that mothers don't generally know that sort of thing. It's still on her, of course, but I'll bag it for the lab. It looked expensive, exclusive. Maybe Homicide can find out where it came from."

Jesse nodded.

Angela didn't like telling the next part. It was what bothered her most of all. "There was a box of chocolate-covered strawberries on the bed beside her. One was missing. I'll be able to tell you later whether she ate it, or if perhaps her killer did."

Jesse's stomach squirmed. He couldn't immediately answer, and didn't want to envision how she would find out.

"There was also an opened bottle of champagne on her bedside table, half-empty."

Jesse finally swore.

"I wasn't able to find any wounds whatsoever except the gunshot," she went on with deliberate dispassion. "The bullet shattered her left temporal parietal skull and exited the other side. That's what they're looking for there." She nodded at a group of cops searching the opposite side of the room.

Jesse thought about that. "Her *cheek?*"

"The side of her head," she corrected. "Probably the bullet was meant for her temple, and she tried to avoid it at the last possible moment." She had to close her eyes then, although that was almost worse. She could still see the woman as they had found her. "That was the only sign that she had even remotely put up a fight. From the angle of the shot, I think her killer would have to have been seated on the bed beside her."

That did it. Jesse left abruptly, veering to the bathroom.

She stared after him, bemused. When he came back, he looked pale.

"She had more fun just before dying than she ever had in her life," he said hoarsely, a halfhearted explanation.

Angela nodded helplessly.

He tunneled his fingers through his hair. He'd done all he could do here, Jesse realized, and he knew he should leave. For the sake of his own psyche, if nothing else. He'd done damage control with the press gathered outside, giving them one of the brief and none-too-informative statements they hated. He'd spoken soothingly and righteously to Lisette's parents. He'd done all the things a good D.A. was supposed to do before he actually got down to the business of making a case with the evidence. And he couldn't do that part of his job until it began trickling into his office.

He looked down at Angela again, and he didn't move.

"Now what?" he asked. "What happens next?"

"Now I take her back to the morgue as soon as I make sure there's nothing else going on here that I need to know about."

"Will you call me as soon as you're through?"

Angela hesitated, but this was business. She glanced at him briefly. "Okay."

"I'll be at home."

"I never wrote down your number."

No, he thought, she wouldn't have. He wasn't sure if he was irritated or—in spite of everything—amused.

He went back into the upstairs hall, to a small cherry table he'd seen there. It had already been checked and dusted for prints. Everything in the house would be, before this morning was over, whether it seemed likely that the killer had touched it or not.

The center drawer had been left open. Jesse spotted a pad of paper and a fountain pen and took them out, touching nothing else. He held the pad up to the light to make sure that there were no indentations remaining from the last sheet that had been written upon. When he found nothing, he scribbled his number and returned to Lisette's bedroom.

He slipped the piece of paper directly into the pocket of Angela's sweatpants. "Don't lose it."

She jolted when his fingers skimmed her hip. Then a sensation of warmth flooded through her. He left the room. She stepped into the doorway and stared after him, shaken.

His stride was long, arrogant, confident. His black hair was vaguely windblown. Her legs went a little weak. How did the man manage to get to her this way?

The closer he got, the more he touched her, the more he scared her.

Jesse stopped in the living room to talk to Roger Kennery before he left, and a few moments later she trotted down the stairs. She looked like a high-school cheerleader headed for practice.

She paused to speak to one of the lab technicians. Then she tossed her ponytail and went out the door.

If she didn't call him later, he would find her. He figured that between Lisette and the Shokonnet thing, he had plenty of reasons now to contact her. What he couldn't quite fathom was his growing need to keep doing so.

"What?" he asked sharply, looking back at Roger Kennery. "I'm sorry, I didn't hear you."

"Over here." Kennery thrust a thumb over his shoulder in the direction of a small study on the other side of the entry hall. "There's something you need to hear."

Jesse followed him, not liking the tone of the man's voice. A lab technician went with them. Kennery took a latex glove from the man and stepped up to an answering machine. He pulled the glove on, hit a button, and Jesse stared at the thing disbelievingly as his own voice filled the room.

"Lisette. Sorry I wasn't able to catch up with you at the wedding. I'll visit later tonight, if you'll be around."

Jesse felt his blood drain. "I didn't call her."

Kennery raised a brow. "Actually, I have a hard time believing you would, given your well-documented taste in exceptionally good-looking women."

"That's not me," Jesse repeated, scarcely hearing him.

"Oh, it's you all right," Kennery replied.

"*I didn't call her!*" He realized belatedly that he had shouted.

He worked to get a grip on himself. But the implications of what he had just heard throbbed in his head along with his pulse, making him feel sick all over again.

Kennery plucked the tape out of the machine and gave it to the technician to bag. "I'm sending it to Audio."

Jessed nodded slowly.

"I've encountered this before," Kennery explained. "It's a snap to do with the right equipment. Take snippets of other tapes—a word here, a word there—and splice them together to make the voice say what you want it to say. Then record *that* onto still another tape that's not been spliced. At first glance it looks legitimate. In fact, it takes equally specialized equipment to determine that it's *not* genuine, but we've got it and we'll do it."

Jesse's head was spinning. His anger was building. Had *someone* tried to frame him? Had *someone* killed a pathetic, defenseless woman in order to get to him? Guilt made his skin crawl.

"Or it could have been the other way around," Kennery mused, as though reading his mind. "Maybe someone killed her for their own twisted pleasure, then decided to throw the blame your way."

Jesse thought of the Shokonnet thing. Suddenly, he had a strong hunch that these two incidents were connected. Somehow. Except given the supposed report of negligence turned into the press the Shokonnet thing had probably been aimed at Angela Byerly. This time someone clearly wanted a piece of him.

What the hell was going on here?

"No," he said sharply. "They killed her in *order* to throw the blame my way. I just haven't figured out why yet." He went to the hall again and looked outside. The avid press was still gathered there. He swore succinctly. "Who else knows about this?"

"You, me and that lab kid," Kennery said.

"It can't get out."

"That goes without saying. I'll talk to the lab, keep it quiet."

It wouldn't work, Jesse thought. People talked, if only among themselves. His mouth crooked into a bitter smile. "Maybe somebody's on my side."

"What?" Kennery asked, startled.

Jesse didn't answer, but he thought it would be damned hard to win a mayoral election with something like this hanging around his neck. Unfortunately, it would be equally difficult to take the district attorney slot. He could run for mayor without currently sitting in the District Attorney's position, but he would lose a big advantage over his opponent. Especially with the specter of murder hanging over his head.

His expression grim, he started for the door.

"Where are you going?" Kennery asked.

"My office." *Tapes of his voice.* There were only two places where they could be found. His office, and that little dictating recorder he kept in his briefcase.

Then he would find Angela Byerly again. In spite of the way she turned him upside down, he realized suddenly that he had need of her brain.

He could very well be in deep trouble.

Angela left the refrigerated autopsy room and headed for her office, shivering slightly. She'd dictated her findings onto tape, but she wanted to jot down a few of her more vague impressions while they were still fresh in her mind. They had no place in an official report, but by the same token, they might prove important later.

She turned into her office and stopped dead.

This time, she couldn't have avoided the reaction for all the tea in China. Her mouth dropped open and her pulse rate soared. If Jesse rarely appeared at crime scenes, then he had *never* showed up in her morgue before.

"I'm really having a hard time avoiding you these days," she said when she finally found her voice.

He'd been sitting with one hip on her desk, leafing through a forensics magazine he'd found on top. He put it down and pushed to his feet, then crossed slowly toward her where she stood rooted in the doorway.

"I need you, Doctor."

"I beg your pardon?" Her heart jolted up into her throat. She stared at him disbelievingly. For a minute, she thought he actually blushed.

"I need your help," he clarified, then he scowled. "What's all that?"

She'd already pushed her hood back as soon as she'd left the autopsy room. It tended to be hot and confining, but she couldn't risk any of her own hair or skin cells mingling with what the victim carried. She took her face shield off, as well, along with a pair of orange-tinted glasses.

"It's a big, bad world out there, Counselor," she answered, wondering why she felt like laughing at his expression. He looked utterly horrified and not at all arrogant or confident at the moment.

"I don't follow you."

"AIDS. Tuberculosis. Meningitis. Hepatitis. Shall I go on?" She held up the glasses. "As for these, they help me see in non-light."

He recovered a little. "You're worried about all that with Lisette? AIDS and whatnot? That's who you were working on, right?"

Angela nodded and moved carefully around him to sit at her desk. She removed the rest of her protective equipment and laid it all neatly atop her blotter. "You of all people should know that nothing is ever really the way it seems," she responded. "Even the Lisettes of this world sometimes have secret lives we'd never guess at. I can't take chances."

"No. I guess not." He had, in fact, never thought about it until now. His job had never entailed risking his health or his life. He wasn't sure how willing he'd be to do it if it did, and that shamed him a little.

Shame was something he hadn't experienced in too many years to count. He did what he had to, and he assumed he did it pretty well.

"So what did you find out?" he asked at length. "About Lisette?"

She hesitated. "It was an exceptionally clean job. She was killed by someone who took a great deal of care not to leave much of himself—or herself—behind."

Jesse sat on the edge of her desk again. Too close, she thought, and had to fight not to roll her chair back.

"So you don't know *anything?*" he asked.

Angela shook her head fretfully. "I didn't say that. The Magic Beam—"

"The what?" he interrupted. "Oh, the cable." It *was* a piece of technological magic. Using fiber optics, it could see things the human eye would never possibly find. In utter darkness—the non-light she'd mentioned—it gave fingerprints a fluorescent glow and made things like fibers and saliva light up like neon.

Angela nodded. "It picked up a single hair between the third and fourth fingers of her left hand. I bagged them—her hands—so it made it over here intact and in place."

His gut clenched. "Whose?"

"Pardon me?"

"Whose hair was it?"

She gave him an incredulous look. "There's no way I can know that at this point."

Jesse almost flushed again. "So let me rephrase my question. What *kind* of hair?"

"Head hair. Reasonably short—two and a half inches long. Black."

For a moment, the air seemed to leave the room. Jesse couldn't breathe. "*Damn* it," he growled, pushing to his feet again.

"What?" Angela asked, alarmed by his tone.

"What else did you find?" he demanded without answering.

"Not much at all. She was neat as a pin except for the holes in her head."

He flinched at the images that brought to mind.

"She wasn't sexually assaulted," she went on. "In fact..." It was her turn to wince. She covered her face with her hands. Part of her fought to cover her emotion again with some cold and professional facade, and another part couldn't see the point in bothering. It was just Jesse now.

And that feeling floored her.

There was nothing "just" about Jesse Hadley. There was no reason, no sanity at all, in trusting him with her emotions.

"What?" he demanded harshly.

"She was a virgin," she managed to reply.

"Oh, God," he muttered. And in that moment, he was not even a little bit arrogant. In that moment, his expressive green eyes showed a wealth of regret, sorrow, pity.

Their emotions moved her even as she told herself she was a fool to allow it.

"I know," Angela whispered. "It got to me, too. She never even had the chance to be in love with someone." And that had touched her deeply, personally.

"Anything else?" he asked hoarsely. "Anything else I should know about?"

Angela gave him a quick glance and shrugged. "She was the one who ate the strawberry that was missing, and she died mere minutes afterward. She'd also had a good bit of that champagne. Depending upon her body's familiarity with alcohol—and based on the condition of her internal organs, I'd have to say that it was minimal—she consumed enough to make her drowsy and uninhibited, less capable of putting up a defense, maybe even less likely to have realized that a defense was even needed until the danger was right on top of her."

Jesse noticed that her voice had become clipped, short, precise. Void of emotion. And he knew that it would have to be that way for her, that she would have to pull her heart back into some remote place inside herself to do what she did for a living. A part of him hurt for her, though her profession was her own choice.

"Other than that," she continued, and he forced himself to follow what she was saying, "there was absolutely nothing. Cause of death was the gunshot, of course."

"Do you know if they found the bullet?" he demanded.

"They hadn't when I left. It's possible that it didn't imbed in the wall or any furniture, and the killer was able to retrieve it. In fact, it's looking like that was the case."

"What did you do with the hair?"

She scowled at him, at the quick pace of his questions. "I've got it packaged to send out for DNA testing."

"It's mine."

She couldn't possibly have heard him right. She stared at him.

"It's probably going to turn out to be mine," he repeated grimly.

She shot out of her chair, horrified, backing up until her spine hit the wall behind her. "What are you saying?"

It struck him then, belatedly, that he was entrusting her with something a hell of a lot more explosive this time than the fact that he didn't want to run for mayor. He was giving her information that could blow the entire Hadley empire sky-high—or at least rock it off its neat foundations for a time. And she didn't like the Hadleys.

He'd been doing it instinctively, without conscious thought, which was not how he ever did things at all. This woman was making him act in ways he hardly believed possible. Or maybe she just elicited a hidden, repressed part of himself. That possibility disturbed him.

Whatever was happening, it felt right to trust her. He thought she would be open-minded, fair, even righteous, with any atrocity that landed in her lap. He remembered her idealistic speech about SIDS that first day. If something was wrong, he knew innately that this woman would do whatever she could to fix it, to set it right.

He rubbed at his growing headache and told her about the tape Kennery had found in Lisette's recorder. She'd find out about that through other channels anyway.

When he was done, she only continued to stare at him.

"I stopped by my office on my way here," he added. "Maybe half a dozen of my dictation tapes are missing. We keep them for thirty days as backup to our computer records. It's my office's version of your protective mask there."

Angela's gaze went blankly to her equipment. "Protection?" she whispered after a moment.

"In the event that someone says I did or ordered something that I didn't do or order."

"I see."

"Someone stole those tapes from my office to make another tape, one that made it sound as though I was going to Lisette's last night to...well, to arrange an amorous meeting, so to speak."

Angela recovered. A bit. "Lisette had to know when her killer got there that he wasn't you." Then she wondered why she believed so implicitly that he *hadn't* killed the woman. So he was the D.A.—so what? Stranger things had happened. Greater power than his had been abused.

It was just her instincts. His eyes said he was innocent.

"One would think so," Jesse answered neutrally. "I've known her all my life. Unless the tape was planted afterward and she never even heard it."

Angela pushed away from the wall and began pacing. "No. I don't think so. There's that champagne. Now I have to wonder if it was *hers*." Her mind was racing. "Maybe the killer didn't get her tipsy. Maybe she was *already* tipsy. Try this. She was out somewhere, came home, found that message. So she popped open a bottle of bubbly because she was excited, or—" she waved a hand expressively ''—or maybe she was getting in a soft, romantic mood, something that might not come naturally to a woman like her. So she drank it before her killer even turned up. When he got there, Lisette was already too intoxicated to do anything about the fact that it wasn't you. Or maybe she didn't care.''

''Thanks,'' he muttered.

She looked at him, surprised, then a smile flicked across her face, so fast he almost missed it. ''Sorry, Romeo. It works. If she didn't get a lot of male attention, she might have been grateful for any guy coming along.''

''This is assuming she heard the tape.''

''Right. Except I'd think that if she was expecting you, and someone else turned up, that might have alarmed her.''

He gave her a pained smile. ''Maybe she thought she'd hit a bonanza. Maybe she thought he'd just stopped by, and I would be coming by later. Two for the price of one.''

Angela groaned. ''We'll probably never know.'' Her inference was clear. Lisette was the only one who could tell them that.''

This was exactly why he had come to her. She was intuitive. She was creative and brilliant. Her mind picked up where his currently felt incapable of going on. ''Why did you take this job?'' he asked suddenly.

She scowled at him. ''We've already been through that.''

''No. *This* job. The FBI is a pretty lofty employer.''

''Oh. That.''

He grinned, enjoying her discomfiture. It distracted him for a moment. ''Yeah, that.''

She flushed. ''The federal budget is even worse than the city's. I'm paid more here. And I have more authority, more control over my own domain.'' She hesitated. ''What does that have to do with anything?''

Money, he reflected. Authority and control. Interesting priorities. God, she intrigued him. He wouldn't have thought such things important to the kind of woman she appeared to be on the surface.

''I really admire the way you think,'' he answered finally.

She flushed again. She turned away quickly so he wouldn't see it. It was bad enough that he touched off reaction in her. She was damned if she was going to let him know it.

''Is it connected?'' she asked hoarsely, as much to change the subject as anything else. "This and what someone's trying to do to me with the Shokonnet case?"

"I can't imagine how." He'd been thinking about it. "Can you?"

She shook her head, her ponytail swirling from side to side. "No. I mean, why would anyone go after *both* of us? We had no earthly reason to connect closely until the Shokonnet thing happened. *That* was what linked us." She yanked the band out of her hair, tried to run her fingers through it and failed. She gave up, swearing. "Unless someone's trying to bring down the entire criminal justice system of Philadelphia," she mused aloud. "You know, knock me out, then you. Maybe the police commissioner's next. Wouldn't that be wild?"

"No," Jesse said flatly. "It wouldn't be my idea of a fine party."

But his pulse kicked. That, too, was something he hadn't considered, and he was impressed with her all over again.

"If the DNA matches yours on that hair," she went on, "then the killer must have planted it. But how could he have gotten your hair?"

"Any number of places. People shed, Doctor. You know that."

"I'll check her hand again for fingerprints. I'll look closer. In order to have placed it there, he would have to have had some contact with her."

"I'd guess he wore gloves if you didn't notice prints the first time around. The beam would certainly have picked them up."

But he was touched at how ferocious she sounded, how determined she was to go back and find something that would exonerate him. He had been right about trusting her.

"I'll look again," she repeated stubbornly. Then she let out her breath. "But the killer really didn't leave much behind at all."

"Could he have worn a hood of some sort?"

Her fingers plucked fretfully at the one at her neck. "Could be. Makes sense. But I'd think that would have frightened her sooner."

"As for *my* hair..." He thought of the one of hers that had clung to his lapel on Saturday. "It could have come from one of my suit coats, my hairbrush, my pillow, anywhere."

"You're thinking this guy was in your *house?*"

"Could be. He was in my office," he returned grimly. "Those tapes were locked in my secretary's filing cabinet."

Angela hugged herself. She didn't want to ask, and it had to be asked. *She* had to know. She believed him so instinctively, and that wouldn't, couldn't be good.

"Where were you last night?" she asked quietly.

"Home."

"Alone?"

"Of course, alone. The household staff had the night off. They're generally off from Saturday evening until Monday morning, unless I give a party or some event. And I don't like them living in. As for the woman I've been seeing, she ran off to Milan with another man, and my bedroom hardly has a revolving door."

He didn't seem the least bit upset by the woman's defection, Angela observed, only that she had asked. Was he that cold, that shallow?

She couldn't think about that now. "Did you drink anything?" she persisted.

"Drink?"

"Alcohol, Counselor."

"Oh." He looked nonplussed. "I had a little brandy right after dinner."

He was big, tall, she calculated. His body could certainly handle that without fuss. "How much is a little?" she asked to be sure.

"One snifter." Suddenly his jaw dropped. "You're thinking that I *blacked out?* That I don't *remember* killing her?"

She shot him a hard look. "It had to be asked. Besides, if that hair is yours, and there's no alcohol content to the root, then it *had* to have been planted if you drank last night. It would have to have been taken from you at some other time. We can check for that."

He let his breath out. In truth, he would have thought less of her if it hadn't occurred to her. Then he shook his head. "It won't fly in court."

"Why not?" Then she understood. "Your staff of domestic help wasn't working. So nobody actually *saw* you drink that brandy. It's only your word that says you consumed it. Oh, God, Jesse."

She said his name on a gasp, and in spite of his dire predicament, it made his skin rise into something like gooseflesh. "My sentiments exactly," he replied wryly.

Angela closed her eyes. There was another question she had to ask, and she couldn't believe she was actually going to do it. But it was another instinct, and asking didn't necessarily mean that she would follow through on his dictates. She just had to...know.

"What do you want me to do with that hair?"

He stared at her, then his jaw went rock hard. "What are you asking me, Doctor?"

I'm trying to figure out what you're made of. "I just...need to know where you stand on this."

"Neck-deep in alligators comes to mind."

Incredibly, she felt another smile try to pull at her mouth. "That's true."

"You have no choice but to send it out," he snapped angrily.

"No, I really don't."

"So do it."

Angela couldn't believe how relieved she was, how thoroughly, inordinately relieved. His uncle would have seen to it that that hair got lost. She uncurled her hands from the fists she had made of them and couldn't imagine why it should matter to her so much whether Jesse Hadley was honest or not. She couldn't imagine why it should matter so much that his response made her tremble.

Jesse raked a hand through his black hair. "Send it," he repeated. "It'll take at least six weeks for the results to come back, right?"

"Right. Probably eight if I don't put a push on it."

"Would you be adverse to doing that, to giving me some time?" he asked carefully.

She wanted to stiffen and couldn't. What he said made all the sense in the world. And she never put a push on things anyway unless her office or the P.P.D. was breathing down her neck for some reason. Perfect, comprehensive work took time. The faster the lab worked, the more mistakes were possible.

"No, I wouldn't." She sighed. "That's fine."

"So theoretically I've got six to eight weeks to get to the bottom of this," Jesse muttered.

"Yes. As long as the killer didn't leave any other little goodies lying around, anything that would point another finger at you."

This was ludicrous, impossible. It overwhelmed him that they were discussing it, that it was even happening to *be* discussed.

"You said he *didn't* leave any other goodies."

"Not at my end," she answered honestly. "There was just that one hair. But I don't know what all they found at her house after I left."

Jesse shook his head. If there had been more than that answering-machine tape, Kennery would have told him.

"So..." She let out a deep breath. "Assuming there's nothing else I can do for you, I'm going home." She gathered her equipment from her desk again. "I'll let you know, of course, as soon as I get any lab results back."

"There is one other thing," he said suddenly.

Something about his tone had changed. She looked at him, surprised then wary. "What?"

"Have dinner with me."

She dropped everything. In one moment, she had it piled neatly in her arms, and in the next, the mask slipped. She hitched a shoulder and moved her arm to try to catch it, and everything else followed, clattering to the floor.

"Put on something incredibly lovely," he went on anyway, "and—"

"I don't have anything incredibly lovely," she interrupted, frantic.

He thought of fake carnations and turquoise shoes. "So buy something."

She inched backward until her bottom hit the desk. "Why are you doing this?"

"Inviting you to dinner?"

She nodded spasmodically. For a second, she couldn't find her voice.

"I'm not interested," she lied, and wondered if her face looked as hot as it felt. "Is that what you came here for?" she demanded, trying to get back the upper hand. "Was all this stuff about Lisette and the hair a...a...?"

His face hardened. "It was a request for information. Trust me, I don't have to come up with excuses to see a woman. If I want to, I ask. I'm asking."

Her head hitched. *"Why?"*

"What *is* it, Angela? Why the hell are you so leery of me?"

She didn't answer. There were too many answers to allow her to give him any single one. She shook her head, feeling lost and confused.

"Look," he said slowly, "it's been a horrible day. It's been a pretty bad couple of *weeks*. Someone besides me released that Shokonnet kid's body—"

"So you say," she countered desperately.

Jesse swore. "All right. Forget Shokonnet. Someone's trying to frame me for murder."

She made a strangled sound.

"I'm scared," he admitted. "And I'm very, very angry. They killed a woman I've known all my life. They did it in an exceptionally cruel way, preying on the poor woman's weaknesses. She's in there—" He thrust a thumb toward the hallway that led to the autopsy rooms "—and I don't even want to know what condition she's in right now. This is *ugly*. It's more inherently painful than anything I've had to deal with in a long while. And I don't have a flowered dress."

As soon as the words were out of his mouth, he knew that that was exactly why he wanted this dinner. Angela Byerly—and her dresses and shoes and hats—shook up his cold, orderly world. He needed desperately to be distracted for a while. And no one could do that quite like this woman seemed to.

"Please," he said more quietly.

"I can't," she managed to respond helplessly.

"We'll go somewhere where the lighting is low. And candles. I need civility and good wine. I want to go somewhere where people talk quietly and no one gets killed. I need to balance this mess, Angela. And you're available. Aren't you?"

She let out a choked sound of laughter. "At least you're honest."

"In most cases, and always with myself." He moved toward the door. "I'll pick you up at seven."

"You don't even know where I live."

"I can find out. My limo picked you up the day of the wedding."

"I can't—" she began again.

The sound of the door closing cut her off.

She had to run after him. She had to tell him no. It wasn't just him. It wasn't just that she had learned never to get too chummy with any man she didn't fully intend to sleep with. It wasn't just that.

She didn't trust herself. Even if she *wanted* to get to know him better, spend time with him, she knew that disaster would follow.

She had to catch him and straighten this out. She stood rooted to the spot.

Chapter 6

There was a good fifteen minutes' worth of voice mail waiting for him when Jesse got home. As he began to listen to it, tension tightened his muscles again. He heard Angela's voice. As long as the killer didn't leave any other little goodies lying around...

But none of the calls were from Kennery or the P.P.D. Most of them were from social acquaintances expressing horror at what had happened to Lisette, but probably, Jesse supposed, just wanting the inside scoop from the D.A. himself. The only call he returned was his mother's, and that was more from a sense of obligation than anything else.

"Horrible!" Isobel cried. "I just shudder. Poor Abe. Poor Gwen."

"Poor Lisette," Jesse murmured, suddenly tired.

"Do you want the guest list?"

"What guest list?"

"Lisette was *here* for the wedding. And all those horrid people..."

"And you think one of *them* killed her?" he asked incredulously.

"Where else would poor Lisette encounter the sort of person who would...who would do what was done to her?"

Crazily, out of the blue, he heard Angela's voice yet again. *Meaning that the people she knew don't kill each other? Anyone can be incited to murder....*

"I tried to do right by your sister," Isobel complained, "but I don't understand why she insists upon doing the things she does with her life."

Going to the Police Academy after law school had been the worst of it, Jesse reflected. Isobel had still been recovering from that when Tessa had gone to work for the police department and married a detective named Matt Bryant. Then a year and a half after she'd been widowed, she'd married Gunner, another detective.

"Most of those people Gunner invited were *cops,*" Jesse stated levelly.

"Well, of course, but that doesn't preclude—"

"Goodbye, Mother." He took a page from Angela's book and hung up quickly.

He wasn't sure why he was so aggravated with his mother. She had not behaved any differently than she ever did. She had been lamenting Tessa's choice in men for years. But today she made him feel a little wild, as if he would actually enjoy punching something.

Sweatpants and a Grateful Dead T-shirt popped into his mind, as though by way of explanation. That shook him a little, too. But he couldn't deny that the contrast between Angela's volatile idealism and Isobel's icy propriety was great.

He reached for his briefcase, deliberately clearing his mind. He worked for a while, dictating and sorting through paperwork. Then he went upstairs to shower and change. By the time he came down again, his footsteps were moderately lighter.

He drove his Mercedes to the garage where he kept his cars. Society Hill didn't leave much room for parking. And even there, if he left a car long enough at the curb, he would eventually find it missing pieces.

He changed the Mercedes for the old Cobra, telling himself that it had nothing to do with the fact that something about Hadley money seemed to set Angela off. It had nothing to do with the fact that the Cobra was a quirky car that was due for a paint job and needed a few hard-to-find parts, while the Mercedes was new and all Hadley elegance. The Cobra was a hobby car, all rumbling power, and he told himself that the growl of the engine matched his mood.

Except his mood continued to lighten the farther south he drove. He grew more and more confused, as well. He was surprised by Angela's neighborhood. He knew that she could also afford to live in Society Hill if she chose to. He parked, then stood on the curb for a moment, eyeing the teenagers who were loitering just down the block. It was a clean street with neat homes, but it had always been his experience that kids loitering anywhere spelled trouble, and this really wasn't the best of areas.

Then Angela's voice rang out. "If so much as a chip of paint is missing when we come out, just remember I know all your names!"

Jesse looked sharply up her stoop to her door. She was leaning outside, looking at the boys herself.

"A limo and now these wheels?" one of them shouted back. "You're traveling high class, Angie! La-di-da!"

Jesse was impressed. Despite its condition, they knew the Cobra was nothing to sneeze at. Then his attention turned again to Angela.

"Don't you forget it," she hollered. She laughed, then sobered abruptly as she looked at Jesse. "Come in," she said stiffly.

He got as far as her foyer before he allowed himself to stop and stare. Oh, yeah, he decided, she was just what he needed tonight.

He had seen her looking cool and provocative in that short red dress at the wedding, while her eyes had said she was scared to death. He had seen her looking young and innocent in sweats and no makeup at Lisette's home, while her eyes had shown she was fiercely determined to find out what had happened to the woman. He'd seen her draped in protective equipment with a haunted look in her eyes, and now she was heat and smoke and fire.

Now she could make a man imagine wild and incredible things with just a glance. There was nothing—absolutely nothing—outrageous about her tonight, except perhaps her impact, her sheer beauty.

She wore midnight blue that shimmered. Her dress was short again, revealing those miles of legs. It was sleeveless like the one she had worn to the wedding, but this had a loose, scooped neckline. It clung and slid and shifted over her skin when she moved.

He wondered what, if anything, she wore beneath it, and he felt like someone had punched him.

Her hair was caught up over one ear with something silver, and tonight her eyes were golden again. She wore silver shoes.

She made him think of a treasure chest, of opening one up to find a thousand glimmering jewels inside. He wondered what was inside *her*, what was going on behind those eyes that watched him warily, defensively.

She stepped back to let him into the foyer, then she planted her hands on her hips. "We need to be clear on something here," she said immediately.

"What?" He realized his voice was surprisingly hoarse.

"This is *not* a date. It's a..." Her voice trailed off and she looked vaguely confused for a moment, as though trying to figure out exactly what it *might* be. "Maybe I needed something like this, too," she finished on a breath.

"Then why can't it be a date?"

Because if we call it that, you'll ruin everything. And I'll fall apart. Because if she deluded herself, played games with herself, maybe they could both enjoy a respite, she hoped. If he thought it was a date, he would expect too much from her. He would think he had the right to touch her.

She was out of her mind. She shouldn't be doing this.

"I just wanted to make sure we understood each other," she said awkwardly, And there was certainly safety in that. "I just figured...well, what could I have done? You'd have been here at seven o'clock whether I liked it or not."

Whom was she trying to convince? "Probably. Let's go."

"Yes. Sure." Still, she hesitated a moment, and Jesse thought she swallowed carefully.

He followed her outside. The car was intact, paint and all. One of the kids on the corner gave a wolf whistle. Angela winked at them.

"They like you," he observed when they were in the car. He watched out of the corner of his eye as she crossed her legs and he felt something shudder deep inside him.

"Well, I'm safe as far as adults go," she returned. "I fall into a gray area. I went to school with most of their parents. But by the same token, I'm nobody's parent."

"Do you want to be?"

She looked at him, startled. "What?"

"A parent."

"Oh." Something, maybe just her breath, seemed to go out of her. "I haven't really considered it in a very long time."

"How long?" he asked, curious. "And why?"

"Maybe fifteen years."

She said it casually, but there was an undercurrent of something there, he suspected, some tremor to her tone.

"When exactly would I have time to be a mommy?" she rushed on. "In the wee hours of the night when I actually get to sleep if I'm lucky, if no one important has had the audacity to die at such an inconvenient hour?"

She was talking too fast. Nervously, he thought.

"I'm on call twenty-four hours a day," she reminded him.

"But you don't take every autopsy, visit every crime scene yourself."

"No, of course not. That's what my deputies are for. But my schedule is still very iffy. At any given moment, something could happen that would demand my personal attention."

"That's what daddies are for, right? To pick up the slack?"

She made an odd sound. He glanced over at her. Her face was expressionless.

"You've never married, either?" he pressed, not even sure why he was doing it. He already knew all the rumors that said she hadn't.

"No," she said shortly. "Same thing. No time."

They pulled up at the restaurant. Angela looked quickly at the facade. It was one of those small, low-key places in the center of the city, on the corner of a block that abutted a residential neighborhood. Even the awning shouted understated elegance—hunter green, with just a hint of gold trim. There was a doorman.

Jesse turned his keys over to the valet. By the time he got around to Angela's door, another employee had opened it for her. He noticed with some chagrin that the kid paid a hell of a lot of attention to her legs.

He was surprised by the possessive surge that hit him. He moved impulsively to take her hand and help her to her feet himself before they went inside.

After they were seated, she counted only twelve tables. They were all occupied, but there were no startling bursts of sound or conversation. Everyone seemed to lean toward each other, talking urgently and quietly. There was a lot of dark wood, and the hunter green color scheme extended to the interior—wallpaper, table-cloths, all with just a hint of gold. It was a place that suited him, she decided.

The maître d' unfolded her napkin onto her lap. Angela jerked back to give him ample room to do so without inadvertently touching her. When she looked up again, Jesse was watching her closely.

Her heart skipped. "What?" she asked warily.

"You never answered my question. Do you *want* kids? You told me all the reasons you shouldn't, but not what you feel."

"Oh. Are we still on that?"

"We never changed the subject."

"I'm happy the way I am," she said finally.

He got the impression that she was merely closing the conversation rather than being entirely honest with him this time. He let it go for the present, but he sensed more stories left untold.

The wine steward took his order. A flashbulb went off somewhere, and Jesse swore.

Angela looked around, confused, then she understood. "Oh," she murmured as the photographer retreated through the restaurant door. "How do they *do* that?"

Jesse's face was grim. She thought she saw something tick at his jaw.

"I made reservations," he said.

"So?"

"So they keep on top of things like that. They check periodically. 'Anybody interesting dining with you this evening?' That sort of thing. And when the answer is yes, they hang around outside and take their picture. Don't worry about it. Nine times out of ten they don't end up using mine. I'm mostly fill."

"Fill?" she repeated.

"If someone more important or more colorful hasn't done anything worth mentioning recently, and they have space to kill, they might use that picture."

She thought she'd seen him in the newspaper—and magazines—a lot more often than that. He was rich, attractive, single—American royalty, and a bachelor to boot. Angela began to get an odd, disassociated feeling, as if she was wearing something, doing something, that didn't really fit her. What in the world was she doing here with this man?

"Traveling with you is certainly interesting," she said at length.

His eyes seemed to narrow on her face. "Where would we be tonight if the choice had been yours?"

One corner of her mouth quirked. It seemed a self-mocking reflex. "I wouldn't be with you at all."

"But you are. Why?"

"I told you earlier."

"Ah, the old he'll-show-up-whether-I-like-it-or-not excuse."

Her heart skipped. Suddenly, she was no longer comfortable—not that she really had been even once since he had appeared on her sidewalk. But now there was something too provocative about his voice. He watched her as if he genuinely wanted to know every little thing there was to know about her. Those eyes again, she thought. Damn his eyes. They said he would challenge her to tell the truth.

"We'd be in Gunner's hunting cabin in the Poconos," she blurted.

Something in his eyes flared. She regretted her honesty even as something in her belly curled at that look.

"Interesting. And what might we be doing there?"

She had much more sense than to think about that in too much detail.

"We'd be roasting hot dogs in the fireplace," she managed to answer finally. "We'd have a six-pack of beer on ice." She sipped the wine the steward had brought, then couldn't help but close her eyes in appreciation. "Oh, but this is good, too."

She found, wildly and improbably, that it reminded her of him—deep and rich, dark and smooth. When she looked at him again, she had to wonder if her thoughts showed in her eyes because there was something that fairly simmered in his own now.

Oh, God, what was happening here? She couldn't let this happen. She drank again quickly because her mouth went dry.

Jesse leaned back in his chair. "I have a country place."

"You do?" Then she realized she wasn't surprised. She remembered the calluses on his decidedly un-white-collar hands. Maybe they came from chopping wood or some such thing. She found herself able to believe that he'd want to do those chores himself. "And do you rough it there?"

"Sort of. I don't have servants."

She startled herself by relaxing enough to laugh aloud.

"Why do you live where you do?" he asked suddenly.

She looked into his eyes, taken aback. "On Oregon Avenue? Because I'm home there."

"You could afford better."

Her eyes narrowed. "I don't want better."

"Why not?"

"What would I *do* with it?" She looked genuinely bewildered, then her eyes cleared. She threw the question back at him, deliberately, he felt. As though to steer the conversation from herself.

"Why do you live where *you* do?"

"I—" He broke off. He honestly didn't know.

She watched him, waiting.

"It's—" He stopped again. What? he asked himself. "Quiet," he finished.

"Ah, so we're back to that again."

"I like peace. Orderliness."

"Do you? Or are you just inured to it?"

"What's that supposed to mean?"

"It's human nature to gravitate toward that which a person is most accustomed to. Change rattles all but a few reckless, outgoing personality types."

"You're a psychiatrist, too?"

She gave a wicked smile. Somehow, she realized, she was rattling him.

"Rotations," she explained. "In medical school. They give you a little taste of everything. Are you most accustomed to order?"

He thought about it. He could not remember one single instance where a voice had been raised in his childhood home. "We lived as though the voters were always peering in our windows," he heard himself say.

She looked amused. "What if you had to burp?"

"We didn't."

"Everyone burps."

"Not Hadleys. Never Hadleys."

She actually laughed again. And, impossibly, she relaxed even more.

The food was just as wonderful as the wine. She tried to eat with some restraint, but could barely keep herself from smacking her lips. At his suggestion, she ordered a leek and shrimp salad with carrot vinaigrette, a combination she never would have otherwise contemplated. It was delicious. They shared pasta with lobster and tomatoes for the main course, and as he had promised, it was rich and filling. If there was something intimate about sharing, something very warm and soothing about the low hum of their own conversation, then she chose not to think about it too closely.

They did not talk of Lisette.

"The owner here—and chef—is from Porquerolles," he said when the plate was empty of everything but the garnish. Angela picked up a curly leaf of escarole and popped that into her mouth, too. His eyes widened only marginally. "I suppose I should have expected that," he said after a moment.

"Hmm. Waste not, want not." She chewed. "Porquerolles?"

"It's the largest of the Îles d'Hyères just off the French coast southeast of Toulon."

"I knew that."

And he guessed from her tone that he had finally told her something she *didn't* know. He grinned.

And then he ruined it. "What did my uncle do to you?" He hadn't meant to ask, but the question slid out of him almost with a will of its own.

Angela felt the pleasure drain out of her. It left a cold void. "What makes you think he did anything?" she hedged.

"Gunner said so."

She would kill him. She wasn't sure if she was angrier that Gunner had betrayed her, or that she had found out about it now, spoiling the evening. But then, she had known that the spoiling was inevitable. Somehow. If not in this way, then he would touch her.

And then he would know.

"Nothing," she said shortly. Then, because it was pointless to lie, she added, "It's really not important."

"Your eyes say otherwise." He had begun it, he realized, however unintentionally. Now he wanted to know. "I could find out."

"I'm sure you could." She took her napkin from her lap and laid it neatly beside her plate.

"So why won't you just tell me?"

"Because I don't like to talk about it."

"My uncle doesn't remember you."

She felt something painful settle into her chest. "Never once," she answered slowly, "have I ever believed he would."

"What does that mean?"

"I want to go home now."

"Fine. But leave the silver."

Her eyes widened. He wasn't sure if she was going to laugh or take offense. He watched, fascinated, as she ducked her head to collect herself. When she looked up again, her beautiful eyes were more or less unreadable.

"Too fancy for my taste," she said simply, and rose to her feet.

He hadn't intended to laugh, either, but he did.

He paid the bill then took her elbow as they left the restaurant. He more than half expected that she would pull away from him, but she didn't, although he did feel her stiffen beneath his touch.

"I'm not my uncle," he said when they were back in the car.

"Maybe not."

"But?"

"You're close enough." She had to keep believing that, or she was in very deep trouble indeed.

"You didn't have to join me for dinner."

Her head snapped around and her eyes found his. The color was deep again, and there was turmoil there. He could see it even in the dim light of the moon shining through the windshield.

"I wanted to," she said, and her tone told him that she was both startled and upset by that.

"I'm glad."

"*Why?*" she asked helplessly. "Why *me?*"

What was it? Jesse wondered. Because she was a challenge in subtle ways, and what man alive didn't enjoy one? Something about her shouted, "Stay away!" even as she wore clothing that demanded attention. He'd told her that she intrigued him, and that was certainly true.

More than once tonight, he'd imagined peeling that shimmering dress off her. He thought again of what might lie beneath and

something inside him clenched. She was beautiful, almost inno-
cently provocative, and he was a perfectly normal warm-blooded
male.

She made him...feel things, he realized. Until that very moment, he had never admitted how rarely he allowed himself to
feel. He wondered if he was afraid that if he let the internal bar-
riers down, if he looked into his own heart too closely or let it
loose, he would be appalled at how utterly lacking his life really
was.

He reached over and caught one of her long blond curls around
his finger, as though that could give him the answer. It twined
there like a serpent, seemingly winding around his flesh of its
own accord, as though to ensnare him.

"I want you," he said quietly.

She paled. And then the fear, the terrible fear, came back.

"Don't," she whispered. "Don't say that. *This isn't a date.*"

He scowled. "I don't care what we call it. We're both well
past the age of consent."

She laughed hoarsely. "So it would seem."

She wanted to think he was only talking about a quick cou-
pling, mutually gratifying sex, no strings. That was bad enough,
but for some untold reason, she didn't entirely believe it. And
any more than that would never, ever work because he was a
Hadley.

She was clinging to that beyond all reason—like a weapon with
which to ward him off. Because she had spent fifteen years avoiding men, and now, more and more, somehow she kept forgetting
to keep her guard up with this one. Because the only thing she
could really find wrong with him was his last name.

She realized that her pulse was skittering erratically, and she
recognized its tempo intimately—it was all confusion and panic.

Jesse opened his mouth to say something more. The valet
tapped on his window, motioning that there was another car behind him. Reluctantly, he released her hair and drove.

They spoke very little on the drive back to South Philadelphia.
He wondered what she was thinking. *Don't,* she had said. *Don't
say that.* Why? He knew, suddenly, that he had not even begun
to figure her out yet.

But he would. Oh, he would. He could no more turn around
and walk away from this woman now than he could change who

and what he was. Unfortunately, those two things—her and who he was—were apparently at odds. Because of his uncle.

He turned onto Oregon Avenue and heard her startled cry at the same time his own breath rushed out of him. *Now what?* Her street was alive with flashing color—blue and red lights winking off windows and concrete.

Four P.P.D. cruisers were parked in front of her house.

Chapter 7

Jesse poked the Cobra's nose into a small area near the curb left by two of the squad cars, turned off the ignition and was out before Angela could say a word.

"What?" she cried finally, scrambling from the car behind him. *"What?"* It seemed the only response she was capable of.

He jogged up the sidewalk to the stoop. A cop stood just outside her opened door. Light spilled out into the night—the kind of abundant light that Jesse would forever associate with late-night places where something had gone wrong. The cop's gun was drawn, but he held it loosely at his side. Jesse didn't think he could be more than twenty-one.

"What's happening here?" he demanded, then he heard Angela's footsteps hurrying up behind him.

He turned to look at her. Her eyes were wild. She was breathing hard. She looked as though an unexpected noise would make her fly apart.

"What are you doing?" she yelled at the cop. "What are you doing in my house?"

The cop looked as bemused as Jesse felt. "Well, your alarm went off, ma'am."

She shook her head frantically, in denial.

A sense of invasion swept through her, making her shake even more. It left her with a raw, violated feeling that she was all too familiar with.

Jesse watched her closely. She seemed more upset than the situation warranted, he observed, at least now that they knew what it was.

He looked back at the cop. "So did you catch this trespasser?"

"Uh...Jergens and Manilla are inside now."

"What does that mean?" Angela cried.

"Well, we got here and your front door was open," the young cop answered nervously. "Me and my partner, Joe Perriman, caught the call. I called for backup."

"Three cars' worth?" Jesse demanded.

"Well, she's Code One."

Angela couldn't stop trembling. None of this was making any sense.

Oh, she understood the Code One. That meant the police force, or any chief city official. Code Two was for her deputies and, she imagined, the investigators in Jesse's office. But she still had no idea as to who had been in her house or why.

"Doctor?" Another cop had come out the front door. "We need you to have a look-see and tell us if anything is missing."

"But who *did* it? Who was here?" she asked irrationally.

"We're still investigating, Doctor."

Which meant, she thought helplessly, that they didn't have a clue.

She went inside. Jesse took her elbow, but she shook him off absently. "I have to see."

She had to look. She had to know. She could find no words to tell him what it felt like to have someone force their way into something that was *hers*.

He watched her drift from room to room, almost in a daze now. He finally left her and found the cop named Manilla—an older man with a good bit of gray in his hair. His chiseled face wore a haggard, I've-seen-it-all expression, but his eyes reacted when he recognized Jesse.

"I wasn't able to get anything out of the kid outside," Jesse began.

Manilla scowled. "That's mostly because there's nothing to tell. Dr. Byerly's alarm went off. He and his partner got here and the door was open. No sign of forced entry. He called for backup anyway because of the code. Any chance she forgot to lock up on her way out?''

Jesse shook his head. "No." In fact, he had been vaguely startled by the sheer *number* of locks on her door. And she had meticulously turned every one of them.

"Well, then, I can't figure it," Manilla went on. "By the time we got here, whoever it was had taken off. And we got here pretty quick. I was only four blocks away when the request for backup came in."

Jesse nodded, frowning at all the locks.

"Nothing seems to be out of place or disturbed," Manilla said. "But I guess we won't know for sure until she tells us so."

Jesse stepped into her living room, off to the left of the foyer. He hadn't gotten this far inside earlier.

There was a lot of clutter. That seemed characteristic. Yet for all the disarray, there was also something warm and comfortable about the place. Unlike his own favored parlor, this was a room where he could take his shoes off and put his feet up on the table. And he wasn't entirely convinced that the disarray wasn't intentional, at least in part—maybe another obscure attempt at defiance, the way her clothing seemed to be.

There was a butter yellow sectional sofa littered with a lot of pillows. Red pillows. Blue pillows. Gray and green ones. Bookshelves and an entertainment center lined one wall. Paperbacks and hardbacks were shoved between textbooks and periodicals. There was no rhyme or reason to any of it.

There was a half-finished glass of cola on a coffee table, whose top looked to be antique marble. Even as Jesse glanced around, a grandfather clock in the hall chimed the hour. Good sound, he thought, then he jumped a little, turning to it and staring as a porcelain bird erupted from the top of it.

There was nothing proper, predictable or bland about anything. Jesse actually smiled, relaxing again. He started up the stairs to find her.

Angela moved through rooms that were as familiar to her as her own skin, and something in the pit of her stomach clenched painfully. She had no tolerance for invasion of her personal spaces. She knew that about herself and accepted it. She did not allow strangers to touch her. She rarely allowed anyone she did not know into her home. If once she had been merely shy, a little self-conscious about herself because she was too thin, too tall, a bookworm, then when Charlie Price had gotten through with her, she'd become self-protective to a fault.

This house was hers. The things in it were *hers*. And someone had walked through here as she was doing now, perhaps touching things, and *she had not allowed them to do so*. Her will, her desire, had not mattered to them at all.

Somehow worse was the fact that nothing seemed to have been moved or taken. She would almost have preferred a robbery, she thought a little hysterically. But this act was stealthy, and it some- how felt evil.

Nothing had been out of place downstairs. Nothing was miss- ing. The television and the stereo and the VCR were all where they were supposed to be, in the living room. The antique grand- father clock in the downstairs hall had appeared untouched. Her jewelry was in her jewelry box in perfect order—which was to say, no appreciable order at all. The little wad of cash she kept for emergencies had been pulled out of the toe of a sock in her dresser drawer. But the money was lying atop the clutter, all three hundred dollars, as though someone had dismissed it as not being worth taking. Logic told her that whoever had been here had gone through fast, because of the alarm. Still, it felt like a mockery.

She left her bedroom, her skin crawling, and rubbed her hands briskly over her bare arms as she crossed the hall. She opened the door to the spare bedroom she used as a home office and peered inside. At first glance, everything seemed normal here, too. The dark computer monitor stared back at her, revealing no se- crets. She started to back out of the room again, then something caught her eye.

She was almost glad to have found *something*.

The deep, wide drawer where the printer was kept was slightly ajar. Angela crossed to it and eased it open a little farther. The printer was there. And so was something else, something that was not hers, jammed onto the shelf right beneath it.

Angela crouched down to look at it and cried out.

She heard footsteps on the stairs almost immediately. She shot to her feet again, slammed the drawer shut with her hip and hurried back to the door.

"What happened?" Jesse demanded.

"Nothing."

"You screamed."

"I didn't scream."

"Damn it, you yelped like a kicked puppy!"

One of the cops came upstairs and stood behind him, concerned. Angela tried to meet the man's gaze and failed miserably.

"Everything's fine," she said, and wondered if anyone else seemed to think her voice sounded strained. "Nothing's missing."

To his credit, Jesse kept silent.

"Well, then," the cop said, "I guess there's nothing more we can do here. Whoever it was is long gone. Probably the alarm scared him off. But I'll write up a report. You can stop in at your convenience and sign it."

It semed an interminably long time before they all left. Angela finally pushed away from the door frame where she had been leaning, hugging herself. She stepped into the hall.

"I need a drink," she said shakily.

"Not so fast."

Jesse caught her elbow and watched something happen to her eyes. Again. It was the same sort of panic, tangled with anger, that showed in them whenever he touched her.

This time, he wouldn't back off. It was an improvement over the wounded-animal look that had lingered there since they had found the squad cars outside.

"This is my home, Jesse," she said tightly. "I don't need permission here, certainly not from you."

"What did you find?"

"Nothing," she croaked.

Before she could stop him, he turned and went back into the office.

Angela cried out again and went after him. A voice inside her head screamed in panic. It reminded her that his signature had shown up on the Shokonnet release—and then he had insisted upon dancing with her at the wedding. That he'd paid her a visit at the morgue, had taken her to dinner—and now this...this *thing* showed up in her printer drawer while she was conveniently out of the house. The closer he got to her, the more treacherous, crazy things seemed to be happening.

A sense of betrayal began to choke her. She caught up with him and clawed at his arm frantically, trying to hold him back.

Jesse shook her off and yanked open the desk drawers, one after another. Finally, he got to the one that contained the printer. He saw the sophisticated tape-splicing equipment jammed onto the bottom shelf. He crouched down as she had done. Angela let her hands fall helplessly to her sides.

For a moment—a second, definitely no more than a heartbeat—he accepted what he was seeing at face value. Some part of him said, *Aha, guilty as charged.* Some part of him believed that what he was looking at was as simple as it appeared, that *she* was the one trying to frame him. She hadn't wanted him to come in here, to find this, after all.

Then he looked up over his shoulder at her.

Her face was too pale, and a fine sheen of perspiration had broken out on her brow. She was shaking her head back and forth, back and forth, hard enough to make her blond curls swirl. She staggered away from him in real horror as he stood again.

His stomach rolled.

"Change your clothes," he ordered hoarsely.

"What?" She was blinking hard and fast, trying not to cry. The sight wrenched at something inside him.

"You're not staying here tonight."

"This is my *home!*" she cried for what seemed to her like the hundredth time. And not one of those times had anyone listened.

"Someone has been in here as conveniently as if they had a key," Jesse snapped. Or a dozen keys, he thought. "Sorry, Doctor, but I'm pulling rank on this one. This particular investigation is not yet closed, and I won't let you stay here at what is effectively a crime scene."

"You have no right—"

"I have every right."

"No!"

"Damn it, do you want to be here if he comes back again with *another* trick up his sleeve—whoever the hell he is?"

"He knew I was out tonight," she whispered. Oh, God, she wondered helplessly, had he been hidden out there in the darkness, watching her leave? Did he somehow have advance knowledge of her plans?

She realized only belatedly that she was having a very hard time holding on to her suspicion of Jesse. She dragged it back forcefully and glared at him. Then something else occurred to her.

"I should have told the cops," she whispered, and was appalled when she started to cry.

Jesse found it very hard to breathe. He had the strong suspicion that if he moved to touch her now, to give comfort, she would fall apart. So he waited, watching her, his body rigid.

"I did the same thing I accused you of doing this morning," she confessed.

Jesse frowned. "What are you talking about? You didn't accuse me of anything this morning."

"I asked you if you wanted me to send that hair! I wanted to know if you...if you..." She shook her head helplessly.

Jesse's eyes narrowed. "You wanted to know if I was honest enough to make sure it was tested, regardless of the effect it could have on my career."

She nodded woodenly, then her eyes flashed his way with a little defiance again. That was better. He went with it.

"And now you think you're using your own position to cover up your culpability? So what are you saying, Doctor?" He was deliberately brutal, trying to snap her out of it. "That *you* killed Lisette and spliced that tape together and now you're withholding evidence that could incriminate you?"

"No!" Her eyes went huge, then they got angry. "Is that what you believe?"

Only for a heartbeat, he thought. Only through that first, booming heartbeat. And that was the difference between them.

He let suspicion go easily when it didn't seem reasonable. She seemed to be clawing for it, *wanting* to hold on to it.

"I believe someone is trying to discredit you," he said carefully, quietly. "Someone left this device here. Having it in your possession makes it look as though you're trying to frame me. Ergo, someone wants me to think that you killed Lisette."

He waited. Her expression didn't change. She remained on the edge of hysteria. So he went on, calmly reiterating what they both already knew.

"He—whoever he is—broke in here to leave this little present, Angela. I'd say that's a given. You'd tell the cops nothing was missing, and they would leave. But I'd stay. The drawer was left open a little bit, wasn't it?" he guessed.

She nodded spasmodically.

"So I'd see it if I helped you look around, check the place over. Which I would almost have to do. Not much of a gamble there."

"But—"

"But I'd guess," he finished for her, "that the alarm caught him off guard. I'd guess the cops weren't in the initial plan. Which tells us something else. He's either stupid, or he's running on the kind of desperation that blots out common sense. Or, another scenario, he hadn't planned to do this *tonight*. We went out and gave him an opportunity, so he had to act fast without being fully prepared."

"I—" she began again. Then she nodded helplessly. "That makes sense." She pressed her fingers to her temples. "I can't even seem to think right now, Jesse."

"That's okay. Just listen for a minute. Hear me out. No matter how it occurred that he ended up here with the alarm blaring, we can pretty much figure what happened next. What was he going to do? Get caught standing in the living room with this machine? Of course not. He shoved it in an obvious place and took off."

Angela managed a watery half-smile. "You're good at this," she said weakly.

"So are you. Normally. You're just freaked out right now. This is what teams are for, Angela. When one guy hits a rocky spell, the other takes over."

She shook her head again, but not really in denial this time.

"Why?" he asked, talking to himself now, thinking about the splicer again, Angela answered anyway.

"I don't *know!*"

He moved closer to her, cornering her against a dresser. And he wanted badly to touch her, to draw her into his arms, to comfort her, but her eyes still said she'd never allow it.

"The question now is what anyone stands to gain by all this," he went on. "Damn it, Angela, at some point you're going to have to trust me. You've got to let me know if you've got anything, any suspicions. You can't deal with this by yourself."

Her eyes widened and she looked at him frantically. "I can't trust you. I don't even know you!"

He swore ripely, then his voice softened. "Then get to know me. At least give me a chance."

Angela closed her eyes and wrapped her arms around her middle.

This morning, they'd thought that someone was going after him, but they'd been looking at it from the wrong angle. She thought again of that hair caught between Lisette's fingers, and she shuddered visibly. She knew, with a sick sensation, that anyone could—and probably would—logically say that she'd planted it there to set Jesse Hadley up for murder. She hadn't noticed the hair at the crime scene. The fiber optic cable had picked it up during the autopsy. And she had done the autopsy alone. Unassisted. She had no proof that she hadn't planted that hair herself once she'd gotten the body to the morgue. Someone had counted on that.

And if they knew what had happened between her and Jesse's uncle all those years ago, then they would *really* believe she had a motive to destroy him, some long simmering hatred...

Her head spun.

"I don't know what to do," she whispered. What was the right thing under the circumstances? She had to submit that splicing machine for prints. The killer's own could be on it. But then she might only be incriminating herself, because it would be clear she'd had it in her possession. She groaned aloud.

"Did you touch it?" Jesse asked as though reading her mind.

She shook her head.

"All right, then. You just haven't found it yet."

She looked at him disbelievingly.

She needed to slow things down here. She needed to buy herself a breath of time in which to think. They—that collective, authoritative *they* who were made up of the Hadleys and the Glowans and the Prices of the world—could say anything they chose. Their word would always be believed over hers. She *knew* that she could not put any faith in the system. She did not believe that since she was innocent, everyone would rush off to look for the *real* killer. She knew that justice did not always prevail.

"Leave the splicer," Jesse said bluntly. "Just for tonight. For another few hours until morning. We need to think about this, about the best way to handle it.''

Angela nodded, not so much in acquiescence, but confusion.

"Get changed now," he said. "I'll take you to my sister's house. You can stay there tonight."

"Tessa's away," she managed to return.

"I have a key. My housekeeper is supposed to be watering her plants, so *her* housekeeper could use the break to visit her family."

It would be so easy to trust him.

"I'm staying," she said quietly.

His face hardened. "Fine. Then I'm staying with you."

"You're not invited."

"Oh, but I am. Because someone is trying to set you up, to make it look like you're trying to frame me, and that makes this my problem, as well."

She wanted to believe that it was as simple as that. In a way, the stand he was taking made sense. He was powerful and important, and he would certainly want to protect himself. It was an election year, she reminded herself.

She watched him stride angrily out of the room and knew again that there wasn't a damned thing she could do to dissuade Jesse Hadley once his mind was made up. It should have made her feel helpless and frightened and small, but she was only tired and overwhelmed.

"*Now* we need something to drink." His voice drifted back from the hall. "Where do you keep the liquor around here?"

"In the dining room."

She looked out the black window to the night pressing in. Who was out there, trying to destroy her? Goose bumps crawled over her skin.

She decided she was just as glad that Jesse wasn't going anywhere just yet.

Chapter 8

Angela followed him downstairs and took a bottle of brandy from a cupboard in the sideboard. She poured for both of them and carried the snifters to the living room.

Jesse watched her from behind. Tension gripped her every movement. She put his glass on the coffee table, then went to the far side of the sectional. She curled up there, her legs folded stiffly beneath her, and sipped, watching him.

"I don't know," she repeated quietly, as though he had just asked the question instead of having done it minutes ago. "There are a lot of people who might want to discredit me professionally. I just don't know who they might be."

He thought for a moment and nodded. "What about personally?"

The color drained from her face. But then she shook her head. "Not after all this time."

She'd remained in the area for years after the mockery of Charlie's almost-trial. After Gunner had gotten through with him, he'd left her alone. She'd gone to work at Quantico. She had never heard another peep from him. It made no sense for him to suddenly start up again. And certainly not like this.

Jesse scowled. Her response was an admission of something,

though he wasn't sure what. And it was clear she wasn't going to enlighten him.

Yet. He'd get to the bottom of it eventually, he vowed silently.

"I set a few wheels in motion after you showed me that release," he said finally. "Maybe they'll lead us somewhere."

Angela hesitated with her glass halfway to her lips. "What kind of wheels?"

"Regarding the Shokonnets. Regarding the employees in your building. And my own desk logs, to find out who's been in my office the past month and when."

Her eyes widened a little. "You did all this *before* Lisette died?"

He met her gaze evenly. "Someone forged my signature on that release form, then told the press that that release was negligence on your part. Even before bodies started dropping. I wanted to know who. Given these current circumstances, I'd like to find out what's happened with those particular investigations before we make a decision on that thing upstairs."

"There's no decision to be made," she said flatly, and he saw a shiver pass through her body, quickly controlled.

"There are always decisions," he corrected. "When to hand it over to the lab. How. What to do with it in the meantime."

She thought of the device upstairs, crouched in her drawer like some kind of vile presence. It was not simply going to go away.

She gave a laugh that turned into a groan. "We sound like partners in crime."

"If you really believed that, I'd feel better."

Once again, he watched her react. Her body flinched, recoiled.

"Partners generally trust each other," he reminded her.

"Not always."

"We need to, Angela."

"You don't know what you're asking."

It was one of the more honest responses he'd gotten out of her yet, and he knew it. He wondered again what she was so afraid of. He made a sound of frustration. He finished his brandy and put his glass down with a crisp tap on the marble. There were at least four feet between them on the sofa. The distance was obvious, glaring, troubling.

"Would you please come closer, even just a little?"

Her eyes flew to his face. "What for?"

"Because I feel like a leper."

"Then go home. No one asked you to stay here."

He had never met anyone with defenses like hers.

But he'd seen something happen to her face at certain times before. He'd seen her soften, and he remembered what had made that happen. He wasn't above using it. It would not be like the sparrow. He would leave his hand open this time.

"Please," he added quietly, deliberately, and it happened again.

Everything about her wilted for a moment, then he heard her let out an unconscious sigh. And this time her chin actually trembled.

"Whether you like it or not," he said, "we're in this together. As long as someone's using me to get to you, or vice versa, it's my problem, too."

Somehow he didn't think she'd accept the fact that he was in this also because he cared. That he cared so much was something that startled even him.

"Angela, take comfort where it's offered," he suggested. "Take strength when it's there for the tapping. Relax. You're protected tonight. That's all I'm saying."

She hesitated. She thought that she had never felt so confused in her life. Except once.

I didn't invite him. He's lying. I didn't want what happened.

"Angela."

She gasped and her eyes flew open again. She wasn't aware of having closed them.

Jesse held a hand out to her. She gave a small cry and scooted toward him. She almost spilled her brandy. He caught the snifter in time and put it on the coffee table.

It was so hard to keep fighting it, she thought, to keep being so meticulously careful with him, though she knew it was the only sane thing she could do. She knew what could happen when she wasn't careful enough, but his arms were hard and strong around her now, maybe even strong enough to keep all the evil in the world at bay. As long as she made herself clear to him, surely it would be all right.

"I don't want...I mean, just hold me," she whispered deliberately. "I don't want anything else."

She heard him make a strangled sound. ''I realize that, Angela. Trust me, you've made it clear.''

''That never matters.''

He scowled, but then the warmth of her reached him. She relaxed, and she seemed to melt just enough that her body conformed with his. He did what he had wanted to do from nearly the first time he had seen her, and he tangled his fingers in her hair. But he did not, after all, tilt her head back, make her yield. Some innate caution stopped him.

He lowered his mouth to the crown of her head instead, touching her so briefly that she didn't feel it, and even he wasn't sure he had actually done it when it was over. And he felt a new emotion sweeping through him, warm and soft.

Tenderness.

Angela would never have believed that she could have slept under the circumstances. But when she next opened her eyes, sunlight streamed through the living-room windows, making dust motes dance like fairies. And her first reaction was not one of panic or alarm at not being alone, but that she needed to give the place a good cleaning next weekend.

Jesse's breathing was deep and even. His chest moved rhythmically beneath her left cheek. His right hand half curled on her hip. She had been more or less leaning into him at an unnatural angle, and her neck was stiff.

All in all, she thought, not the stuff passion was made of. Maybe because of that, she felt safe and warm and good. Even languorous.

She sat up slowly and looked at him. She touched a cautious, experimental finger to the trace of lines at the corner of his eye. He didn't stir.

''Jesse?'' she whispered, pulling her hand back.

He murmured something and turned his face away from her.

''Jesse,'' she said more loudly.

''Go away.''

Her mouth curved into a smile. ''Wake up!''

He jerked and his eyes flew open. She saw clouds of confusion in his gaze before it cleared.

''Time is it?'' he managed to ask.

"I don't know."

"Then go back to sleep."

"It's Monday. We have offices waiting for us." They had problems waiting, as well, she knew, and her mood, so surprisingly good a moment ago, evaporated.

So many problems.

Jesse finally sat up, scrubbing his face with his hands. He still looked arrogant somehow. He woke with lazy grace, as though no one would dare deny him the time or the luxury. There was something devilishly attractive about him, and when they cleared, his green eyes were expressive enough to touch something inside her.

A day-old growth of beard shadowed his face. And she wanted to touch that, too, to run her fingers over it, to know the texture of it. That compulsion was as frightening as anything that had happened yet.

"I'll get coffee," she said quickly. She got up and fled down the hall to the kitchen.

It was a good five minutes before he joined her. Jesse was under no illusions regarding his morning moods. They weren't usually pleasant, at least not before he had a cup of coffee. But some was percolating, and the smell drew him down the hall. That, and the whisper of her movements in the kitchen.

He stopped in the doorway and merely watched her for a moment.

Her hair was mussed now and thoroughly tangled. Golden curls spilled down her back as she moved. She still wore the shimmering blue dress, and in the morning light she looked like something otherworldly. Her face was too pale, her eyes too dark. He had never before had occasion to wonder what an angel might look like, but given a pair of wings, he thought, Angela Byerly would do nicely right now.

An angel under siege, he amended. Alone and frightened and for some reason determined to handle it all on her own.

She caught sight of him out of the corner of her eye and whirled to face him. She clapped a hand to her heart. "Oh, you startled me."

"You're not used to having anyone creep up on you while you're making coffee." It wasn't a question, and she didn't answer. But he found her reaction enlightening.

He accepted the mug she slid across the breakfast bar at him. He watched her hands shake a little. He took a deep, fortifying swallow, then reached for his suit coat from the stool where he had left it the night before.

He held the mug high in a sort of salute. "I'll return this to you."

She nodded. She wondered what he would do if she told him she didn't want him to take it. Such a possibility had obviously never occurred to him. It was just a mug, and he could probably buy the factory that had made it. She was more bemused than annoyed.

"I'll be in touch before eleven or so," he informed her, "as soon as I know what's gone on with those investigations I mentioned last night. We'll take things from there."

She didn't like it, but didn't know what else to do. Every instinct she possessed urged her to get rid of that damned machine as soon as possible.

"I feel so helpless," she whispered. And she wondered if he could possibly understand that for her, that was the worst feeling in the world. "There's nothing I can do to fight back," she added hopelessly.

"We'll think of something." He saw the torment in her eyes and his voice was hard now, angry, a threat against whoever was doing this to her. "In the meantime," he advised, "sit tight."

"Sit *tight?* I'm going to work."

"I meant emotionally."

"Oh." And then, before she could react, he stepped around the breakfast bar and kissed her.

Shock and panic and denial flew through her. Her hands jerked up halfway to stop him. Instantly. Reflexively. Then they hovered.

His kiss was fast, defiant, planted squarely on her mouth. And even as brief as it was, everything inherent in his personality was there. *Control.* He had the upper hand. *Power.* Touching her had been his decision. *Arrogance.* She didn't think he would allow her to push him away.

She should have been terrified, but there wasn't time.

Her hands finally found his chest, but her fingers only curled into his shirt. Then, as quickly as it had started, it was over. Something flashed inside her at the contact, then lingered. Her mouth still tingled. She stumbled backward a quick half step when he released her, but even as she did, everything inside her kept stirring. She stared at him. She pressed her fingers to her mouth, shaken. "What...why did you do that?"

"I've never spent the night with a woman I've never even kissed. And last night it just didn't seem appropriate."

"Appropriate?"

"I thought about it."

She swallowed carefully. "So this was...planned?"

"No. It didn't seem appropriate this morning, either."

"But you did it anyway."

"I like to break out now and again."

Her eyes widened. "I'll keep that in mind."

And with that he was gone, striding up the hall. Before she could fully recover and go after him, she heard the front door click shut behind him.

Shaken, Angela sat at the breakfast bar, trying to regain her composure.

She *wanted* to feel the terror now, needed to feel it. She floundered for it and couldn't find it, despite the fact that one thing had just become abundantly clear. Despite that veneer of civility, those upper-crust manners, Jesse Hadley was all man. And she had allowed him to get close enough to want her. Hadley or not, genteel or not, he would do something about it.

Finally, her pulse began rioting. But it was as much with wonder as panic.

Jesse was late for work. A good number of his staff were already at their desks when he got off the elevator. It was twenty after eight.

The district attorney's office claimed the entire sixth floor of a stately, redbrick building on Arch Street. The department was cramped. His trial deputies had private offices, but the Trial Division was crammed into one large room chopped up by prefab dividers. The Investigations Division had another chopped up section on the east side of the floor.

It was to this end of the building that Jesse went. As he passed his secretary's desk, Libby jumped up to make sure his coffee was waiting for him when he returned.

Jesse found Eric Zollner on the telephone, his own mug already drained, indicating that he'd been at work for a while. It was one of the things Jesse liked about him.

"Five minutes," Jesse said when the investigator hung up. "My office. I want to know what you found out about the Shokonnets." Then he stepped around Eric's desk to find Jeanette Peckett. "How are you doing with that peek into the M.E.'s office I asked you for?"

"Right here," she said, rummaging through the papers on her desk before holding up a wad of them.

"Good. Come to my office in twenty minutes."

He went back to his own desk. His coffee was waiting for him. He took a mouthful and shrugged out of his suit coat, and by the time he hung it up, Eric was standing in his office doorway.

"Come in," he said. "Sit down."

The young man looked like he'd rather stand. "You're not going to like this. Those kids were in for emergency treatment twelve times."

Jesse swore violently enough to make Eric jump.

"The mother doesn't work," he rushed on to relate. "The father is employed at a gas station down on Catharine and Broad. At present, they have a total of ninety-two dollars and sixteen cents in their checking account, no other savings accounts or investments. No credit cards, no auto loan. No hospitalization, either. They've left open medical accounts all over the city, so it was relatively easy to track the emergency visits. The father was treated once two years ago for extensive lacerations and contusions of the right hand. Records show he was quite inebriated at the time."

Jesse sat down, already tired. "You're right. I don't like it."

"It gets worse. Melissa Shokonnet is pregnant again."

Jesse snarled. "That bastard ought to be castrated."

"I thought of that," Eric said uncomfortably. "*She's* never been in for treatment. But the neighbors say Melissa pops up with new bruises at least once a week."

Jesse closed his eyes briefly. "There's nothing we can get him on now."

"Not unless we can get her to file a complaint."

"She won't," Jesse stated flatly. "Not if she's crying SIDS to cover up what he's been doing to her babies."

"No, probably not. But given their history, we'll get them eventually, sir."

Jesse nodded, his stomach working again. The newborn would show up at some emergency clinic somewhere—at least the mother seemed to get *them* treatment. And when it happened, he would nail Harry Shokonnet.

"Do me a favor," Jesse said. "I know you're overworked and underpaid, but keep an eye on them. When is the baby due?"

"September."

"Well, starting September, post a reminder to yourself to check the hospitals, say twice a month or so. Until it happens. It's the best we can do for now," he conceded, almost to himself. It wasn't going to help Angela.

He couldn't see how Harry Shokonnet could have a grudge against her, not unless she had charged him with child abuse, and she hadn't. No, he thought, little Lacie's body had just been in the right place at the right time, and someone had used it.

Eric left, and Jesse's anger simmered. There would be yet another victim because someone had released Lacie Shokonnet's remains. A defenseless, as-yet unborn infant was going to have to take at least one blow before he could do anything about it. He popped an antacid tablet, and it wasn't even nine o'clock in the morning yet.

Jeanette Peckett's news wasn't much better. She knocked tentatively on his opened door mere moments after Eric had gone.

"What do you have, Jeanette?"

"Nothing."

"Nothing? You just waved the contents of a whole damned file at me a few minutes ago!"

"Full of nice, clean people. The city screens the employees over there. The best I could find was a guy who had a drug problem about eight years ago. He went into detox, and he's been clean ever since."

"What's he do?" Jesse asked.

"Night watchman."

"Did you check the janitors, the secretaries?"

Jeanette nodded unhappily.

"And nobody has an ax to grind," Jesse muttered.

"Well, it would help if I knew what kind of ax you were

looking for. I know a couple of her deputies are irked that they didn't get promoted to her job.''

Jesse shook his head. "I'm not sure what I'm looking for."

But actually, he was. Jeanette had just hit the nail on the head. He wanted to know who over there might resent Angela Byerly enough to try to bring her down.

"Which deputies?" he asked.

"Specifically, Ed Thackery and Brigid Cross. They've both been pretty vocal about it. Thackery has been working in the M.E.'s office for twenty-two years, and Cross is one of those highbrow, silver-spoon types who thinks she should have everything she wants because she wants it." As soon as the words were out, she flushed. She had just described her boss's background.

Jesse waved a hand to dismiss her remark. "Good work. Keep digging."

When she was gone, he went to find his secretary. "Did you ever get those logs I asked for?"

"Right here. The past four weeks' worth. Six now." She dropped two more binders on top of the pile.

Jesse took them. "Thanks."

"I could look through them myself if I knew what you were searching for."

"I'm not sure myself," he said yet again, then slammed his office door.

An hour later, he had a throbbing headache.

No one appeared in any of the log books who didn't have a perfectly legitimate reason for being in his offices. No one from the M.E.'s office had visited, except Angela on the Thursday when all this trouble had started, but she hadn't signed in because Libby had been gone for the day.

Then again, he reflected, stealing tapes wasn't legitimate. And it was entirely possible—even probable—that the break-in had occurred after hours, as well, or while Libby had been away from her desk. Someone in his office, then? His stomach clenched.

"Oh, hell," he muttered aloud. "Not *again*."

He tried calling Angela. He had nothing good to tell her, but he knew she'd be interested in—if infuriated by—the Shokonnet information. And he wasn't adverse to hearing her voice right now.

Her secretary said she was unavailable. He tried not to imagine what she might actually be doing and left a message for her to call him back. Which, he supposed, she might or might not do. If his head wasn't hurting so much, he might have smiled at that. No one could accuse her of jumping to salute.

He touched a finger to his lip and thought about kissing her. He had lied to her. He liked to break out? He gave a hoarse laugh. Not until recently, he realized. Generally, he marched along with the program, with rules both unspoken and carved in granite.

Nor was spending the night with women—with or without kissing them—much in his repertoire. More often than not, after an hour or so in their company, he had no desire to kiss them or sleep with them or anything else. Caro had been a rare exception.

And he hadn't thought about Caro in weeks now.

He got up and stared out his window at the busy street six floors below. He went back to his phone and tapped in a three-digit extension number.

"Eric, I need to see you again," he said when the man answered.

It took Eric less than two minutes to get down the hall to Jesse's office. By the time he did, Jesse's headache was slamming, and his stomach swam in acid. He'd eaten another two antacid tablets.

"Yes, sir?"

"Close the door."

The man did as he was told and waited expectantly.

"There's something else I need you to look into. I want it kept quiet."

"Of course."

"I mean very quiet."

"It won't leave the D.A.'s office."

"It can't leave this *room.* You've got to look into something for me, then forget you ever did it." Just in case, he added silently. Just in case something wild turns up.

Eric swallowed noticeably. "Okay."

"I need you to go back over all my uncle's dockets."

"Which uncle?" Eric's jaw dropped. *"Glowan?"*

"That's right."

"He's been on the bench for twenty-five years! There have got to be thousand of cases!"

"I know it's daunting," Jesse allowed. "If you want to do it after hours, I'll see that you get the overtime." He knew Eric and his wife had just bought a house.

Eric brightened at that. "Any particular place I should start looking?"

Jesse thought about it. "With his work right here in the city."

"That was at least fifteen years ago. I mean, he's been on the superior court for a while now, right?"

Jesse nodded absently. He was remembering something Angela had said about children last night at dinner. *I haven't really considered it in a very long time…maybe fifteen years.* Was there a connection?

"What exactly am I looking for this time?" Eric asked.

"The name Angela Byerly."

"As in the *medical examiner?*"

"Mum's the word here, Eric," Jesse warned again.

"You think she did something *illegal?*"

"Maybe. Or maybe something illegal was done to her. Find out."

"Yes, sir."

Jesse sat back in his chair when the investigator had gone. He swigged cold coffee and grimaced. So he would find out what had happened between her and his uncle. None of the other avenues were panning out. Hell, for all he knew, it could be pertinent. No stone unturned, he vowed, and every day that passed was another day that they were running out of time before that DNA testing came back on his hair. At this point, he was more worried about that for her sake than his own.

But it was more than that. He really had to know what had happened now, for his own protection and self-preservation.

He was falling hard for this woman. And fast. She had him on an emotional roller coaster, when he'd always preferred the sedate ride of a luxury car. He had every right and reason to check up on her.

Why, then, did he feel as though he was betraying her in the worst possible way?

Chapter 9

Angela wore violet. She chose a suit, professional enough except for the color, and the slender bracelet she fastened around her right ankle. And instead of a crisp blouse, she let a hint of lace show between the lapels.

A woman had died, and somehow it was her fault. A man had kissed her, and she had *enjoyed* it. She was bordering on desperate, and, as always, she fought it with color and clothes.

She didn't actually get to the morgue until eleven. On her way out the door, she was paged. An employee at the university library had found a periodical she needed for a lecture she'd agreed to give there. She swung by to pick it up, and in the meantime she heard on the scanner that a ninety-six-year-old man was found dead in his living-room recliner, his television still shouting bursts of canned laughter.

Angela suspected that his heart had simply given out, but since he had died alone and no one could say why for certain, he was a case for the medical examiner's office. Normally, she wouldn't have picked him up herself, but she was already out on the street, and she still had one of the office's six vans from collecting Lisette Chauncy's body yesterday. Trusting that one of the cops on the scene would help her load him, she went by the old man's apartment first.

By the time she got to the morgue, her offices were bustling and all the autopsy rooms were full. She parked in the rear, backing the van into one of the bays to deliver the deceased. She glanced absently at the red bio-hazard warning on the roll-up garage door, and even that made her think of Jesse again. He seemed so squeamish about the trappings of her job.

Remembering that morning kiss, she touched her fingers to her mouth as she went inside, passing two orderlies who rushed to meet the van. She never heard them when they called out good-morning.

Brigid Cross was seated at the receptionist's desk.

"Where's Candace?" Angela asked, surprised to see her there.

"Out sick. You need to fire her, Dr. Byerly."

"Well, it's entirely possible she just needs a flu shot."

"This time of year?" Brigid waved a hand at the computer. "You know I'm not one to squeal, but..."

Her voice trailed off. Angela didn't answer. In fact, Brigid had squealing down to a fine art.

"These data bases are weeks behind," Brigid accused.

"I'll talk to her about it." Angela was almost glad for the innocuous problem. "In the meantime, I need you to do Mr. Ponterelli."

"Who's Mr. Ponterelli?"

Angela told her about the elderly man who had just come in. Brigid brightened. This job would be one of lesser evils. An old man dying naturally beat the devil out of the Lisette Chauncys of the world.

Angela went to her office and found the message from Jesse. She called him back. He was out to lunch.

"Must be nice," she muttered. It was a rare day when she didn't brown-bag it and eat at her desk, although that was largely by her own choice. She hated taking time for lunch, and she hated spending money on something she could just as easily fix at home, no matter how much she earned now. And she *never* broke at eleven o'clock for an extended break.

She stared at her office wall and considered again the vast differences between them. She couldn't help wondering why a man like him would want to spend time with a woman like her.

She flinched at the mental image of him asleep on her sofa and refused to wonder if he had ever slept on anyone else's sofa. More likely in their beds, she suspected, then went to check the autopsy rooms.

She collected the protocols from the completed weekend cases and took them back to her desk to glance over and sign. She came to Lisette's halfway through the pile. She stared down at her meticulous mention of the single black hair caught in the woman's fingers, and her heart pounded.

She closed her eyes, signed the protocol and tossed it into the finished basket. She wished desperately that Jesse had made some veiled mention of that recorder in his message. She needed to know what they were going to do about it.

Then she realized what she'd thought and her breath snagged. What *they* were going to do.

There was no "they," she thought frantically. She could not allow there to be a "they." Okay, so he had kissed her. She *knew* that that wouldn't amount to a hill of beans when the chips were down. He wouldn't protect her if things got really ugly. He would protect her only as long as he needed to in order to take care of his own reputation.

She remembered the splicing machine again, and her pulse suddenly skyrocketed. *What had she done?* He'd kissed her and she'd barely had another rational thought since.

Wildly, she shot to her feet, then simply stood there behind her desk, her hands fisted. She had left for work this morning as he had indicated she should. *Sit tight,* he had said. Her heart thudded. She had walked out of her house and left that device right where it had been, in her printer drawer.

He'd wanted her to leave it last night, too. He'd wanted her to leave it and go to his sister's. *Why?* Anyone could be in there right now, she realized, in her home, planting more evidence. And if someone else tipped off Homicide that the machine was in her house, that would make matters so very much worse. If they found it in her home and she herself didn't turn it in, that would look bad, very bad. It wasn't a piece of equipment that might normally be found in someone's home. It was sophisticated, reasonably rare.

She grabbed her purse and hurried out of her office. Brigid came out of the X-ray room as she dashed down the hall.

"Is something wrong?"

"Yes," Angela gasped, then whipped around to look at her deputy again. "Did you get Ponterelli out of my van?"

"Sure. That's who I was just taking pictures of."

"Thank God." There was no time to try to catch a cab, and she definitely didn't want to take the old man with her.

She raced outside and swung into the vehicle, fumbling for the keys she'd left in the ignition. *Please, let everything be all right. Please don't let him have betrayed me.*

And she knew in that moment that it was too late. If Jesse turned out to be just like the others, she wouldn't be able to bear it.

He had kissed her. And she had liked it.

Jesse got her message when he returned from his lunch with Alvin Carper, the reporter from the *Inquirer*. He had hoped to pin the man down about why he hadn't taped his conversation with the person claiming to be Detective O'Donnell. There had to be more going on there than met the eye. But Carper claimed that the caller had caught him off guard and he'd simply forgotten to record their conversation. The guy had been sweating bullets, too, understandably. He'd left himself wide open to accusations of libel.

Jesse wasn't worried about that. He had bigger fish to fry.

He sat down at his desk, then called Angela back.

"Not in," said a harried female voice.

He glanced at the time of the message. "She called me no more than twenty minutes ago."

"I can't help that. She's gone now, and this place is a zoo. She took off like her tail was on fire, and now this funeral-home guy is here to collect the Chauncy woman, and I can't find any release form for her. Dr. Byerly didn't say anything about releasing that body."

Jesse's blood went cold.

There was no way that Abe or Gwen Chauncy would make funeral arrangements without consulting him. When he'd gone home this morning to shower and change, there had been no less than four messages from the couple, wanting to know when they could possibly bury their daughter. No, he realized, they would not have gone ahead with funeral arrangements before a signed release form had been obtained.

"Don't release her," Jesse snapped, finding his voice again.

"Well, that's all well and good for you to say, but—"

"This is the D.A. And I'm telling you from the top, *don't release her.*"

"Well, I wasn't going to, not without authorization."

"Who is this?" Jesse demanded coldly.

"Dr. Cross. I'm a deputy. Our receptionist is out or I wouldn't have been here at the desk at all," she said, sounding childishly miffed.

"What does the man look like?" he snapped, ignoring her response.

"Who?" Brigid asked.

"Whoever is trying to collect Lisette Chauncy's body!"

"Oh. He's—" She broke off.

"What?" Jesse growled. "He's *what?*"

"Gone."

"Gone?"

"He must have scooted out of here while I was talking to you."

"Weren't you watching him?" Jesse roared.

"No. I had my back turned to give this conversation some privacy. I mean, we were discussing *him.*"

It made sense, but that didn't make Jesse happy. "I'll be right there."

"Something's wrong, isn't it?"

"Very." He grabbed his suit coat again.

Whoever was doing this was foolhardy and brazen. Walking right into the M.E.'s office to take the body! It boggled Jesse's mind.

"I knew it," Brigid was saying. "I mean, the way she ran out of here…"

Jesse came back to the conversation, one sleeve still dangling. "Dr. Byerly ran out? Did she say where she was going?"

"No. But I asked her if something was wrong, and she said yes."

Jesse's blood chilled even more. "Listen to me. I want you to stand beside that body and don't leave it until you see the whites of my eyes. Got it?"

"Yours personally, or one of your investigators?"

"Mine."

"Got it."

Jesse hung up and left his office. The long center hallway was a madhouse. He jostled attorneys, cops and detectives, just barely resisting the urge to run.

"Hey, Jesse."

He looked up without breaking stride, trying to find who had spoken. The voice came from in front of him, and he plowed right into the corresponding body.

"Oh. Hi, Charlie."

Price dropped an irritatingly familiar hand on his shoulder, trying to detain him. "Got a minute?"

"No," Jesse said bluntly, pulling away. "Actually, I don't. Maybe this afternoon. Check with my secretary."

He stepped into the elevator just as the door began to close. He didn't see the man's face redden or the way he changed direction abruptly, going back the way he had come.

It hadn't been touched.

Angela had dragged open the printer cabinet again, and the splicing device was still in the same place. She sank to her knees in front of it and leaned her forehead against the cool wood of the desk, forcing herself to breathe deeply and evenly.

No cops had been here to claim it. No one had tricked her. Jesse hadn't set her up, and no one else had reported it, either. The adrenaline rushed out of her, and she realized she was crying in relief.

After a moment, she leaned back on her haunches and swiped a shaky hand over her eyes. And something odd happened to her heart. Her head was still howling that she couldn't, shouldn't trust him, but her heart began whispering *maybe, maybe, maybe...*

"Oh, Jesse," she whispered aloud. "Please don't hurt me."

In the meantime, she determined, she was going to do what she knew she should have done last night. She was going to get rid of this thing.

She'd go directly to Captain Kennery. He was John Gunner's immediate boss. And he was the one who had found that tape with Jesse's voice on it in the first place. It was not insurance. She knew better than to believe that. She didn't think that Kennery would accept her explanation of how she had come by the machine simply because she was one of Gunner's best friends. He wouldn't do it because she was now the chief M.E. or because she had been with the D.A. when the damned thing had been left in her home. She didn't trust him. He might well arrest her on the spot. But there was no one else she trusted more in that department, and she had to turn this in herself. She wished futilely that John Gunner was in town.

She stood up, then she hesitated, that little voice whispering again. *Maybe...*

Should she call Jesse and tell him what she planned to do? *Were* they in this together? The possibility was overwhelming. She pressed a hand to her eyes.

Maybe, maybe, maybe...

She dropped into her desk chair and reached for the phone.

Jesse had returned from lunch, then he had gone right back out again.

"Well, please tell him that I called again," she told his secretary.

"I'm not sure when he'll be back," the woman said defensively.

"Fine. If I don't hear from him in an hour, I'll call again."

She hung up. She wasn't going to wait an hour. At least she had tried.

She found a box of latex gloves in the medical bag she kept at home. She went downstairs to the kitchen and got a large plastic trash bag from under the sink. Then she went back to the office and slid the device into the bag, touching it only on the edges, having as little contact with it as possible.

She was halfway up Ninth Street when her beeper sounded. She kept driving and fumbled for it in her bag, keeping one eye on the traffic. She checked the number.

Her office.

She didn't dare park the city van with its precious cargo anywhere long enough to use a pay phone. She would call in from Kennery's office, she decided. She kept driving.

"She's not answering her pager," Angela's secretary said fretfully.

"She's probably not near a phone. Give it time," Brigid suggested. Her calm irritated Jesse. Then his stomach moved with a sudden, sick sensation.

Was Angela all right? Dear God, had this nut moved on her? His pulse began to race, and he had to work to get control of it. There was nothing he could do about it right now except wait awhile longer and pray that she would call in.

He turned his attention back to Brigid. "All right, give it to me again."

"I didn't really pay a lot of attention to his personal appearance," she repeated for the third time. "I mean, he was *dressed* like someone from a funeral home. Black suit. White shirt. Dark gray tie. I'd guess he was in his late thirties, maybe his early forties. I told you—what struck me most was his hair."

Greasy, the woman had called it. When Jesse had pressed her for details, she'd said it had been slicked back off his forehead with some kind of "goop."

Jesse looked at the investigator he'd called over from his office to make sure the guy was getting all this down. They'd already questioned all the other employees. The morgue was hectic today, and everyone else had been so busy they'd scarcely noticed one more funeral-home employee hanging around at the reception desk.

No one had noticed any unusual cars in the lot, either. But then, a hearse wouldn't be considered unusual here, and if the guy had been masquerading as a funeral-home employee, then it was a safe bet that that was what he was driving.

Where the hell would he have gotten a hearse? Jesse wondered.

"And you've never seen him before in your life?" he clarified, thinking with another lurch of his gut that that ruled out his original supposition that this was the work of someone in Angela's office.

That left someone from his own office as a possibility, he reasoned. The deputy medical examiners would not necessarily know his own deputies and investigators by sight. He remained convinced that the culprit had inside knowledge or access to one or both of their offices, dating back to the Shokonnet release form he'd forged.

Brigid sat back in her chair, frowning. "You know, maybe it's just because you've asked me that so many times now, but—"

"But what?" Jesse demanded.

"I'm starting to think that maybe I *do* know him from some-where."

He started to ask her where and realized how stupid that was. "Think about it," he said instead. "Think hard."

"If I *did* recognize him, he probably doesn't usually wear his hair like that."

"That's a safe assumption," Jesse said tightly, and she gave him an unpleasant look.

Damn it, the bastard had been *here*. Right here, right under their noses. Jesse thought again that whoever he was, he was bold as brass.

"And you didn't see his paperwork," he said aloud to Brigid again.

"No. I told you. The first thing I did was get the case protocol from Dr. Byerly's desk. She'd signed it, but there was no release form attached. I'd just brought the protocol back to the reception desk when you called. I turned my back to talk to you, and that was when he disappeared.

Jesse swore. Now he had another question. What had happened to make the guy turn tail and run? He couldn't have known at that point that it was the D.A. on the phone. *Brigid* hadn't initially known it was the D.A. on the phone.

The answer hit him like a jolt of electricity. The guy must have seen someone who might have recognized him. Maybe he'd taken off quickly before that person could notice him. Another hint that it was someone who worked for the city?

His stomach burned.

The phone finally sounded on Angela's secretary's desk. He almost lunged for it and restrained himself at the last moment.

The secretary answered and spoke briefly, then she held out the phone to Jesse. "It's Dr. Byerly."

Jesse grabbed the phone.

"What are you doing there?" Angela demanded. "Oh, God, something else has happened, hasn't it?"

Inherent caution rose in him, some instinct not to talk about it over the phone, if for no other reason than he rarely said too much on a telephone. "How far away are you?" he countered.

"Ten minutes, barring gridlock."

"Good enough," Jesse answered. "I'll be here." Then his

voice softened. "Something nearly happened, but we've got everything under control." He remembered how tense, how dazed, she'd been last night. He didn't want her driving in that condition. "Be careful," he added, then hung up. He immediately picked up the receiver again to call his office. He was going to be here awhile. "Libby," he said when his secretary came on the line, "any messages?"

"The medical examiner called a couple of times."

"I've caught up with her."

"And Captain Kennery of the homicide unit called no more than thirty seconds ago."

Jesse's heart skipped. "What did he want?"

"For you to call him back ASAP. He says it's urgent."

Jesse disconnected and called Kennery back. He identified himself and thought the captain's response was slow in coming.

"You want to tell me what's going on with this Chauncy thing?" Kennery asked finally.

Jesse had a sense of a dark, evil net settling over him, around him, ensnaring him. "I'm not following you," he said cautiously.

"The chief medical examiner just left here. She's submitted a tape-splicing machine for evidence."

Jesse's heart stopped.

What the hell was she doing? After his shock came livid anger. *Ten minutes away.* That could certainly have put her at the Police Administration Building. Why hadn't she said anything?

He answered himself in the next moment. Because she didn't trust him. She was still running this show on her own.

"I'll get back to you on it," he said sharply.

"Yeah, well, I'm in no position to force your hand," Kennery snapped, equally as angry. "But if your office isn't planning to charge Dr. Byerly with anything, I'd sure as hell like to know why. I've got six guys working their butts off on this thing. I've got everyone from the commissioner to the mayor breathing down my neck, calling me on it daily. Someone spliced that tape with your voice on it, and while I'm trying to keep that quiet—at *your* request—Dr. Byerly turns up here with the goddamned machine."

"We're not charging anyone with anything at this time," Jesse said tersely. "And I would appreciate it if your office would refrain, also." He grimaced. It was nothing more than a polite warning. If the P.P.D. charged her, he was making it clear that he would not take the case to the grand jury for an indictment.

"Do you have any more evidence that you're not sharing with my guys?" Kennery demanded.

"No," Jesse said honestly. His own investigators hadn't found anything pertinent yet. And Kennery hadn't asked him if he had people on it.

"So how in the hell did she get this? I'm not sure I buy her explanation."

"What was it?" Jesse asked neutrally.

"She said she was out last evening and came home to find someone had broken into her home. I checked and there *is* a police report. That district is sending a copy over to me. She said she didn't find this thing until sometime after the cops had left."

Jesse hesitated only a heartbeat. "To my knowledge that is correct."

"So why did she wait so long to bring it to me?"

"I have no idea."

"And if you knew about it, why didn't *you* tell me?"

"I didn't say I knew about it."

Kennery swore again. "Manilla said you were there last night."

"It takes some time for things to go between the channels of my office and yours," Jesse countered, relenting without actually admitting anything.

"A phone call would have done it," Kennery snapped.

Jesse said nothing. Kennery gave up.

"Well, be in touch. She's a name in this city, a top-ranking officer, and damn it, I *hate* these political cases. And I still have this tape here with *your* voice on it." That seemed to overwhelm him for a moment. He was silent. "And John Gunner likes her, and I like Gunner," he finally finished lamely.

"I understand," Jesse said, and inwardly shuddered at his own repertoire of deliberately-vague comments. His pulse was still jackhammering.

He hung up and heard a noise behind him. Angela stepped into the office.

"What the hell have you done?" he asked with deadly calm, oblivious to the others in the room.

Angela stopped short. She felt the anger coming off him in waves. What had happened?

She cried out when he caught her elbow and propelled her back out of the office. All her panic and inherent fear came alive again, clawing and wild. She hurried to keep pace with him as he headed out the nearest exit, the one provided by the rear bay doors, but as soon as they were outside and alone, she wrenched away from him, breathing hard.

"What's wrong with you?" she demanded.

"Why couldn't you just have trusted me on this?" he snarled. "Do you have any idea what you've done to me?"

Chapter 10

Angela gaped at him. Then she leaned weakly against the van to watch him. He paced with exaggerated care, every turn one of angry masculine grace. He was tense...dangerous.

"Okay," he said finally. "Let's take everything personal out of this for the time being."

She found herself remembering the way he had kissed her only that morning, of how treacherously important it had been to her to go home and find that tape-splicing device, that no one had tipped the cops off that it was in her possession. And she did not think she would ever look at this man without thinking personal thoughts again.

"We won't call it trust," he went on. "We'll call it *cooperation*. You took that machine to Homicide! Don't you think I had a right to know what you were up to?"

"Oh." Her breath caught. Word certainly traveled fast.

He stopped pacing to look at her. "Did it ever occur to you to consult with me first? Did it ever occur to you that I might have thought of a better way to handle it?"

"Then you should have told me!" she snapped, getting angry, as well.

"I might have if you had bothered to call me back!"

"Bothered? *Bothered?* I tried *twice!*"

"I was trying to corner Alvin Carper!" he roared. Then he added more quietly, "I was in and out. I just kept missing your calls."

She flinched back. He shoved his hands into his pockets as though to keep himself from grabbing her. He swore colorfully enough to make even her blush.

"I'm sure your constituents in the gutter would be very pleased to know you can speak their lingo," she said shakily.

His eyes narrowed. "I wish you'd thought about my constituents half an hour ago."

"They have nothing to do with this."

"They have *everything* to do with this!"

Then she understood, and her jaw dropped. "You think I took that splicer in to deliberately muddy your chances for re-election? And you're complaining that *I* don't trust *you?*"

"I don't think you thought of my re-election at all."

It was true enough that she winced uncomfortably. "I don't see what one has to do with the other. It was found in *my* house—"

"Planted there while I was having dinner with you."

"That doesn't implicate you!" she protested.

"The tape was of *my* voice! This *involves* me, Angela. In a highly detrimental way. When it gets out, when the press gets wind of it, my opponent is going to have a field day!"

"I thought you were running unchallenged," she managed weakly. Her mind was racing.

"Not *unchallenged.* Someone else will run. The Republicans will come up with somebody. The party won't just lie down and die. But that's just the D.A. thing. It's the *mayoral* race that worries me. They'll be digging up every scrap of dirt on me then that they can find. And until half an hour ago, I didn't have any."

Angela paled. "But—"

"But nothing," he growled again, then raked a hand through his hair. "I've got to get back to the office. I've got to do damage control."

"I don't know how to play these games," she whispered wretchedly. "Double-checking my every move to see how the public might take it."

"Well, you'd damned well better learn, lady."

"Why?"

Because you're going to be traveling beside me for a while.
The thought stopped him cold. He just barely prevented the words
from spilling out.

She wasn't a politically proper, drape-over-your-arm kind of
woman. That hadn't changed, but he kept finding it harder to
remember. He wanted her. He enjoyed her. She made everything
feel different, vibrant, alive.

"You can't hide in your morgue forever," he said finally, awkwardly. "Whether you like it or not, your job is political, too."

"I'm hired, not elected."

"You were hired by the city politics. And at some point, staying hired is going to require kissing somebody's backside." He
couldn't fathom why this was making him so angry all over again.

Angela shook her head dazedly. "Why are we even talking
about this?"

One corner of his mouth crooked suddenly into a tired smile.
He shrugged. "It took my mind off the splicer," he confessed.

She watched him. He actually seemed...overwhelmed. And
suddenly, her heart went out to him. No matter that he was a
Hadley. No matter that his uncle and a man very much like him
had destroyed her faith, her heart, her self-esteem. The man standing before her now, looking at the traffic moving by, was a man
who might have his future political career snatched away from
him through no fault of his own.

The fault was all hers, though she hadn't invited it upon herself.
Her heart cracked. "I'm sorry," she whispered. "I wouldn't have
tried to...to deliberately sabotage you for anything."

Something about the admission, her voice, rocked him inside.

"But we had to do *something* with that device," she pleaded.

Jesse exhaled. He did it deliberately so that nothing would
show on his face.

We had to do something? It was the first time she had said
"we," and that did something to him, too. In spite of the fact
that he had more trouble on his hands now than ever, something
warm swelled inside.

"I was going to log the thing into my office personally," he
said at length. "With all the proper paperwork. Nice and legal
and aboveboard. I could have had it checked for fingerprints

through my office. Homicide would eventually have to be informed of it, but it might have bought us just a little more time.''

Angela covered her face with her hands. "I never thought of that.

"I was terrified to just leave it sitting there, incriminating me. I mean, if someone told the cops it was there, and they went and found it, and I hadn't mentioned having it..." She trailed off, overwhelmed. "It would have looked so bad for me. I was just trying to protect myself.''

She was back to "I" again.

"Ah, Angela." He moved to her and hooked an arm around her neck, pulling her toward him. She stiffened, but he'd known she would. He waited for her to pull back, but she didn't. She trembled and remained rigid. "I can't make you trust me," he murmured.

"I want to." And it was true. She wished she could. Suddenly, she wished it desperately. She wondered what it would be like to believe totally in another human being, to never doubt him, to know that she wasn't alone.

"And you won't tell me why you can't," Jesse said.

This time, she did pull away from him. She took a deliberate step in retreat. "This isn't the time.''

No, he realized, it probably wasn't. At least a small portion of him was worried that at any given moment another city van would drive up, disgorging contents he didn't really want to see.

"I'll call Kennery back," he said finally. "I'll give him more of an explanation. He can be trusted as much as anyone can right now. I think he'll probably be willing to sit on this, too. It'll be fine as long as the press doesn't get wind of it before we've gotten to the bottom of what's going on, although the more this guy acts up, the more likely some of his antics will get out." Then he told her about the supposed funeral-home employee coming for Lisette's body.

"He came *here?*" Angela cried.

"So it would seem.''

"He's *nuts!*"

"I've always been of the opinion that anyone who could murder in cold blood usually is.''

"But most killers aren't so cunning! They do it out of passion

and then it's over. This guy is..." At a loss, she stopped. "Nuts,"
she said again.

"I'd guess he thinks he's indestructible."

She shivered. She had known at least one man like that. Charlie
Price had thought he could do anything, get away with anything
at all. And he had.

"Are you sure Kennery will go along with us?" she asked
weakly.

Jesse smiled again, but this time it was almost a grimace.
"Roger hates situations like this. He won't touch it with a ten-
foot pole unless somebody forces the pole into his hand and closes
his fingers around it."

She was shivering, though the air was warm. She hugged herself.

He wanted to hold her. He wanted it as much as he had ever
wanted anything, to tell her that it was going to be okay, that he
wasn't angry anymore. But somehow the physical distance she
had put between them again seemed insurmountable.

"Angela, it's not your fault," he said quietly instead. "I'm
sorry I yelled."

"Of course it's my fault."

"No. If we had just managed to connect this morning, it
wouldn't have turned out this way. It was a matter of circumstances as much as anything else. You were busy, and I was out
of the office."

Her shoulders slumped anyway. "Talk about looking on the
bright side."

"I'm an optimist." He hesitated. "Can I see you again tonight?"

She was startled, then something in her heart actually yearned
this time. "It's probably not wise," she managed to croak, her
throat closing.

"To hell with wise."

"There's your image and all that."

"To hell with my image."

"That's not what you were saying twenty minutes ago."

"I've come to my senses." He needed to see her, he realized.

She gave him a fleeting smile. "If anyone does get around to
leaking it to the press that I might be a suspect, you don't want
to be seen with me, Jesse." *So just tell me we'll stay at home.*

The thought came out of nowhere. She didn't realize until that moment just how badly she wanted to be with him. She tried to tell herself that it was just as simple as not wanting to be alone with all this going on. She didn't entirely believe it.

She waited, her breath suspended. God help her, she wanted him to say it. She wanted to be able to tell him about Charlie so he couldn't possibly be surprised by that, too, with all its implications. And she wanted him to believe her when she told him.

"I've got a fund-raiser tonight," he said instead, and her breath escaped her.

"On a Monday?" she asked too plaintively for her own comfort.

"Today's the deadline for official candidacy for the D.A. race."

Her mouth formed a silent, "Oh." Then she added, frowning, "But I've already seen ad spots for your campaign."

"I'm allowed to spend all the money I want before it's official, as long as it's *my* money I spend. I can't take campaign contributions until tonight."

"You don't need them," she ventured.

He laughed, enjoying her. God, he enjoyed her. On one hand, she was intuitive, educated, intimidatingly smart. And she was so sweetly naive that it touched him.

"Everyone needs them," he assured her.

"You travel in a whole different world from me, Jesse."

He thought about it. "No. Not really. We both work toward the same interests. We go after the bad buys."

"Yes, but I don't have contributors. I don't do wealthy people."

"I'm still holding out hope that you'll make an exception for me."

She looked up at him quickly. She was too startled to be alarmed. Then a burst of laughter escaped her.

He wished suddenly, fervently, that he hadn't met her under the bizarre circumstances they were in, with an election hanging over his head, and someone trying to destroy her. He wished he had all the time in the world to dig through her layers, to find out what had hurt her, to fix it and make it better.

"Come with me tonight," he said again. She shook her head.

"We'll put up a united front," he persisted, "in case any of

this does get out.'' But he knew that what he really wanted was
to have her shining like the sun right beside him.

"I won't hurt you any more than I already have," she said
softly. And she thought of who might be at that fund-raiser.

"I'll keep you away from the hors d'oeuvres. I'll take personal
responsibility for it," he said to lighten the moment. He chose to
believe she was talking about her unorthodox behavior at the wedding.

She hesitated, but she didn't smile this time. "I wouldn't be
comfortable."

"So what's the alternative? I'm not sure I like the idea of your
being home by yourself."

It was close enough to her own fears that her heart stuttered.
Then she was angry. She was damned if she did, and damned if
she didn't. There was fear on both sides. Monsters behind both
doors. She was so tired of being afraid.

She thought frantically of odds. Of the path of least resistance.
It was far more likely Charlie would be at the fund-raiser than
someone would break into her home again tonight. Wasn't it? But
at the fund-raiser, Jesse would be beside her. At home, she would
be alone.

Butterflies crowded into her stomach, but somehow she managed a reply. "I...okay."

He let out a breath that he hadn't been aware of holding. This
was a milestone. He knew it intuitively, though he'd be damned
if he could figure out why.

"I'll pick you up at six. Wear something like you did last
night," he added quickly, just in case. An image of that hat leaped
into his mind's eye.

She nodded a little stiffly. Then she looked up sharply as he
stepped closer to her again. "What?"

"Thank you," he said quietly.

There was no chance for the words to melt her this time because he kissed her.

She froze. Every muscle spasmed, then went rigid. For heav-
en's sake, they were outside in full view of traffic. Then she
realized just how safe that was.

Something warm and slow seeped through her, melting the ice.
Maybe it would be like this morning, she imagined, and everything inside her would stir sweetly and pleasantly. Or maybe it

would be like it had always been before, and something inside her would slam down like jail doors closing.

Suddenly, she needed to find out. She told herself that if there was no real, lasting attraction between them, if it happened once more and everything inside her recoiled, then there was no reason to tear herself up inside over trusting him.

She ought to be sure. That was what she told herself.

She came up onto her tiptoes, leaning into him when he didn't retreat this time. She thought he might have caught his breath, but she was too frightened, too aware of her own pounding heart, to be sure. The last thing she saw was a look of surprise on his face that turned to something hungrier. Then her eyes drifted closed.

It was not fast this time. And no steel doors came clanging shut.

He held her arms just beneath her shoulders in a feather-light embrace, and she had the crazy feeling that it was deliberate, that he was letting her know that she could pull away at any time. But he couldn't know that she needed that.

His mouth claimed hers, but for a moment that felt like eternity, their lips simply clung. No pressure, emotional or physical. Just...sweetness.

She'd expected panic. She'd hoped for pleasure. Instead, something pounded suddenly through her, something she could neither identify nor name. It was needy and desperate, and she found herself threading her fingers into his hair, holding him, wanting more.

Jesse groaned. And then his mouth opened and his tongue skimmed her teeth. Something shuddered inside her. He drew back a little to nip her lower lip. Oh, he was good at this, she thought wildly. And she had never felt like this before in her life.

She found herself pulling him back, straining into him now, afraid and exhilarated, stunned and greedy. This time, his mouth was harder on hers. His tongue drove deeper. She met it tentatively, then with more abandon, and his hands moved, tangling into her hair, pulling her head back, making her open her mouth wider.

Then, suddenly, his hands were gone.

Jesse swore—though she couldn't understand why—and dropped his hands abruptly to his sides again. When she opened her eyes, she could not read his expression. He looked confused, and she couldn't believe that that was an emotion a man like him might be prone to.

"I still want you," he said quietly, "and when this is over, when we're not distracted by this other mess, I'm going to do something about it." It was a warning. And a promise.

She watched, dazed, as he turned away and went to his car. A black Mercedes this time, she realized, polished to a high gloss.

She stared after it as he left the parking lot, finding herself unable to even walk to find a place to sit down.

Chapter 11

She wore something that might have been lavender. Or silver. Or a pearly pink. Every time she moved and light spilled over her from a different angle, the dress shimmered and its color changed. It wasn't short. It was ankle-length. But there was a pretty incredible slit up the front, reaching to a point midway up her thigh.

Jesse was still surprised that she had come with him. He was more surprised that he had invited her. And he was glad he had, and it had nothing to do with their trouble this time.

She still didn't drape well over his arm. It wasn't her style. But she held her own and she held it well. Only her eyes gave her away, he found. Only her eyes revealed that she wasn't entirely comfortable here. They moved constantly.

Jesse kept his own on her as he moved with polished ease among the people gathered for the fund-raiser. He shook hands, laughed when it was appropriate, and once in a while he clapped an appreciative hand on someone's shoulder. Normally, he enjoyed these functions, and he had no qualms about admitting it. But tonight his mind was elsewhere, on someone holding a flute of champagne on the opposite side of the room.

"Hey, Jesse!"

"How are you?" He caught another hand and pumped it.

"Heard anything yet from the Republicans?"

"No. At four o'clock they still hadn't officially registered a candidate."

"Keeping us in the dark until the last moment," someone said sagely.

Jesse nodded. It was a tactic he was familiar with and thoroughly appreciated. It was not so different from the way he held off on going to the grand jury until the last possible moment. Once he did so, he was obliged to turn his evidence over to the defense. He liked to keep them in the dark, guessing and worrying and possibly making tactical errors, until the eleventh hour.

As of four o'clock this afternoon, the Republicans had been doing the same thing to him. They were going to run *someone* against him, and rumors had been running rampant for months as to who it might be. Three or four names had been bandied about, and those same three or four names had spoken publicly of their desire and intention to run against him. It was no secret that if Jesse got in again as D.A., then the city would probably soon have a Democratic mayor, as well. And that was something the Republicans did not want to see happen.

Assuming he ran for mayor, Jesse thought.

His smile faded as he made his way back to the table he shared with his parents, his uncle and one of the cousins who sat on the Senate. He was more than mildly startled by the…well, the rebellious thought. He would run. He had to run. There were few ways he could get out of it, none of them easy.

His eyes searched for Angela again.

She was speaking to a city councilman—one of those, Jesse remembered, who had been at the forefront of the drive to hire her away from Quantico. Jesse realized that of all the women he might have brought with him tonight, any of those from his past, only Dr. Angela Byerly knew enough of the people present that she had no need to cling to him. It was something he should have anticipated and hadn't. Nor had he guessed that it would please him so.

When he moved, Angela excused herself from Joe Campenelli and headed over to join him. Jesse didn't know if he was amused or relieved that she hadn't remained with his family when he'd gotten up to circulate.

He sat and she slid smoothly into the seat next to his. He touched her hand briefly.

"What?" He turned sharply as he realized that his uncle was speaking to him. He felt Angela stiffen beside him.

"I said that the faces missing tonight are the ones I find most interesting."

Jesse looked around. "I hadn't imagined that Abe and Gwen would be interested in attending under the circumstances."

"I wasn't speaking of the Chauncys."

Jesse's eyes moved back to Wendell. "Who, then?"

"Charlie and Monica Price are conspicuously absent, as well."

This time, he felt Angela jolt. He looked at her curiously, but she wouldn't meet his eyes.

Jesse looked back at Wendell. "Actually, I can't say that I'm surprised." Price's had been one of the names tossed about as a possible Republican candidate. The man had conveniently changed his party status a few months ago.

"But it *does* seem revealing that he's not here," Ryan, Jesse's father, joined in. "He's never missed one of your fund-raisers, Jesse."

Jesse nodded and got to his feet again. He reached for Angela's hand. It was ice-cold.

"I still think you look familiar, dear," Isobel said, glancing up at her. "But I simply can't place you."

"He was dancing with her at Tessa's wedding," Wendell supplied, winking at Angela.

Her gut churned.

Isobel's face lightened. "Yes. I remember now."

"You hold some significant position with the city, don't you?" Ryan asked hopefully.

Angela fought for her voice. "I'm the chief medical examiner."

"Oh, how dreadful!" Isobel cried. "How could a woman do that sort of thing?"

"She's a doctor, of course," Jesse supplied, suddenly enjoying himself. "And a lawyer, as well."

"You are?" Isobel looked doubtful. "Who is your family? Are you from the city?"

"Yes. But you wouldn't know them," Angela replied thinly.

Jesse started to turn away, pulling her with him, then he thought of something else. He decided to enjoy himself even more.

"Angela is a very good friend of John Gunner's," he offered.

They watched together as Isobel's face went pale, then got pink. As they walked off, Jesse was laughing to himself. He squeezed her hand.

"I've been waiting weeks to do that," he murmured.

By nine o'clock, Angela was running on pure adrenaline and nerves. She agonized over her decision to come and wished desperately that she had stayed home.

She had worried that Charlie Price would be here. Naively, perhaps, it had never occurred to her that Wendell Glowan would be, that the Hadley clan would come out for this affair in their virtual entirety.

Glowan still didn't recognize her. Tonight she was relieved.

Jesse worked his way through the crowd, pulling her with him this time, and Angela felt herself nodding, smiling, murmuring whenever anyone spoke to her. Then they reached the dance floor and he drew her into his arms.

She had the most absurd thought then. *Ah, safety.*

"You're terrific," he said, his voice low against her ear. "You're doing great."

She decided to let him think so. She looked up at him and dredged for a smile. "There are table scraps in my handbag and Joe Campenelli tried to grab my backside the last time we danced."

Jesse chuckled. "What did you do?"

"If you'll look closely, you'll see that our esteemed councilman is limping."

He laughed outright, then sobered. "No problem with my uncle?" he asked neutrally.

She stiffened. "Not yet."

What the hell had Wendell done? Jesse wondered again.

Angela looked Glowan's way and remembered.

She'd quit school for that one semester. She'd been too distraught, too destroyed, to study anyway, at least until the case came to trial and it was over. She'd been sure that if she could just have some sense of closure, of justice, then she could go back to Princeton and she'd be fine. She'd thought she would heal. And maybe she could have, if it had been anyone but Charlie Price, if anyone but Glowan had been on the bench.

It had started at the end of August, right before she'd been about to return for her senior year. She'd spent September, October and November at home, as well, and by then she'd known that there would be no closure. During the months she'd spent in the city, she had walked into her bedroom on numerous occasions to find Charlie there, waiting for her. She'd pulled open her shower curtain, and there he was. He came in windows and through the basement. *Into her own home.* Whenever he chose. Without warning. No matter what she'd tried to do to stop him. She put extra locks on her doors and windows, so he loitered outside. He'd let days go by without an appearance, and then he would be there constantly, everywhere she turned, for days more.

At some point, even as terrorized as she'd been, Angela had known that his actions were a deliberate method of torturing her. He had a plan. It was a means of keeping her off balance, of making her afraid to even sleep for fear he'd come back, or that he was out there, watching her windows. He'd wanted her to know that he could do whatever he chose, and she would not be able to anticipate him. He'd been slowly and systematically driving her mad. Above all, he'd been making damned sure that he discredited her. And it had worked.

Then the photographs of what Charlie had done to her had disappeared from the evidence room. The people who had heard her scream decided not to testify. And Glowan had chastised *her* and had let Charlie Price leave his court a free man.

The song ended. She kept dancing and stumbled a little when Jesse didn't.

"Are you sure you're all right?" he asked.

"I'm fine," she lied. Maybe she'd make a good politician after all.

"Not much longer now," he promised. "Maybe an hour or so."

"Good," she murmured. And *that* word was heartfelt.

As it turned out, it was nearly two in the morning when he dropped her off at home. There were no cops at the door this time.

"Let me take a look around inside," Jesse said, parking.

She wouldn't argue with him. Her home, her sanctuary, had been violated, and she thought that it was going to be a very long time before she felt completely safe here again. He covered the ground floor while she checked upstairs. They met back in the foyer.

"Everything okay up there?" he asked, watching her face. He thought she looked inordinately pale.

"As near as I can tell."

"I want to stay again." The words were out before he thought them.

"No." Angela shook her head. This afternoon she had *longed* for him to stay. But now she felt enervated, dazed, exhausted. The night had been an ordeal.

She'd spent half the time feeling like an impostor. She'd wanted to scream at Glowan—and wouldn't that have brought the house down? *Look at me! I wasn't good enough fifteen years ago for you to hear my case. Now you're winking at me!* The rest of the time she had been simply praying for a way to blend into the wallpaper, struggling mightily not to give in to the urge to fade back and away, to let them all make her cringe.

She needed to be alone now, she realized, as scary as that still was. All her resources were used up. With the release of the night's tension, she could barely keep her eyes open. If anyone came tonight, she'd sleep right through it. Besides, the night was half over.

"Jesse, I'm tired," she managed to groan. "I just want to sleep."

"And you won't do that if I'm here," he said for her.

She almost smiled. "No."

"You did last night."

"I shocked myself. It won't happen twice. And I woke up with a stiff neck."

Still, he hesitated. "Make sure the alarm's on."

"I will."

"And put my number in your speed dial."

"I'd call 911 first."

She had everything under control, it seemed. So why was he so reluctant to leave her?

He wasn't so much worried about danger, he found, as he was loath to have the evening end. He'd barely had a chance to exchange five sentences with her all evening, what with Wendell and his father and a hundred or so supporters pressing in on him. And oddly, as the evening had worn on, he'd begun to feel like an impostor. They were all watching the old Jesse Hadley. But inside was a man who had begun wanting badly to call it a night, to be done with politics and handshaking and glib responses, to be alone with her to watch the expressions play over her face. He wanted to explore more feelings than he had ever allowed himself to know before.

He cleared his throat. "Well, then...good night."

Her eyes came up to his, a little wide, a little wondering. He realized that she hadn't entirely expected him to respect her wishes. It was hard, damned hard, but he would do it.

He caught her chin in his hand. Gently. Still, he could almost feel her vibrate. Her eyes fluttered closed. He watched her beautiful face for a moment. Watched the color come back into her cheeks. He touched his mouth to hers and felt her sigh against his lips.

Not good enough. He wanted more. Needed more. And again something warned him not to take it even as his hands framed her waist and his tongue dipped and the scent of her filled his head.

He stepped back, away from her, before she could respond one way or the other, not trusting himself to be able to stop if he kept on.

"I'll call you in the morning," he said hoarsely and went out.

He left her empty and wanting. As soon as he'd touched her again, she'd been filled with want. And she didn't know what to do about it, didn't know how to deal with it, because when he turned and walked away as she'd always wanted every other man to do, he left her aching.

Angela groaned, set the alarm and went upstairs to bed, her feet dragging.

Jesse woke Tuesday morning feeling more groggy than usual. He felt drained even after a shower. His eyes felt grainy and his muscles were stiff.

His first thought was to wonder if Angela was okay.

He went barefoot down to the kitchen, a towel hitched around his waist, his hair wet and disheveled. He picked up the phone, then replaced it again. It was barely six o'clock.

A cup of coffee first, he thought. At least then he would have a shot at sounding coherent.

And he wouldn't come off as seeming...smitten. Hooked. Ensnared so far beyond reason that he was calling a woman at six o'clock in the morning to see if she was all right, when he had only left her four hours ago. It was something he had never done before in his life.

He wondered what she looked like in the morning when she had slept well and deeply—not half-sitting up, in her clothing, on the sofa. He wondered what she might look like in the morning if she'd spent the night being well and truly loved. His blood rushed suddenly and hotly, with no slow buildup, no warning. He swore at himself and put on a pot of coffee.

When he'd called her that first Sunday morning and her breath had sounded short and gasping, he'd actually thought it was because she had been loving someone. Now that he knew her better, he doubted it.

She'd kissed him yesterday like a woman shocked to find that she enjoyed it. But oh, she had enjoyed it. She'd sighed her way into his arms last night, a bare beginning, inviting more.

Everything inside him moved more hotly again, gathering at his groin this time. He called himself a few choice names and went out to the front porch to collect the newspaper. This was another priority on his list for today—something he *should* be thinking about. This morning he would find out for certain who'd be his opponent in the D.A. race.

He flipped through the city section while he waited for the coffee to brew, stifling a yawn. And then he found it. Charlie Price. He'd put his bid in late yesterday afternoon.

"Surprise, surprise," Jesse muttered. "Hope you're up for the fight of your life, pal."

He poured a cup of coffee and drank without waiting for it to cool. The major problem with Price was that he had a great deal of family money to back him up. Not Hadley money, but a good bit just the same. He could mount a colorful, emphatic campaign. Working somewhat against Price was the fact that he was an ACLU attorney. He'd spent years defending the rights of the downtrodden, often in the interest of criminals who felt their own had been violated. He had a reputation for being soft on crime.

Jesse wondered why the man would make such a switch, from defending people to putting criminals behind bars. Money? He shook his head. The district attorney's job didn't pay that well, at least not considering the family income Price already had.

Jesse decided he wasn't worried. He looked at the wall clock. It was nearly six-thirty. *Now* he could call Angela.

He reached for the phone just as something else in the paper caught his eye. Even in a grainy, black-and-white newspaper photo, he knew the golden sunshine of her hair. He scowled and stepped back to the paper on the kitchen counter, pulling the society page toward him this time.

"Damn it," he muttered. It was the photograph that fool had taken the other night at the restaurant. The caption stunned him.

He read it again. *A consortium of enemies.* He finally found the accompanying story a little farther down the page, part of a gossipy column written by Alvin Carper.

Alvin Carper. Again.

Jesse's eyes flew over the words, then he went back to read them a second time aloud. "'At first appearance...jut a handsome couple enjoying an intimate dinner at Langoustier on Sunday evening. But he's the district attorney, now officially running for re-election, and the lovely lady is none other than Dr. Angela Byerly, chief medical examiner for the City of Brotherly Love. We'll speculate that there's no love lost here, however...a matter of little-known public record is that Dr. Byerly once loudly and passionately cried rape—*date* rape, no less—in The Honorable Wendell R. Glowan's court of law. For those of you not up on your Hadley history, that's our D.A.'s uncle. Judge Glowan had the good sense to throw the case out. We have to wonder just what these two could possibly have been discussing over lobster and wine. Perhaps for our M.E., old grudges still simmer. She doesn't look happy. We'll keep you posted.'''

Jesse stood immobile, rocked to his soul.

He looked at the picture again. His pulse began slamming with rage.

Angela didn't look happy. She looked uncomfortable. Skittish. Wanting, and not wanting, thawing but trying not to. Her eyes were a little haunted, something he hadn't recognized then, not entirely. He remembered every word they had exchanged that evening, and now he knew precisely why she had looked, why she had behaved, the way she had.

Rape. Date rape.

He felt sick with anger.

He straightened away from the counter and shoved the paper away from him. Then he gathered it and crumpled it savagely in his fists before hurling it toward the recycling bin.

He had known, he realized dazedly. Of course he had.

Not about Wendell. Not about his own family's involvement in the mess. He hadn't made that connection—yet. But he'd certainly known that she was broken, had felt it, sensed it, had seen it in her eyes. He'd tasted it in the way she'd kissed him. It had been there in the way she always held herself slightly apart. It was why he had been reluctant to hold her too tightly, to kiss her too roughly, to make her yield. It was why, when his hands had gotten away from him yesterday afternoon and had tangled in her hair with a will of their own, he'd pulled himself back hard and fast and instinctively.

It was why he had not tried to sate himself with her. Pure instinct, but strong.

No, she wouldn't tell him, he saw now. Especially not if Wendell had allowed the bastard to walk off scot-free. *Why?* Why in the hell would Wendell have done that?

What was it John Gunner had said at the wedding? *Your uncle screwed her over.* And Jesse knew, grimly and with a sick feeling, that the victims always felt that way when something went wrong. They blamed the system, the judge, the lawyer, whoever had been forced to let them down by virtue of their country's own laws. But Gunner was a cop. He should have known better.

So there had to be more to it.

Date rape. He knew firsthand how often it came before the court, and he knew how the victims could be raked over the coals by the defense. He had handled only a few such cases in eight years, because the women nearly always backed off when their own reputations were torn to shreds.

Angela hadn't done that. Something moved hard in the area of his heart. She had made it all the way into court. She had dragged her courage around her and had gone to Wendell seeking justice, and for some reason she had been turned away.

His stomach filled with an oily, hot feeling. "Oh, angel," he said aloud.

He wouldn't call her. He would find her. She would probably be devastated when she saw the paper.

But first he had to find his uncle.

Chapter 12

As a general rule, Angela preferred to have breakfast and read the paper at work. Hers was a business in which a lot of developments occurred at night. She had learned over the years that if there was going to be a problem, it would invariably occur first thing in the morning.

At six-thirty, she finished dressing, choosing a more somber blue today. The skirt was a series of clever patches of gray and indigo with a hint of mauve stitching. She topped it with a short-sleeved indigo sweater. The tension of last night lingered in her head like a bad hangover. She knew in her heart that if anything else happened today, not even a clown suit would help.

She wrapped a bagel and stuck it into her purse, then grabbed her medical bag and the newspaper on her way out the door. Instinctively, out of habit, she carefully inspected the cabdriver who pulled over for her before she actually got into his car. Once it might have been Charlie, and for some reason those memories seemed fresher than ever now.

She found the article on his candidacy on the first page of the city section as she thumbed through the paper on the drive to work. Her blood rushed. Her fingers and toes went icy and numb. She wondered wildly if she was going to pass out.

"Pull over," she told the driver, her voice a croak. He looked back at her in the mirror. "Pull over!" she shouted.

She thought she was going to be sick, but she wasn't. She got out on legs that wobbled and leaned heavily against a mailbox, struggling to breathe evenly. After a few minutes, she felt somewhat less light-headed, but her heart still thrummed.

He was running against Jesse. Charlie Price was running for district attorney. He was crazy, twisted, abominably cruel, but she was one of the few people in the world who knew that. And he was a Price, and somehow he had passed his bar exam and now he was going to run for elected office.

She had wondered for fifteen years if something like this would ever happen. Like the Hadleys, many of the Prices were involved in politics. Even while she had been in Virginia, she'd subscribed to the Philadelphia newspapers. Just to know. Just to be sure. Outside of his representing an ACLU case now and again, or attending some social gala, she had rarely seen his name in print.

Suddenly, now, she understood Jesse's father's innuendos last night. She'd been so tense then that they'd scarcely registered.

"No, no," she whispered aloud. "This is so *wrong*."

He couldn't possibly win, she thought frantically. Could he? Against Jesse? No, God, no. The only thing more powerful than a Price was a Hadley.

Unless someone—unless *she*—destroyed Jesse's good name.

The realization stunned her. She clapped a hand over her mouth, afraid once again that she might be sick.

"Lady?" the driver called out.

She couldn't answer.

"You want I should just leave you?"

"I...no. No, I'm coming."

Angela returned to the car, shaking. The man drove off again. Even now that the truth had occurred to her, it still seemed unbelievable. Then she thought again of all the things Charlie had done to her in the past. The taunts, the games, the cruel manipulation. The terror. The craziness. And his constant, unflagging belief that he could never be caught or punished. He had told her that so many times, laughing at her frustration, at her fear. She had known even then that he was psychotic, though no one believed her. But that was part of the definition of the term, wasn't it? He was a man who gave a smiling face to society, championing victims' rights and the constitution, appearing so utterly normal and admirable. Underneath all that, Charlie Price was a monster.

The cab stopped in front of the morgue. Angela wasn't aware of it.

"This was where you wanted, right, lady?"

She looked dazedly out the window at the building. "Yes." She pushed money at him and got out.

The morgue was deserted except for one night watchman. "Hey, Doc," he called out. "Nothing happening here. We only had three come in last night."

"Well, it's a new moon," she answered vacantly. And it really was true that loonies came out of the woodwork and wreaked havoc on a full moon.

Except Charlie Price. He had done it whenever he pleased. No one had believed her then. No one would believe her now.

"Dr. Byerly? Are you all right?"

She stopped walking. The night watchman had followed her into her office. Somehow she had come to stand behind her desk without even realizing it.

"I'm fine," she managed to reply.

"You don't look fine. You know, there's flu going around."

"I know. It's not that."

Lisette's body. Suddenly, she had an overpowering, inexplicable need to make sure it was still in the refrigerator. She tore past the startled man, into the hall again.

Anything could have happened last night. Anything. If this was all Charlie's doing, he was capable of any abomination at all.

She used both hands and all her weight to haul back on the door to the huge walk-in. She moved frantically among the gurneys, checking name tags. As usual, they had a full house. There were too many bodies and not enough drawers. She found Chauncy, but wasn't satisfied. She opened the bag to make sure the correct face was inside.

It was Lisette's. Angela started to breathe again, then she noticed that there was a note tied around the woman's neck. Angela swayed.

She worked it free. Her fingers fumbled and trembled. Her eyes burned with unshed tears of frustration. She took the small piece of paper out into the hallway to read it where the light was better, blinking furiously.

Keep your mouth shut. Next time it could be you.

Angela moaned.

"Doc, you're really worrying me."

She spun around to find the night watchman still following her. "Who was here last night, Leo?"

"Here? Nobody."

"For God's sake, you just said we had three cases come in!" she cried.

"Well, yeah. But nobody other than that. I mean, nobody who shouldn't have been here."

"Did you come on at midnight?"

"Yeah."

Think. "Where are the three? Who exactly came in?"

He pulled open the refrigerator again. "Right there. On the left side."

Angela stumbled back into the coldness. She checked all three new bags. There was nothing outlandish or peculiar about any of them.

"Okay," she breathed. "Okay."

"Okay what?"

"I need the paperwork."

"Sure thing. It's all on my desk."

She followed him woodenly to the back of the building. His desk was sensibly located near the unloading bays. No one used the front door at night.

Had Charlie come in *that* way? No, she reasoned. Impossible. That door would have been locked for the night. The alarm would have gone off.

I will fight back this time, damn you. I will fight until my last breath. I'm not twenty-one anymore. I'm not a kid on a scholarship anymore. And maybe, just maybe, I might have a stand-by-my-side pal in the D.A.

Angela froze in midstride. That, she realized, was exactly what Charlie was afraid of. It was why things were escalating so suddenly, so wildly. He'd made a big jump from the forged release form to murder. Because that release form had started her and Jesse working together.

He wanted to discredit Jesse, of course. He was trying to throw a pall of public suspicion over him even if it was never substantiated. But more than anything else, Charlie feared *her* position now. He was afraid she was going to talk about what he had done to her. *That* was why he was trying to discredit her. Again. Just like before. So no one would believe her this time, either.

Except this time, the stakes were obviously higher. This time, he needed to use more subterfuge and he was opening the floodgates to a million horrors.

She had to find Jesse.

She forced herself to move again, to collect the paperwork on the incoming cases. She took it all back to her desk and studied it closely. Everything matched what she had seen in the refrigerator. Angela sat back in her chair, shaking. She wasn't sure what she was looking for. *Think it out,* she instructed herself again. She picked up the papers once more.

In order for him to have put that note around Lisette Chauncy's neck, Charlie had to have been here in the morgue. In order for him to have been here in the morgue, he would have to have dropped off one of these bodies. Which one? Did it matter?

Yes, she thought, yes. At this point, everything mattered.

She stood up, feeling stronger, more determined, and went back to Leo's desk. "Who dropped these people off?" she asked, careful to keep her voice even this time.

"The cops brought the accident case in. Ed Thackery caught the gang-fight thing. And Nelson Thomas brought in the old lady."

Nelson was another of her deputies. Okay. That meant that Charlie had probably been masquerading as one of the cops. *That* was terrifying. It reminded her that Charlie Price was capable of any audacity.

Angela groaned and went back to her office. Jesse would believe her. Surely he would. *Dear God, he has to.* This wouldn't be like before.

She sat down again at her desk and found that she was not only praying for someone to help her stop Charlie Price this time. She was praying that Jesse really was the kind of man she was beginning to think he was and that he would stand by her.

She realized, incredibly, that both prayers were of equal importance. She was going to put her trust in him now. All of it.

"He's not in," Jesse's secretary said.

"It's after nine o'clock!" Angela cried. And this was her third call.

"I can't help that," the woman snapped. "He's not here."

"Where is he?"

"I told you before. I don't know."

"Isn't he generally in by now?"

The woman hesitated, and for the first time Angela heard concern in her voice. "Almost always."

Something was wrong. She felt it.

She hung up slowly and wished desperately that she had that slip of paper Jesse had pushed into her sweatpants' pocket last Sunday. She'd left it at home after putting his number into her speed-dial memory last night. Now she was sure something had happened to him and she had no way of finding out what.

She picked up the phone again. She called Captain Kennery and could only pray that she was doing the right thing. But if Jesse was hurt, if he was lying injured somewhere, if Charlie had done something truly atrocious...

If she was right, he had already killed once. He had murdered Lisette. If she was right and he had done something to Jesse, then he was out of control.

"It's Dr. Byerly," she gasped when Kennery picked up. She thought she heard him groan.

"Now what? A smoking gun?"

She ignored that. "It's Jesse Hadley."

Kennery paused. "What about him?"

"I can't find him," she blurted, then, after another long moment, she added, "Are you still there?"

"You want to tell me why that's so alarming?"

"Well, he's..." Suddenly, she felt foolish. "He's not in his office."

"He's a very busy man. But something tells me you already know that."

"He hasn't *been* in his office yet today. I don't think that's normal."

"And you think something's happened to him." It wasn't a question.

Angela let out a shaky breath. "Yes."

"Can you tell me how you've come to this conclusion?"

Angela glanced at the newspaper again and closed her eyes. "I...no. It's just a hunch." Jesse might believe her. She did not think Kennery would.

"Let's try this. What exactly is it that you'd like me to do?"

"I don't know." She thought frantically. "Can't you call whatever district he lives in and have the officers check his house."

"I can do that," Kennery said slowly.

"Please."

"All right."

"Call me back. Please call me back as soon as you know anything."

Kennery grunted something noncommittal and hung up.

Angela laced her fingers tightly together and waited. It was all she could do.

It took the better part of an hour for Kennery to call her back. In the meantime, she paced her office. She called Jesse's secretary three more times until the woman virtually hung up on her. Every once in a while, one of her deputies would peer into her office to watch her worriedly or to ask a question. She managed to give orders and point them all in appropriate directions, but beyond that she couldn't think.

Charlie.

Jesse.

When her extension rang, she lunged for it. "Dr. Byerly."

"It's Roger Kennery." The man sounded very, very tired.

"What happened?" she breathed. "Did you find him?"

"No."

"No?" Oh, dear God. What did that *mean?* She didn't even know if it was good or bad. On one hand, it probably meant he wasn't in any area hospital or involved in a police call. And he definitely wasn't in her morgue. But where *was* he?

She felt panicky, terrified. Not at the thought of fighting Charlie alone. At the thought of *being* alone again, without Jesse's smiling eyes, his strength—even his arrogance and the charisma that hadn't allowed her to push him away. The thought of losing him was suddenly staggering.

When had she started caring so much?

"Look, I need you to come over here, to my office, as soon as possible," Kennery said a little angrily. "Something is obviously going on here, and I'm running out of patience. I want in on it."

Her heart stopped thundering and subsided to a dull roar. She began thinking with some coherency again. She shouldn't have called him, she saw now. She had overreacted. Maybe. Probably. She felt like a fool.

"No," she began, "I'm swamped here. I need to—"

"Dr. Byerly, you're not hearing me. This isn't a request. It's time to start consolidating our forces here." Kennery spoke as though he was ticking things off on his fingers. "We have a dead woman. We have a hair that was found between her fingers, which no one but you seems to have noticed. A copy of your autopsy report came in this morning, and it mentions this. And what do you know—it's black. We have a tape of Jesse Hadley's voice seemingly making a date with Lisette Chauncy. And then you trooped into my office yesterday and dropped a tape-splicing machine into my lap. You need a lawyer, Doctor."

"I *am* a lawyer!" she cried inanely.

"Then I hope to God you know what and what not to say in my presence." His voice changed, going tired again. "Look, Dr. Byerly, just come over here. Let's see what we can do to straighten this out. And maybe this time someone can fill me in on what the hell is happening here—up to and including why you felt you had to call me and tell me that Mr. Hadley might be in trouble."

"Okay," she whispered helplessly, "I'm on my way."

But when she hung up, she only slid bonelessly off the edge of her desk, where she had been sitting, and dropped into her chair. It was happening again. Charlie was doing it again. Changing things, twisting them, making a mockery of her. Controlling her life, discrediting her.

Already, Kennery's respect was merely a formality.

This time, Charlie wouldn't be content to simply walk away from a mistake looking blameless, she realized. This time, he would go one step further and see her behind bars.

It was her worst nightmare come back to life. And she wondered where in the name of God she was going to find the strength to fight it all one more time.

And then, like the answer to her prayers, Jesse entered her office.

Chapter 13

Her first impulse was to run to him. She needed him. She needed to touch him and see for herself that he was really all right. His arms would be protective and strong around her, and he would comfort her and reassure her and make this horror go away.

But there was something different in his eyes. Angela clenched her fists and kept her distance, feeling sick.

"Rough morning, huh?" he asked. "Are you okay?" Then he held out his arms to her.

Angela hurried around her desk. They came together.

"Easy," he murmured.

She wrapped her arms around his neck and buried her face against his shoulder. She felt his hands at the small of her back. Then one coasted upward, kneading the rock-hard tension out of her shoulders. The other smoothed her hair back. She felt his warm breath at the top of her head. After a while, she stopped shaking.

"Are you all right?" she managed to ask. "Really all right?"

He frowned. "Why wouldn't I be?"

"I couldn't find you."

It pleased him that she had been looking. That in a moment of horror, seeing that picture in the paper, she had tried to turn to him. Then he thought about where he had been, trying to get hold of his uncle. Wendell had stayed one step ahead of him all morning, moving from court to this meeting and that one, until Jesse had thought it was more important to find Angela.

And then, of course, all hell had broken loose.

"I just talked to Kennery," he said after a moment. "I called in for messages and there were a ton from him. He said you'd...been in touch. He's a little upset." He paused. "Angela, I think this would be a real good time for that united front I spoke about yesterday."

"Thank you," she choked. Her response surprised him. He'd expected an argument.

"Shh." He put her away from him a little. He saw tears clinging to her lashes and something shafted through him. He touched one with his fingertip and felt another shudder pass through her.

"I know who's doing this now," she whispered. "I've figured it out."

Everything inside him went still, then his heart thumped. "Who?"

She closed her eyes, swaying a little without his support. "You're not going to believe me."

Someone passed by out in the hallway. Jesse left her abruptly to shut the door.

When he came back, she was trembling again violently. "Try me," he said.

She kept her eyes closed. She drew in a deep breath, and it seemed to him that she was shoving the words out forcibly when everything inside her wanted to keep them buried. She couldn't look at him.

"Charlie Price."

Jesse felt shock knife through him. "I beg your pardon?"

"You heard me right."

"Charlie *Price? Why?*"

Her eyes were open now. She was looking at him bleakly. "You don't believe me."

Something about the tone of her voice told him that that might well be the worst thing that had ever happened to her in her life.

He caught her face in his hands, sliding his thumb up over her cheek to catch another tear. "I didn't say that. I asked—like any good district attorney would ask—how and why you've come to this conclusion. You're leaving a lot out here, angel. From where I'm standing, it looks like a huge jump.''

She drew in another deep, shuddering breath—more at the endearment than anything else. But it gave her courage. She fought again to force the words out. ''He raped me.''

Jesse felt the room seem to go bright, then dark. He was that stunned. ''It was *Charlie?* Charlie Price did that to you?''

Angela looked at him pleadingly. And then his words sank in and made her go cold inside. ''You knew,'' she muttered hoarsely. ''You knew that that was what happened between me and your uncle.'' She wrenched away from him and backed up, staring at him. She felt sick. She'd been betrayed. She felt like a fool. *''All this time you knew!''* she cried.

''No.'' He thought it prudent not to mention right now that he had told Eric to look into the mystery. Eric hadn't gotten back to him with anything yet anyway.

''No? But you just said—''

''I saw the paper.''

For a moment, he thought she was going to pass out. Her eyes went unfocused. He closed the distance between them again and caught her shoulders.

''The paper?'' she returned weakly.

''Didn't you?'' he asked carefully.

''Of course. That was how I knew Charlie was running against you.'' She shook her head fretfully. ''I should have understood last night. Your father, your uncle... But I was nervous. I was...'' She couldn't finish. Nothing she had felt last night compared to this.

Jesse's heart thumped. She hadn't seen it all, then. ''No, Angela. Not that part.''

His voice was soft and gentle, and it touched her physically. She dug her fingers into the front of his shirt and held on to him, dreading what he was going to say, knowing before he said it.

''Where's your newspaper?'' he asked.

''In the cab,'' she whispered. ''I left it in the cab.''

''Okay. Come on. Let's sit down.''

She let him guide her to her office sofa—a cheap, vinyl thing as hard as a box of rocks. She crumpled onto it.

''That picture was in there,'' he said slowly. ''The one that was taken the other night at the restaurant. Do you remember?''

"Fill?" she murmured, looking at him, her eyes searching. "The one you said they'd only use if they needed fill?"

"Well, fill apparently had nothing to do with it this time. It was the work of...whoever is doing this. They're stirring the pot."

"Charlie?"

He took a deep, careful breath. They'd discuss *that* in a moment. There was no easy way to tell her that her private hell was all over the city now.

"It was in the paper this morning," he said. "About you. And my uncle. About what happened. That's why I came over here. That, and Kennery's raving."

She gasped and her face drained of color.

"That's how I knew," he said again.

"They put in there that *Charlie* raped me?"

Jesse shook his head. "No. The only names mentioned were yours, mine and my uncle's." And now, finally, he had cause to wonder about that.

She startled him by jumping to her feet. If her face had blanched a moment before, now twin spots of hot color burned into her cheeks.

"Of course." She laughed crazily. Her hands curled into fists. Her gaze flew around the room, settling on nothing. "No," she went on, "it wouldn't say that Charlie was the one who did it. He wouldn't want *that* to get out. He's trying to intimidate me into keeping my mouth shut. Because now maybe, just maybe, someone might listen to me." She spun to face him again. "He's trying to discredit me so if I *do* bring it all up again now that he's running for D.A., no one will believe me this time, either. They'll think I'm a lunatic and a murderess out to avenge myself against your family after all these years."

"Angela," he said slowly, "if I'm following you, then you're saying he's doing all this to discredit you in case you drag all this up during his campaign."

She nodded frantically.

"That doesn't make sense," he said very carefully. "His case was thrown out of court, right? So effectively, he was never charged. He can always come back with that. It's not worth...all this." He waved a hand to indicate everything that had been happening.

Angela's eyes went wild. "How can *you* of all people say that?

That doesn't matter! Yesterday you were worried about how my turning in that splicer would affect *your* campaign and reputation!''

He opened his mouth and closed it again. She had a point.

She swerved suddenly for her desk and snatched up the piece of paper she had taken from Lisette's neck. She thrust it at him. Jesse took it.

'''Keep your mouth shut. Next time it could be you,''' he read aloud. It was typed. He turned it over. It wasn't signed, of course, and there was nothing on the back. ''Where did you get this?''

''He left it on Lisette.''

''He did *what?*''

She was shaking badly. ''He was in here. Last night. It's just like before.''

''Angela, look at me.''

She stared at him, her eyes almost glassy now.

''You've got to calm down. Our brains are all we have here. Our *rational* brains.''

She flinched. ''You think I'm being irrational?''

''No. Not necessarily. But I'm not following you. You're reaching out and saying things so fast I can't make sense of them.''

She took a deep breath and finally nodded. His voice was reasonable, she told herself.

''Come back,'' he said, motioning to the sofa. ''Sit down. Start from the beginning.''

She made an involuntary movement, as though he had hit her. ''You mean...with what he did to me?''

''Okay.'' It was as good a place to start as any, though he wasn't at all sure he could stand hearing it. And that made him wonder, too, but not about Charlie Price.

Angela came and sat stiffly beside him. ''I met him at school.''

''College?''

She nodded tautly.

''He went to Princeton?'' Jesse asked, trying to draw her out.

''Yes. M-me, too. On a scholarship.''

''Okay.''

Suddenly, she looked confused. ''He's older than I am, but we had a lot of the same classes.''

''We graduated from high school together,'' Jesse said thoughtfully. "He had lousy grades. I think he took a year off between high school and college." And, if he remembered correctly, there had been rumors of wild parties and other such things. The elder Price had sent his son abroad later that year, ostensibly to sow his wild oats. Jesse wondered if it had also been to clean up some messes.

But Charlie had allegedly raped Angela *after* that, after whatever those messes might have been. And if they had existed at all, they had been carefully buried.

Then he realized what he'd just thought.

Allegedly? He felt nausea swell in his stomach. How easy it was to fall into legal traps and lingo, even for him. Charlie Price had raped her. He accepted that. He believed her. But whether or not Charlie was doing this to them now... Jesse found he wasn't quite able to swallow that. But he didn't dare tell her so. Some instinct made him know that his belief in her was all she had to hold herself together with right now.

The responsibility made his stomach burn even more. Not because he was uncomfortable with it, but because he couldn't bear the thought of what might happen if he failed.

"I skipped a year in high school," she continued. Her hands were clasped rigidly together in her lap. Her voice was tight and controlled. "That could account for some of the time. And I know that he...there were a couple of classes he didn't pass in his junior year. That was when he came to me for tutoring. That was how I met him. We worked together three nights a week. I got to know him fairly well."

"You dated?"

Pure pain flashed over her face. "That was what your uncle called it."

"And what do you call it?" he asked evenly.

She looked at him sharply. Not once, not ever, had anyone asked her that question, not even the old D.A. She'd told him of course. But to them the fine line between dating and tutoring hadn't seemed pertinent. At least, no one had ever seemed interested.

"Tutoring," she spat now. "I never saw him outside the library until that...that last night. And that was *here,* in Philly. Not at school."

"Go on."

"He made me nervous. Toward the end of our junior year, I thought...it had started to seem like maybe he wanted more than tutoring. He was...he had started to make a lot of comments about my appearance." She shuddered. "And my body. Finding reasons to touch me. I never particularly liked him. I would have stopped tutoring him, but I really needed the money. And he paid well. And every time I tried to suggest that he find someone else, he'd offer me more. The best I could do was always make sure that we met at the library. In public. But then he contacted me before we went back to school that fall. He had been taking summer courses. He had a final. He needed help studying for it. That was what he said." She closed her eyes. "The money. I needed the money."

He squeezed her hand and knew grimly that Wendell would never have understood such a thing.

"I told him I would meet him at the city library. At seven-thirty. At seven o'clock there was a knock on my door. It was him."

He saw her eyes go distant as she relived it. Something caught him around the throat. But he had known this wouldn't be easy.

"You lived at home?" he asked, his voice tight.

She gave a quick shake of her head. Her curls danced. "No. I rented a small house on Front Street with two girlfriends. There were...problems at home. That was why I needed the money so badly. I was supporting myself. I actually worked for the M.E.'s office that summer as a receptionist—I guess that's how they knew my name all these years later. But my salary wasn't enough, not for everything. Rent, books..." She shrugged helplessly.

"So he came to your house." Jesse gently picked up the thread again.

"It was the first time," she whispered.

Jesse felt an unseen force slam into him. "The *first* time? He raped you *repeatedly?*"

Her gaze flew to him. "No! Oh, no. It was the first time that he...that he did what he wanted. The first time he took matters into his own hands. He was there just because he had decided to be. Because he wanted... I'd said the *library,* but he decided no and left me no choice." She swallowed carefully. "I left school after that. For a semester. I filed charges."

"With Paul Coniglio?"

She nodded stiffly. ''Yes. He was the D.A. then. But someone else...one of his deputies actually tried the case.'' She laughed shrilly. ''A new guy. No trial experience. Tells you what Coniglio thought of my case. Anyway, it took the better part of three months for it to come to trial.''

''In my uncle's court.''

She began trembling again. She wouldn't look at him now.

''Angela, if Wendell didn't have the evidence—''

''*No!*'' she shouted, twisting around on the sofa to face him. ''No. That's only what he said. *The truth was that Charlie made sure there was no evidence!* And your uncle believed him because he wanted to.''

''Why?'' Jesse demanded angrily. ''Why in the hell would Wendell do that?''

''Because Charlie was as rich and powerful as you Hadleys are! Because you guys stick together!''

Jesse flinched. Oh, yes, he understood now.

''That's not fair,'' he said quietly.

Panic and confusion crossed her face. She didn't address his comment, but let it go.

''Charlie spent those months before the trial driving me insane. Deliberately making it look like I was on the verge of a break-down. Sort of like he's doing now.'' She told him wretchedly about the bathtub, about the basement. ''I'd...I'd open the pantry, and he'd b-be standing there, grinning that grin. *Surprise!*'' She threw her hands up in bitter parody. ''At first, of course, he'd just pick the locks, jimmy the windows, be there waiting for me when I came home from somewhere. So we found a locksmith to make that impossible, and Charlie found a way in through the basement. We fixed that, and he came right in while we were home if we forgot to barricade ourselves in. So we stopped forgetting. It was like living under siege. We'd lock ourselves in, then we'd glance up to find him peering through the window at me. So we'd draw the blinds, but in a way that was even worse, because then we could never be sure if he was out there or not.''

She took a steadying breath. ''Every time he turned up,'' she continued, ''it wasn't enough to just be there, to prove to me that he could enter my life, invade my privacy, at will. He would t-touch me. And I'd call the cops. Or my roommates would when they heard me scream. But we were three *women,* Jesse. There was nothing we could do to physically hold him there until the cops arrived. If he was outside, he'd be gone by the time they got there. We took pictures of him to prove he was there—those instant snapshots—and the cops acted like we were nuts. What did they prove? He was always *smiling* in them. Lock him in a room? Sure, we tried that, too. He crawled out through a window because of course there was no way we could lock the window from outside, and he was too smart to go into a room without one. I knocked him flat with a frying pan once, but I don't think the police ever investigated if he was bruised or not. He was Charles Price's son. In the absence of some cold, hard evidence, they just acted like I was some lunatic out to drag his name through the mud. The authorities just seemed to look the other way. Like the word had already come down from the Commissioner or whatever. 'This woman is nuts. Would Charlie Price do these things? Of course not. So just humor her.'''

Rage flowed through Jesse's blood until it almost literally colored his vision.

"So by the time we got to court," Angela went on, "there were thirty-two instances on record of my calling the cops. And not once in those thirty-two instances did the cops ever find their 'proof' that Charlie had been there. I think even the D.A. thought I was nuts. The defense attorney said that I was...mentally unbalanced.

"We had photographs taken...of my...my bruises after he raped me, too, but they disappeared from the evidence room before the trial. Neighbors saw me open the door to him that night and heard me screaming later. But then they declined to testify, or they changed their stories.

"The defense attorney said that all along I wanted more than just to tutor Charlie. He made...he made a big deal of the fact that I was at Princeton on a scholarship, while Charlie was rich and quite the man about campus.

"He lied even more. He said that I had invited Charlie to my house that night. And when he got there, and realized that tutoring wasn't what I had on my mind, he politely tried to extricate himself from the situation. The defense attorney said I cried rape because Charlie rejected me and I wanted revenge."

She looked at Jesse, her eyes pleading. They hurt him. "It wasn't like that. But it was his word against mine. Your uncle believed him. And he chastised me for my behavior, for wasting the court's time.''

Jesse felt something both painful and amazed move inside him. He'd thought this morning that most women would have backed off from pressing charges—especially given who the defendant had been. He knew all too well how it happened, the sort of interrogations the victims were subjected to during depositions. The police would keep at it, off the record—the insinuations, the dirty intimations, the leering remarks—until the women's eyes went from haunted—as Angela's were now—to unsure to stricken. Until *she* started believing that she had done something wrong.

But there was nothing unsure in Angela's eyes. Nor was there a trace of apology in her voice. She must have gone through hell, he realized, and it had broken something inside her; it had shamed her, but she wouldn't accept guilt. What had she said that day in the limo? *Keeping your attention in line is* your *problem, Counselor.*

She was an extraordinary woman.

Jesse came up off the sofa. "I'm sorry." And he heard his own words and was sickened all over again. As though they could change any of what had happened to her. He began to pace. "I need to think."

"About what?" she demanded. "You don't—"

"I believe you," he interrupted harshly.

"But?" Her voice sounded suddenly like a whip cracking. He stopped to look back at her.

"*But* this is a delicate, highly complicated situation."

"Because you're a Hadley," she said flatly.

"Get off that, Angela. *Now.*"

His voice turned to ice, frigid with warning. It frightened her a little. She stared at him.

"Because I'm the district attorney," he clarified tightly, "and because this bastard is running against me as of late yesterday afternoon. And every move I make now, every word I utter, is going to be put under a damned microscope. And what about you? You can't fight back blindly or you'll come off looking crazy again! Even that note is something you could have planted yourself. It's *typed.*"

She swayed. "Yes," she admitted, and her voice was stricken.

"Whatever method we use to deal with this has to be absolutely, one hundred percent above reproach or it's going to backfire on both of us."

"Yes," she acknowledged again. And, oh, the *we* sounded so sweet, so good now. It was all she had.

Charlie had once again stripped everything away from her. Except this man. He *would* stand beside her. She believed that until Jesse spoke again.

"And while I don't doubt for a moment that the creep did what you say," he added, "I keep coming up against a brick wall when I try to consider him doing this to you now."

She flew off the sofa. "Fine. Get out. I'll deal with it myself."

"Over my dead body."

She laughed shrilly. "Watch what you say, Jesse. I already have one corpse in the fridge, thanks to him."

"He's known Lisette Chauncy all his life!"

"He'd psychotic!"

A knock sounded on the door. They both jumped and clamped their mouths shut at the same time.

"Are you all right in there?" Angela's secretary called out.

"Yes," Angela returned. "Everything's fine." She looked at Jesse. "We were shouting," she said, dazed.

Jesse cleared his throat. "Sorry."

She shivered. From the very beginning, his ability to do that, to apologize and express gratitude, had touched her deeply. Because it was not a well-known Hadley trait. And that made her honest. *Honest?* she thought wildly. She was about to bare her very soul.

"I need so desperately for you to believe me. I cannot, *will* not, stand silently by while that man runs for district attorney. He terrifies me. But I have to *do* something."

Fresh respect washed through him. He stared at her.

"I'm not foolish enough to think that anyone will believe me this time, either," she allowed hoarsely. "I will be ignored, ridiculed and made to look like a fool."

Jesse watched her, unable to say anything. His heart was moving hard. He knew that she was asking for something immense—at least to her. It was somehow a thousand times more intimate than if they had tumbled together onto that sofa and made love.

He was both terrified that she was going to say it and holding his breath in something very close to pain in case she might not.

"You asked me to trust you," she continued, her voice shaking. "And now you know why it doesn't come easily to me. But I'm trying. God knows, I'm trying. I'm giving this to you, Jesse. I'm asking you to believe in me. *Help* me. Stand by me. Please."

He chose his words very carefully. "Would you have me go along with you blindly?"

"What do you mean?" Her eyes narrowed.

"Would you have me believe you without question? Or do you want someone sensible, someone armed with concrete facts, on your side?"

"I don't understand," she whispered.

"We can rush out of here right now if you like. We can go out there and point our fingers at Charlie Price and make our accusations. At which point the Wendell Glowans of the world—" he winced briefly at that "—are going to ask us for the connection. For the *proof.* And at least some of the people are not going to believe me any more than they'll believe you."

"But you're a Hadley," she objected.

"Doesn't matter. Because we have no visible thread between what he did then and what's going on now. We have supposition, a motive and that's all. We need *proof,* Angela."

He waited. He was appealing to her mind. He was praying that she was reachable beneath her justified anger and resentment and panic. When she nodded slowly, he let himself breathe.

"I don't have any proof that he's doing this," she admitted quietly. "But there's not a single doubt in my heart."

"Worse, Price has at least one bit of ammunition to prove that *we're* all wet," he added.

She paled. "What?"

Jesse spoke the things that bothered him most about her theory. "Angela, Charlie Price is a reasonably well-known man in this city. Don't you think that if he was the one who tried to relieve your office of Lisette's body yesterday, then Brigid would have recognized him?" He paused, thinking that Brigid had thought maybe she had. And Charlie's picture wasn't really in the papers that often. Only someone who religiously read the society pages *might* have known him.

He'd work on that later.

"Don't you think that that reporter—Carper—would have recognized him?" he asked her. But Carper hadn't *met* with the man, he recalled. He'd merely encountered a voice on the phone. "At the very least, my secretary would have done so, if he was in my office to take those tapes out of my cabinet. She's met him before." Unless, he thought, Libby had not been at her desk at the time. If it had been after hours Price wouldn't have logged in. And Jesse had only looked at the logs for the past six weeks. There was nothing to say that he hadn't been there *seven* weeks ago.

Jesse rubbed his forehead against a headache that was getting worse by the minute.

"We need facts. Proof," he said again, more to convince himself.

"He won't allow it." She groaned. "He's smart. Shrewd. Manipulative."

"And you're smarter. I'm shrewder. And I can manipulate with the best of them."

"Oh, Jesse," she breathed.

He reached out a hand, thinking to soothe the frown from her forehead. Then he hesitated. "Can I touch you?"

"You've never asked before." Angela flinched and her eyes filled. "It's not...like you."

He felt shamed at the truth of that, and small.

She hugged herself, then sighed. "Do you know," she asked slowly, "that I don't think I ever really believed you'd consider me to be...tainted? Or even to be the kind of woman your uncle thought I was?"

He was more curious than surprised, but his heart thumped. "Why?"

"Because we danced at Tessa's wedding."

Her mind was leaps and bounds ahead of him again. "So?"

"When I pointed out that we had stopped dancing, that we were just standing there, you apologized. Like I deserved... respect."

He was a little shocked to realize that he remembered that, too, and that something so small and innocuous had stuck in his brain. Then again, he had been noticing the most infinitesimal things about her from the beginning. And the biggest things about himself.

"You're not a real Hadley," she declared.

He was almost amused. "I'm not sure my father would be pleased to hear that."

One corner of her mouth moved, but she didn't smile. "I'm sure not."

"So how did you come to *that* conclusion?"

"Because you also told me that day that you didn't want to be mayor."

He gave a bark of ironic laughter and she lifted one shoulder in a careful shrug.

"Also, I figured that anyone who got physically ill over what had happened to Lisette Chauncy couldn't be all bad. You *did* throw up that day, didn't you?"

He felt embarrassed. "I have an ulcer."

"Because you work too hard and take it all too much to heart."

"Now you sound like my sister."

"What I can't figure out is…" Angela's heart was thrumming hard now. She wasn't sure she wanted to ask again, and knew that she needed to know. Because somehow they were turning a corner here. They'd gone from reluctant acquaintances—at least on her part—to some sort of friendship, and then he had kissed her. And she had liked every one of those occasions very much.

Now she had all but begged him to be a man she could trust.

"Why me?" she blurted.

Jesse frowned. "Why not you?"

"Because the last time I saw your picture in the paper, it was with that West Indian model."

"Caro," he said blankly.

"Yes. And before that, it was Sabina Rousseau. The actress." He was uncomfortable. "So what's your point?"

"I don't hold a candle to either of them."

He looked at her, incredulously at first, then with some discomfort. He'd once thought the same thing himself.

He'd been wrong.

"I don't like to be touched," she confessed.

"Understandably." Then he realized that she was waiting for him to go on. "It's your mind. I was first attracted to your mind." And then it was her strength, he decided. And her desperate pride. But her intellect—*that* had come first. It was, he remembered, one of the biggest reasons he had gone to her office on the morning Lisette was killed.

Angela gave a quick, breathless laugh. ''Sure. That's why you were staring at my legs that day in the limo.''

''Believe me, I've noticed everything else, as well.'' Until holding back had gone from vague instinct to a deliberate, painful effort. ''But your wariness is one of the first things a man...I don't know, *feels* about you,'' he added. ''And that's a challenge.''

He thought suddenly that that was probably what had happened to Charlie Price, all those years ago. Charlie had wanted her. She would have remained aloof even then—she'd said she hadn't liked him. The fact that she was a poor student on a scholarship, while Charlie had everything wealth and position could offer, must have inflamed him.

Price had gotten to her before they'd even gone back to school that year. He'd probably spent that entire summer obsessing about her, Jesse guessed, and then he had erupted. She'd had the audacity to try to prevent him from having something he wanted.

Anger spurted through him again, the kind of anger that needed a target, the kind that almost demanded he throttle something. Then he realized that she was still watching him closely. And it touched him all over again that despite her defensiveness, her brittle independence, she needed his assurance.

''You're all layers,'' he finished. ''Contradictions. Flowers and death. That hit me right off the bat. And it intrigued me.''

''Oh,'' she said in a small voice.

''You're a relief.''

''A relief?'' she echoed uncertainly.

''When I talk to you, I don't have to explain things twice.'' He smiled briefly. ''And your eyes didn't glaze over with boredom last night. It's pleasant, though I'd be the first to admit that I never expected it to be. Angela, those other women can't hold a candle to *you*.''

''Ah.'' Her heart skipped. ''Ah,'' she said again, pleasure swelling. She laughed nervously. ''Well, I don't think I've ever been wanted for my mind before.'' Mostly it intimidated men, she found. That, and the fact that she could never respond to them physically.

Because she couldn't trust them. And she realized then that

she'd responded to Jesse so far, almost from the start, because her heart innately did. He was strong. And while she feared masculine strength, she also knew that, deep down inside herself where it counted, she also needed it. Deep down inside, she ached for someone she could lean on occasionally, someone strong enough to bear the weight, who would never use that strength to overpower her.

The phone rang, jarring both of them.

Angela recovered and moved quickly to her desk to see that it was her own personal extension, not her secretary putting through a random call. She knew who it was before she answered.

"Hello, Captain," she said evenly.

"Doctor, I've got to reiterate that it's in your best interest—" Kennery began.

She cut him off. "I've thought about what you said. I agree— I think I'd do better to bring an attorney." She looked up and caught Jesse's eye. He held her gaze.

And then he smiled.

Chapter 14

Roger Kennery was built like a barrel. He had large, meaty hands and a florid face. At the moment, his features were even more splotched with red than usual. He was clearly frustrated and angry.

Jesse took over.

His stride was aggressive as he entered the office. "I'm not pressing any charges," he said flatly before he even sat. "Given that, I'm not sure what we're doing here."

Kennery's gaze moved to him. "Now, see, *this* is my problem," he snapped. "Are you going to tell me why? Something's going on here, and I've got a good portion of my unit working on this murder case. If you've got evidence—"

"We don't," Jesse said shortly. "What do your guys have?"

Kennery glared at him. "I share, and you close the door?" he growled. For a moment, Angela expected him to close up, as well. Then he let out a hefty breath. "Okay, okay. We've got tread marks on Lisette's driveway. They're consistent with a late-model Mercedes sedan."

Jesse flinched. "Fancy that." But Price drove one, too, he recalled.

"Does your office have anything that would support or shadow that?" Kennery asked pointedly.

Jesse was quiet, then he conceded, "Not yet."

Kennery swore. Jesse leaned forward in his chair.

"Look," he relented, "if I sat here and gave you an earful of what I suspect, you'd no doubt have me committed. The only physical evidence that I have and your guys don't is something that was only discovered this morning." He told him about the note.

He'd sent it by messenger to Eric, Angela knew, hoping that maybe they could trace the typewriter, a staggering long shot.

"One of my investigators is working with a copy," he finished, "with instructions to send the original to the crime lab for possible fingerprinting. I'll make sure your guys get a full report."

"That's something, I guess," Kennery muttered, slightly mollified. "Get Homicide a copy as well, though. Let's see what they can do about tracing it, too."

Jesse hesitated so infinitesimally, Angela was pretty sure she was the only one who caught it.

"Of course," he said stiffly.

"I want the bastard who shot that bullet into the woman's head," Kennery said gruffly.

"I honestly can't help you there," Jesse replied. "I have nothing on that."

Kennery leaned back and laced his fingers together behind his head. "I'm going to hate this, aren't I?" he asked sourly.

Jesse almost smiled. "That's a safe assumption." Roger didn't answer. "All I'm holding back from you are a few guesses, Roger, which at this point are nothing more than shots in the dark. Making accusations at this point could be more dangerous than not doing so."

Kennery thought about that. "Hell," he muttered. "First Benami in January, and now this."

"And you don't even know the half of it," Angela muttered under her breath.

Kennery heard her anyway. He looked at her sharply. "I also got the preliminary report back on that splicing machine an hour ago."

Angela held her breath. "And?"

"Your prints aren't on it."

She breathed again.

"Unfortunately, no one else's are, either."

Jesse swore. "That would have been too easy."

"Yeah," Kennery agreed. "Well, I've still got a plan here, whether or not you want to let me in on what you suspect. Tell me if it might help. It'll make *me* feel better, anyway."

Jesse nodded. His cool amazed Angela.

"I think the doctor should make herself scarce for a while."

"Scarce?" Angela repeated blankly.

"I like it," Jesse said immediately.

"Well, *I* don't!" Angela cried. "You're talking about my going away somewhere? No! I have a job to do!"

"Oh, you'll do it," Kennery said. "You'll be at work. Other than a select handful of people, I think everyone else should just assume that you're going about your business as usual."

Jesse saw from her expression that, for once, she was not catching on. She was too personally involved, he felt, too threatened.

"Angela," he said quietly, "what Roger is saying is that we can put a stop to this lunatic. We might not catch him, but at least we can exonerate you. We can clear up that end of it and take the public hassle off Homicide as to whether or not Roger's going to charge you with anything. And if this guy can't discredit you, we've also taken away his motive."

"You're saying that if he does anything else, then my own whereabouts at the time would be covered." She looked at Kennery. "You'd be able to say for certain that it couldn't possibly have been me."

Kennery nodded. "One of the things that bothers me most about all this is that we have no way of proving that you're not involved. You can't provide any alibis. So we'll give you someone. We'll put one of my detectives on you twenty-four hours around the clock. Something else happens, and this time we'll have a bona fide witness to say you were otherwise occupied."

Her heart scurried. The implications of what they were saying finally dawned on her. She looked at Jesse again. She hated it, but her eyes filled.

"I can fight back this time," she whispered.

"Sure you can."

"But not in your home," Kennery continued.

She looked back at him quickly, feeling the first fingers of panic curl around her stomach. ''Why not?''

''It would be too hard to keep it tight. Anybody even looking in your window would know what we were up to.''

''Anybody looking in my window will know I'm not there,'' she pointed out desperately.

''He'd have to sit there and watch the place twenty-four hours a day to be sure of that,'' Jesse said. ''You're a busy woman. We'll just have to gamble that he's not going to be able to do that. We have to gamble that he'll assume you're going in and out while he's not watching.''

''Whereas if he looks in once and sees a detective watching over me, he might guess what's going on,'' she admitted reluctantly.

''We need a center of operations anyway that's not your home,'' Jesse pointed out, ''or your office, or my home, or my office, for that matter.''

Kennery raised a brow at that, then apparently decided not to question it. ''Can you put your lights on an automatic timer?''

''Actually, I have two automatic timers.''

''That's even better,'' he said. ''Have one set do the lights one way tonight, then have the other set do them another way tomorrow.''

''For this to work,'' Jesse said quietly, ''this guy has to be tricked into doing something during the period you're covered.''

Angela finally nodded. ''Okay.'' She would do anything to beat Charlie Price at his own treacherous games. And this time she had help.

Her throat closed suddenly and hard. Jesse must have read something in her face, because his hand came back, covering hers where she gripped the chair arm.

''We'll put you in a hotel,'' Kennery said. ''Four people will know of it. Us, and whatever detective I put on you.''

''A woman,'' Jesse said without inflection.

Angela squirmed. *I'm not fragile. I'm not broken.* But in truth, she knew she would not be able to sleep, would not be able to eat, would not be able to do *anything* while a man she didn't know hovered around her, watching her most intimate behavior and daily routines. She finally looked at Kennery again and knew in that instant that he had seen this morning's paper, as well. Her face flamed.

Jesse wanted to kill Charlie Price all over again. Then he wanted to get his hands on that reporter. And his uncle was still pretty high up on the list.

"Fine," Kennery answered. "I've got a few women on board. In fact, Melanie Kaminsky is on a couple of cold cases right now. I can spare her."

"Good," Jesse said, standing. He reached for Kennery's phone.

"Where will you put her?" Roger asked.

"The Four Seasons. And we're going to use a fictitious name. Just to be safe."

Angela sucked in a harsh breath. "For God's sake, Jesse, that place is upward of two hundred and fifty a night! I'm not spending that!"

"You can afford it," he said quietly. "Give up your vacation in Rome."

And then she understood. She wasn't twenty-one anymore. She wasn't on a scholarship anymore. Charlie Price had nothing she needed.

His smile was not one she ever wanted to see directed her way. It was almost...feral. But in spite of everything, though she never would have dreamed it possible, Angela laughed hoarsely.

Kennery watched on disconsolately. "Fill me in someday," he muttered.

Jesse finally moved his gaze from Angela to the homicide captain. "Roger, I'll do it personally, just to see your face when you understand."

"Now what?" Angela asked a little breathlessly as they got back into his car.

"A few things," Jesse answered. "And the quicker we do them and get this settled, the better. I don't want too much of a break in your regular routine."

She shuddered. "You think he's watching me."

"I'd bet on it. And I'm not a gambling man. But like I said back in Kennery's office, he can't do it around the clock. He's an attorney who's running for D.A. He's got to take care of appearances too, that's our edge.''

He realized that while he had been shocked this morning, things were beginning to click unconsciously into place. But he wondered again why Charlie would risk ruining himself now. If Angela brought the whole thing up again, he could come right back with the fact that the case had been thrown out of court.

Of course, as Angela had said, that might not matter. It probably wouldn't matter any more than the fact that Jesse hadn't killed Lisette Chauncy. Even the hint of a scandal was often enough to topple a campaign.

Still, murder seemed excessive. He laughed wryly at the understatement. Angela looked over at him sharply.

''I'm inclined to think there are some stakes here that we don't know about,'' he speculated aloud. ''There has to be something else going on that makes this risk he's taking worthwhile. Even before I knew all this, when I was reading the paper this morning, I was wondering why he'd make the switch from defense to prosecution. Now I've got to wonder why he wants my D.A. seat so damned badly that he's going to all these lengths.''

''Maybe he always planned to run for office,'' she whispered. ''Then I came back to Philly eight months ago like a skeleton falling out of his closet.''

He understood better now why she had. Courage, he thought. A refusal to cower, to give way to helplessness.

''I think,'' Jesse said slowly, ''that between the two of us, Charlie Price might just have finally met his match.''

Angela swallowed carefully and closed her eyes. She was sure of it now. No matter what he said about concrete evidence, he believed her. ''Jesse,'' she asked quietly, ''is there any possibility that I can take the rest of the day off?''

He looked at her sharply. ''I'm not your boss.''

She combed her hair back with her fingers. ''You know what I mean. Tactically.''

He considered her request. ''Actually, I think it would be brilliant. It'll please him. He'll think you're distraught over this morning's paper.''

''I am.''

He looked at her. ''What can I do, angel?''

Her throat closed all over again. "Nothing." She shook her head. "You're doing so much."

"You're not alone this time, angel. I'm not going to toss you to the wolves and walk away."

Tears threatened. She covered her face with her hands and groaned.

He was overwhelmed. She was strong, yet fragile. She was brave, yet scared. And she was thoroughly shaken by the simple idea that she had someone on her side. How had she been duking it out on her own for so long?

Angela sniffed and dropped her hands again. "I'm fine." She took a deep breath. "I'll be fine. Let's trap this jerk. I'm ready."

She wasn't fine.

"I can't do this," she complained half an hour later. "It's impossible. I can't get three days' worth of clothes into a medical bag."

"If you walk out of here with a whole suitcase, he'll know something's up," Jesse countered reasonably.

"I hate it when you're reasonable."

"You drive me crazy when you're not."

They grinned at each other, then she turned back to her bedroom closet. Jesse watched her from the door, one shoulder leaning lazily against the frame. He pushed away from it and came up behind her. He looped his arms around her waist. She stiffened, then relaxed, and he thought possibly the whole process took a little less time than it might have a few days ago.

"What about the dress you wore to the wedding?" he asked.

"It was *red*."

"I definitely remember that," he murmured, half-smiling again.

"I can't make red look different three days in a row."

"Maybe not, but it was...uh, small. You could cram that into your bag and use up minimum space. Have it ironed when you get to the hotel. Wear it on Thursday." He reached around her and pushed through the hangers until he came to a plain black skirt. "What's this?"

She craned her neck around to look at him. "What does it look like?"

"I can't picture you in it."

She sniffed. "I bought it for a funeral. I didn't want to offend anyone."

"That explains it." Gradually, he felt tension filling her again. "What's wrong now?"

"If I wear that to work, then he's even invading the way I dress," she said in a small voice.

"No," he said sharply. "*You're* playing with him *this* time. You're temporarily altering those things that are within your means to alter. The power has moved over onto your side, angel. You're not just sitting blind, taking blows."

Angel. She realized that she really loved it when he called her that. It made her feel like someone good, pure, worthwhile.

"Okay," she said, "the black skirt. I can wear it with this yellow blouse tomorrow, wear the red on Thursday, then switch back to the black with flats and this great big T-shirt thing on Friday." She looked over her shoulder at him. "Friday is dress-down day."

"In my office, too."

"The mayor hates it. City image and all."

"Well, he won't be around all that much longer." He grimaced.

She didn't see the reflex. "Sandals," she decided, bending to grab a pair. "Not flats, but sandals."

Jesse backed away from her carefully. When she bent over like that, her bottom moved provocatively against him, and everything inside him heated and responded.

Do you know I don't think I ever really believed you'd consider me to be tainted? Her voice came back to him, soft and seductive with its own vulnerability. He did not consider himself to be anyone's hero, or even a man above reproach. He did *not* consider her to be tainted, and was even angered by the term she'd chosen. He was infuriated by what Charlie had done to her, both during and after the actual act, but he was not put off by it.

It only...quelled him.

He wanted her. And for the first time in his life, he honestly didn't know what to do about it. He could not just rely upon his own innate male responses. He thought that with any other woman, he might have laughingly grabbed her and pulled her back against him. And he wondered, too, if his physical reaction, if his need, would be as urgent and demanding with any other woman.

He had always held a piece of himself back in his relationships, giving only what he wanted and had time to give. Until he'd met someone who held back from him for the very necessary sake of emotional survival, who forced all his emotions to come boiling to the surface.

She had straightened away from the closet and was thrusting the sandals into her bag. She paused at his expression. "Jesse?"

He shook himself. "It's nothing. I was just thinking about all this."

He saw panic flit over her face, and it hurt him. "In what respect?"

"Charlie," he answered, not quite lying. "Putting him behind bars for a long, long time."

She hesitated, then nodded.

He went to the phone beside the bed and punched in a number. She got the impression that he was talking to Kennery, and she was right.

"Melanie is already at the hotel."

"Good."

"We're going to have to part ways now, angel. I don't want to drive over there blaring horns and waving banners. In fact, you might want to change cabs on your way, maybe stop at your office briefly. Don't go straight to the hotel. Don't lead him there."

She understood. If he went with her, someone might remember his face, while they probably would not recognize hers as easily. Or Charlie might be watching them.

"Let me leave here, then I'll catch up with you later," he added.

She wondered if he meant that literally, if he'd come to the hotel or simply call. She nodded again and gathered up her bag, realizing that she very much hoped he would come by in person.

Chapter 15

Jesse had reserved her a suite.

Angela slid her card key into the door to unlock it and stepped inside to find Melanie Kaminsky curled up on the sofa like a cat might with a pile of feathers before it. The woman had a soft drink in one hand and a bag of chips in the other. Her eyes were glued to the television.

"Hi there," the detective said, standing reluctantly and looking her way. "Want something to drink? The refrigerator is loaded."

Angela gave a little laugh as she looked around. "They probably want six bucks for a can of soda."

Melanie stopped dead and stared at her. "Do you think so? Nah, no way."

"I'll bet you a dollar."

"You're on."

And that simply, that easily, they were friends.

"Wait until you see the bed," Melanie said as they dug through the refrigerator. "It's the size of Kansas."

Angela found some cheese and crackers. "I'd like it all even better if I wasn't paying for it," she muttered, standing again and looking around.

Melanie put her can down quickly as though it had scalded her. "*You* are?"

Angela smiled. "Don't worry about it. I'm going to submit the bill to the city as soon as this mess is over."

"In that case, there's guacamole on the room service menu. Fourteen bucks with tortilla chips of gold."

Angela managed to laugh. "Let's get some."

They ordered and ate, watching afternoon talk shows. Angela felt her eyes growing heavier by the moment.

"You ought to rest," Melanie said finally.

"I think I'd like to." She was exhausted, she realized, drained.

"Would you mind leaving the bedroom door open?" Melanie suggested.

Angela looked at her quizzically.

"I've had my experience with defense attorneys. When this blows up, I want to be able to say I literally never took my eyes off you. Your toes will suffice. You can't easily go trekking around the city without your toes."

Angela nodded, then she scowled. "So when are you supposed to sleep?"

"I'm a homicide detective. I'm not supposed to need to."

Angela laughed half-heartedly.

"When you go to your office, I'll catch some shut-eye," Melanie explained. "Of course, then it will be your responsibility to make sure others have you present and accounted for at all times. Like your secretary, for instance, or your deputies. Your co-workers in general. Whatever you do, don't take any crime scenes by yourself until this is over."

"But there are plenty of other people at crime scenes," Angela protested.

"But not driving to and from. That's all the time this guy might need to say you were elsewhere."

Angela groaned. It was overwhelming. She had never realized before how easy it could be to frame a person. Who wasn't alone at some point during a day?

"I want this guy," she said. "I want this to be over."

Melanie nodded sympathetically. "Get some sleep. I'll wake you up if anything happens."

"*Anything,*" Angela repeated fiercely.

"I promise."

Melanie was as good as her word. Angela felt as though she had barely fallen asleep when the woman woke her. She was curled on her side, her hands clasped in front of her face. Even in her sleep, she realized dismally, she was warding off blows.

She became aware of a presence standing above her, then Melanie cleared her throat.

"Dr. Byerly?" she said softly. "I think you should see this."

Angela sat up groggily. "What is it?"

"The news. Hurry."

Angela got to her feet and followed Melanie into the living room. She sat down on the sofa, studying the television blearily. After a second, her vision cleared and Jesse's face swam into view. He was giving a press conference.

Charlie must have been at it again. *Now what?* At that moment, she felt incapable of watching, of absorbing any more.

"Your bad guy must have tipped off the media this afternoon," Melanie said. "They said this was taped a short while ago."

"What time is it?" Angela asked.

"About five. You didn't sleep very long."

Angela listened. Jesse's handsome face was granite, but she thought she could see that nerve ticking in his lower jaw again.

"Is it true that a device used to fake a tape of your voice was found at her home?" someone called out.

"No comment."

"Where is this machine now?" someone else asked.

Jesse's expression broke for a moment almost too quickly to be noticed, but Angela caught it. He very nearly smiled. Her heart thumped. She knew what he was thinking. If the question had been asked, then Charlie hadn't leaked the splicer's whereabouts to the press. Because Charlie didn't know that. He didn't know she had turned it into Kennery's office.

"We've been told it was found in Dr. Byerly's home," someone shouted again.

"That's absolutely not true," Jesse said. "The authorities didn't find a tape-splicing machine in Dr. Byerly's home."

"We've also been told that Dr. Byerly was not in her office today. Has she fled the city?"

"I would have to doubt that," Jesse said shortly. "She would have no reason to."

"So where is she?" someone demanded.

"I have no idea where she is at this time."

Melanie gave a bark of laughter. "Sure. You could be in the living room, in the bathroom. For that matter, you could be down in the lobby. Damn, he's good."

"Yes," Angela whispered.

"What about the hair?" another reporter called out.

"What about it?" Jesse hedged coldly.

"We're told that no one actually saw it on the body except Dr. Byerly. Could she have planted it?"

"You've gotten erroneous information. I saw it there, as well. I was present for the autopsy and it was there when Dr. Byerly unbagged the victim's hands."

Angela stared at the screen, stunned. He *hadn't!* What was he saying? What was he *doing?*

Throwing his own reputation over hers to cover it, to protect it, she realized. She had asked to be able to trust him. He had given her something beyond precious. He had lied for her.

"Oh, dear God," she moaned aloud. She was overwhelmed. She couldn't breathe. She forced her attention back to the TV. There was a brief, stunned silence from the media. Then their voices rose, tangled and excited. One was louder and more insistent than the others.

"Where?"

"We've been told that it was *your* hair!"

Jesse's eyes sharpened as he looked for the person who had last spoken. His gaze was lethal, Angela thought, shivering.

"Apparently, you know a whole lot more about this than the rest of us," he said too quietly. "Since both my staff and Homicide are actively looking for evidence, perhaps you'd like to step back into my office and share your information with me."

The man shut up. Melanie whistled. "Hey, I'll vote for him."

Angela managed a pained smile.

"There are no DNA results on that hair at this time. We don't know whose it is. Is there anything else?" Jesse demanded. "If we're through here—"

"Are we to gather that your office is *not* going to ask for an indictment against Dr. Byerly?" someone interrupted.

"That's correct," Jesse snapped.

"Do you have any suspects in the Chauncy murder other than yourself or Dr. Byerly?" someone dared to ask.

"What an *imbecilic* question," Melanie grated.

"We have no suspects, period," Jesse said shortly. As Angela watched, his palm came up and covered the camera lens. "That's all, people."

In the next moment, the screen switched back to the anchor in the studio. Angela let out her breath and covered her face with her hands.

"What am I doing to him?" she murmured.

"Not you," Melanie answered firmly. "From what Captain Kennery told me, I'd say it's the jerk who's orchestrating all this. That's who we ought to blame. And I wouldn't worry too much about it. Jesse Hadley's going to come out on top."

Angela spread her fingers to peer at the screen again. He'd certainly been strong, arrogant, powerful, just a touch condescending. A true Hadley, if only when it suited his purposes.

Her purposes, she corrected herself.

"Honey, that is one man who knows what he's doing," Melanie said consolingly. "And he's on your side."

Jesse did not know what he was doing. As he had told Angela earlier, he felt as though he was just spinning his wheels and it infuriated him. He got as far as Eighth and Vine before his cell phone went off. He grabbed it. It was his father.

"Where are you headed?"

"Home," Jesse said shortly. He didn't add that he then had every intention of changing and turning around to go back to the city center, to the Four Seasons.

"Come here first," Ryan Hadley responded. "We need to confer on this."

Jesse knew that tone and he was in no mood to deal with it. Then he reconsidered. Wendell would almost certainly be there.

"I'm on my way."

He made a detour to his father's law offices. Wendell was indeed present. Jesse took the offensive. He felt as though he had been on the offensive all damned day and he wanted the day over with.

"You didn't *remember* her?" he immediately demanded of his uncle. He shrugged out of his suit coat, slung it over the back of a chair and took a cup of coffee from the tray his father's secretary had left on his desk. "Even if she was forgettable, I can't imagine that Charlie Price was."

"Charles Price III was innocent," Wendell said mildly.

Jesse snarled a single word to show what he thought of that.

"The case was in and out of my court in a single afternoon. It was a good many years ago. It was not something that locks into one's memory."

"Did his father pay you off?"

Silence. Jesse felt that was telling.

"Did Price pay you to drop it?" he demanded.

"That's neither here nor there at this point," his father answered.

Jesse rounded on him. He thought it was pretty damned pertinent under the circumstances and barely refrained from saying so. He realized, stunned, that what hit him just now was the fact that he didn't particularly trust his own family. Not at this moment.

He rarely had, not emotionally. He rarely spoke to any of them about what was in his heart. And after a while, even he had begun ignoring his heart. It had never bothered him before. Now it left him chilled.

"What I can't believe is that you didn't tell me about this," he said more quietly. He looked at Wendell again. "You must have been burning with the secret when Price announced his candidacy. It sure as hell gives me a way to discredit my opponent."

"I haven't been able to reach you all day," Wendell replied calmly. "And I only learned of his candidacy this morning."

"Yeah," Jesse grated. "I spent a good bit of time looking for you." His uncle had been avoiding him, Jesse realized.

"Mudslinging has never been the Hadley style anyway," Ryan broke in evenly. "And since Charles was never convicted, this doesn't give us honorable leverage."

Honorable leverage. Dear God, *was* there ever such a thing? Jesse just didn't know anymore.

"It's not important," Ryan repeated. "What's pertinent—and untenable at this point in time—is your aligning yourself with this woman. For God's sake, Jesse, why aren't you bringing charges? You sounded only too eager to protect her!"

His father's voice had escalated to the roar that had taken more than one witness apart over the years. Jesse stared back at him implacably.

"You're throwing your reputation right down the tubes along with Angela Byerly's," Wendell joined in.

"Are you finished?" Jesse demanded.

Something about his voice alerted his father. With a raised brow, Ryan sat slowly back in his chair. "No," he said more evenly. "You never mentioned that hair to me. Is it yours?"

Jesse watched him. "Probably." He had the pleasure of seeing his father's blood drain from his face. For the first time in Jesse's memory, Ryan Hadley could barely speak.

"Dear God...did you...it's not...what—"

Jesse felt more coldness settle over him. "I can't believe you even have to ask me that."

"Forewarned is forearmed. I—"

"I don't know how it got there," he said, and oh, the anger hurt now, his temples pounding. His stomach was awash in fire. "Needless to say, my office is actively working to find out."

"Dear God," Ryan said again, "Price will latch onto this and—" He broke off and got a visible grip on himself, ready to do damage control. "Price is no competition in this D.A. thing. He couldn't beat his way out of a paper bag. But I got word this afternoon that he's planning on leapfrogging from the D.A.'s seat into the mayor's office. And this concerns me."

Jesse felt his blood chill. Then there was a hot, sudden burst of adrenaline.

Now Price's panic made more sense. He'd probably had these plans for a while, just as Angela had figured. Then she had come back to town, throwing everything into jeopardy. He wondered what Price might have planned for him, to have gotten him out of the way, if Angela hadn't complicated the issue. He was sure there would have been something. But she came back, allowing Price to use one of them to destroy the other.

"I'll be damned," he said aloud.

"I'm worried that this is going to follow you clear through to the mayoral campaign, no matter whom you run against, and you can rest assured that Price will use it in this first election," Ryan continued as though Jesse hadn't spoken. "My sources tell me he's in a very unstable position with the ACLU. Apparently, he botched two cases badly."

Jesse stared at him. "*Nobody* gets fired from the ACLU."

"Which is precisely why Price is trying to move on now before he gets dumped.'' Ryan gave an unpleasant smile. ''His parents would never be able to hold their heads up in this city again. That boy was always trouble. He's never come up to their expectations. I imagine that Charles, Jr. and Sr., are putting pressure on him to stop screwing up and make something respectable of himself before it's too late.''

For an odd, brief moment, Jesse almost felt sorry for the man.

''You've got to disengage yourself from this woman now,'' Ryan insisted. ''Press charges against her, align yourself on the side of justice, and distance yourself from this mess immediately. You've had no identifiable involvement yet. There are just rumors. By the time the mayoral campaign begins, people will barely remember that you might have had something to do with all this.''

''I'm not running.''

He hadn't planned to say it. He was as stunned as anyone else in the room.

Was he doing this to protect Angela? No, he decided, not entirely. He didn't want to be mayor. He wanted to be the D.A. And dropping out of the mayoral campaign wouldn't stop Price. The man still needed to run for D.A. His situation was not unlike Jesse's. Price couldn't easily get to the mayor's office without holding an elected post first. He needed to leapfrog. *That* was why he was changing his colors, both from Democrat to Republican, and from civil liberties attorney to district attorney. So declining to run for mayor wouldn't take the heat off Angela, unless he declined to run again for the district attorney seat, too. And that he wasn't prepared to do.

They'd have to beat this bastard some other way. They could do it, he thought, if they did it together.

''I beg your pardon?'' Ryan asked. His voice cracked.

''I'm not sure I'm running for mayor,'' he clarified. He shot a look at his uncle. And then he knew the real reason. ''The day I start selling out and letting guilty parties walk is the day I quit this game, gentlemen. Dr. Byerly is as sane as you or I. On the other hand, I've got reason to believe that Charlie Price is a raving lunatic.''

''Even so, you can't use her old accusation now that he's announced his candidacy,'' Wendell said pointedly. If Jesse had insulted him, it didn't show. ''It wouldn't look good.''

Jesse felt disgust wash over him. He picked up his jacket and moved for the door.

"You're making a treacherous mistake here, Jesse," his father warned.

"What exactly is going on between you and Goldilocks?" Wendell asked harshly. "I admit she's attractive, but—"

Jesse interrupted him as he opened the office door. "Her name is Angela Byerly," he said quietly. "Use it." He shut the door with a resounding crack.

It was a long moment before either Wendell or Ryan spoke. Ryan broke the silence first. "We've got a problem."

Wendell got to his feet, bypassed the coffee and went to the liquor cabinet to pour himself a shot of very good Scotch. "Well, you know what I always say. If you can't beat 'em, join 'em."

"Is she unstable?" Ryan asked shortly.

Wendell drank. "I had reason enough to think so at the time."

"What do you think now?" Ryan asked, because past indiscretions never bothered him.

"It doesn't matter. Our rising star thinks she's innocent and he's refusing to charge her."

They looked at each other. Ryan finally nodded. "And that's the bottom line," he said.

It was nearly seven-thirty before Jesse got home.

He paused in the parlor for his usual brandy. For weeks now, he had been moving under the impetus of emotion, and that was so stunningly unlike him that he couldn't seem to get his bearings. Today he'd let gut instinct and impulses drive him. It was time to sit down and really *look* at it all.

When he had finished his brandy twenty minutes later, he did not like the conclusions he had come to.

He admitted, for the first time since Angela had dropped her bombshell on him this morning, that he didn't *want* Charlie Price to be Lisette's killer. It wasn't that he particularly liked the man. He didn't. He remembered running into him yesterday morning. He'd seemed impatient to see him, even irritated. Charlie Price always wanted something. And he always wanted it to come cheap.

That the man should turn out to be a rapist and a murderer

wasn't a personal disappointment, Jesse realized. It was a political nightmare.

With or without proof, there was no way he could allow this man to become the next mayor, or even the district attorney. Aside from what was happening now, he believed Angela. The man had raped her fifteen years ago. Even if Jesse did not want the post as badly as he did, it was critical that such a man not take over the job of prosecuting Philadelphia's criminal element.

With or without proof, he believed, too, that the man *had* killed Lisette Chauncy.

In the quiet of his home, in the dim golden light of the single lamp in the parlor, Jesse felt sickened. The lamp threw an arc of light over the Cézanne and the fireplace wall, and Jesse stared at it. He wasn't soothed this time. Too much fit too neatly into place.

Angela had said that Lisette had not put up any sort of a fight until the last possible moment. Probably because she had not believed until the last possible moment that she was actually going to die. And she hadn't believed it because she had known and trusted her killer.

Yes, Charlie's face was vaguely visible to the public. Not as a politician or lawyer—the ACLU rarely made it into the news—but as a member of one of Philadelphia's oldest, and gilded, families. With this election, his voice would become more recognizable, as well. But what unconscionable risks had he really taken with that? He had made only a couple of personal appearances—all at the morgue. Where only Angela was likely to identify him, and if she had, if she had said so, he'd already fixed it so that people would think she was out of her mind. Brigid Cross thought she might, just *might,* have recognized him, but she couldn't put her finger on where she knew him from.

Eric and his investigators had finally run Alvin Carper to ground again late this afternoon. The photograph from Langoustier, along with a typewritten paragraph, had allegedly been delivered to the *Inquirer*'s mail room yesterday morning. No one remembered exactly who had dropped it off. But they immediately called in an expert and the type matched that of the note left on Lisette.

The press conference this afternoon had been prompted by another typed missive left at the desk of KYW-TV. Same thing with the type. But no one had seen who left that, either. And, interestingly, no one had tipped *those* bloodhounds off to the society-page blurb, and by some miracle, none of them had seen it. Because those reporters would have looked into it more deeply and asked a lot more questions.

Price would not want that to get out. He'd used that blurb sparingly, with only Carper. Jesse suspected, his nerves tightening, that money had to have changed hands here, too. Eric had reported that Carper had seemed tense and skittish when he had talked to him. Jesse would not be surprised to learn that Price had greased his palm to keep that tidbit out. Any good reporter would have dug into it, to find out who Angela had charged. Any good reporter would have checked his facts against public record.

He did *not* believe Price would have paid the man off in person. Still, Carper would have put two and two together, would know by now that he was playing a high-stakes game with some powerful people.

No wonder he had seemed nervous.

Jesse swore, drained the last of his brandy and rose to his feet. He went to his office, got his briefcase and sprang it open.

The first logs that Libby had given him hadn't amounted to anything, but tonight he had brought home the sets from the end of April, going into early May. He sat down at his desk, and flipped through them. He found what he was looking for almost immediately, leaned back in his chair and closed his eyes.

"*Damn* it."

Eight weeks ago, Charlie Price had stopped by his office. He had been helping his wife out with a Cancer Society fund-raiser, had said he was going around to friends and business acquaintances, selling tickets. Jesse had bought two and never used them.

He tried to remember if he had left the man alone that day for any reason, but it was too long ago for him to be sure. It was a safe bet that he had. And that Libby, too, had left her desk at some point during the visit. Jesse imagined that a release form and possibly even some dictation tapes had left his office on that afternoon. Or maybe he had come back for the dictation tapes at a later time.

Either way, it threw a whole new slant on this. It became a matter of premeditation. A *lot* of planning and preparation had gone into this scheme. And that made the killing of Lisette Chauncy murder in the first degree.

Pennsylvania had reinstated the death penalty last year. It was his decision, as D.A., whether or not to ask for it. It was a decision he did not want to have to make.

Ambition, he thought. It had all been done in the name of ambition, family pressure and desperation to *be* someone. Unseating Jesse in the D.A. race would be a long shot. So he'd used Angela to muddy his name, discrediting her in the process, as well, killing two birds with one stone. Just in case she talked. Just in case she thought about opening old cans of worms once he announced his candidacy. Which he had done at the last minute. After a good bit of damage had already been done to her reputation.

It wouldn't give a sane man motive, Jesse reflected. But Charlie Price wasn't sane. He wanted something for nothing. He wanted to win the easy way, as he had been doing all his life.

There was one more thing Jesse needed to check, just to be sure. He called the medical examiner's office. Brigid Cross was on call tonight. The night watchman gave him her number and Jesse phoned her at home.

"It's Jesse Hadley," he identified himself. "Dr. Cross, I need you to do something. Do you still have this morning's newspaper?"

There was a short silence. "I'm sure I do." She called out to a roommate or husband, for someone to bring it to her. "Is this about Dr. Byerly, about that picture of you two?"

"No. It's about the man who wanted to take Lisette Chauncy's body out of the morgue yesterday."

Brigid breathed a quiet, "Oh." A moment later, she added, "Okay, I've got it here."

"Turn to the first page of the city section." He waited. There was the rustle of paper, then he heard her gasp.

"That *could* be the guy," she said, her voice excited. "I mean, he looks different without his hair all slicked back. And that mole underneath his right eye wasn't there. I would have remembered that." She hesitated. "And my guy had a mustache," she finished.

"You didn't mention that yesterday," Jesse said sharply.

"It was small, scraggly," she explained. "Like he was trying to grow it. I didn't remember it until I saw him looking so clean-shaven here."

He recalled, in retrospect, that Charlie might have been sporting the thin beginnings of a mustache yesterday, too, when he had run into him briefly on his way to Angela's office. It hadn't seemed odd at the time. He hadn't yet talked to Brigid.

He tried to remember the condition of the man's hair and failed. He'd been in a hurry. But it had probably been combed forward again, greasy or not, or Jesse *would* have thought something was odd.

Jesse was sure of one thing. He'd upset some kind of applecart when he'd dashed out of his office. Charlie had no doubt turned tail out of the morgue, covered the two blocks between there and Jesse's office, while he had been talking to Brigid.

Why?

To establish an alibi, Jesse realized. Now he knew two things. Someone *had* recognized Charlie Price yesterday morning, or they had come damned close.

"Keep this quiet for the time being, Dr. Cross," he said finally. "It's your job."

"You don't have to threaten me," she said stiffly.

"Good." He hung up, rubbed his temples and stood up to go change. It was time to find a pair of hip boots. Hadley or not, the mud was getting deep, and he had no alternative but to start slinging it or sink in it.

Chapter 16

By the time he stood in the hallway outside Angela's room, Jesse felt like a fool. He knocked once, sharply, and Melanie Kaminsky's voice came back to him.

He identified himself.

"Put your ID up to the peephole," she called back suspiciously. "It doesn't look like you."

He wished he could believe that she was getting carried away with this. Unfortunately, she wasn't. He stuck his opened wallet up to the hole. A moment later, he heard locks clicking and the door opened. Melanie took one look at him and cracked up.

"*Jesse?* What are you *doing?*" Angela gasped from behind her.

He was dressed in black jeans—nothing odd about that. But he had on a red Phillies baseball jacket that was marginally too small. He wore a pair of reading glasses that she had never seen him use. He hadn't shaved, at least since this morning, and it gave him a deliciously disrespectable air, like the one he'd had after spending the night on her sofa. But the kicker was the hat—a fisherman's cap.

"It's not...you," she managed to gulp, fighting the almost overpowering need to laugh, as well.

Jesse grimaced. "The jacket and cap are Gunner's. I swung by my sister's place on my way. I couldn't find anything close to what I needed in my own closet."

"But *why?*"

"Because I've put it all together. And I didn't want to be followed here. You were right, and the lunatic does seem to have eyes in the back of his head."

Angela felt her legs fold. She sat hard on the sofa. "I'd thought you believed me all day."

Jesse looked at Melanie without answering. "Take a break, Detective. Burn off some of the cabin fever. Take as long as you need, and if the Do Not Disturb sign is still out, don't come back until it's gone."

There was a click as the woman let herself out and the door closed behind her. Angela got to her feet again. She fisted her hands at her sides, her heart thudding too hard, too fast.

"What are you up to?" she asked, her voice thin.

He shrugged out of Gunner's jacket and threw it over a chair. The hat and the glasses followed. He dropped down onto the sofa and looked up at her.

She was the best thing he had seen all day.

She wore shorts—of the sweatpants variety again—with a drawstring waist along with a short T-shirt. Her feet were bare and her hair was wild. Her toenails were painted crimson. She looked like a cheerleader again, and the sight was refreshing, wholesome, clean—just what he needed right now. He wondered about that. How could a woman who was able to take on so many flavors with a simple change of clothing always manage to be just what he needed at any given time?

"Will you come over here?" he asked. "Will you stop standing there staring at me as if you expect me to grow horns? I've got them under control."

Angela shook her head helplessly. *If the Do Not Disturb sign is still out, don't come back until it's gone.* Her muscles felt stiff, brittle at the way he gave orders, blithely, without any consideration that his wishes might not be the only ones. "You should have asked me first," she whispered.

He knew what she meant and didn't pretend not to. "Should I have? Really?"

His voice was soft, caressing, and she understood. She'd been afraid that his behavior toward her would change now. Yet she was still panicked when it didn't.

She let out her breath. "I don't know," she said miserably.

"You can bring the sign back in yourself if you like," he said evenly, and she wondered just how much more patience she could expect this man to possess. She hadn't even seen him put the sign on the other side of the door. She'd been more preoccupied with the way he looked.

She shook her head again.

Jesse reached up and caught her hand. She gave a small gasp. But he didn't pull. He didn't demand. He urged and she settled onto his lap, facing him.

He felt her muscles go rigid. He placed a hand deliberately on each of her thighs. Her skin was warm.

"This has been the most miserable day I can ever remember having."

Angela hesitated, then nodded. "It's been a doozy."

"And this almost—*almost*—makes it all go away. I don't want anything more from you than this, Angela." It wasn't true, he realized. Not at all. "Until you're ready to give it," he added.

She met his eyes and thought he was probably lying. Something trembled inside her that he even cared enough to bother.

"You never saw that hair." It was out before she had known she was going to say it. But it had been tormenting her all night.

Jesse tilted his head back against the cushions and closed his eyes. For a moment, she didn't think he would answer.

The fact was, he wasn't used to explaining himself, he realized. He was even less familiar with wanting to.

"Angela, I was there in your office the day you did the autopsy," he said finally. "I told *you* that the hair was probably mine. I thought you were genuinely shocked. And I trust my own perceptions of people. That wasn't a court of law out there today. I didn't take an oath. It was just twenty or so bloodthirsty people who would have loved nothing more than to rake you over the coals and destroy your reputation. Mine, too. At the instigation of Charlie Price. I thought a hair worth splitting. So to speak."

"Oh, Jesse. If it ever goes to court, you'll have to tell the truth and they'll remember this—they'll have it on *tape*—and they'll know that you lied." *For me.* It was both beautiful, and so very dangerous.

He opened one eye to look at her. "Spoken like a true politician. Better watch yourself there, angel. You might become one of us whether you like it or not."

"But that's exactly what will happen!"

"I'll roll with it if and when the time comes."

She had never known anyone as strong, as steady, as this man. The depth of his strength struck her hard. She couldn't believe he had done this for her. At *election* time.

"In the meantime, there's probably something else you should know," he added.

She stiffened instinctively, warily.

"I probably would have split that hair for anyone under the same circumstances. I would have split it if you were a man, if I had seen that same reaction on your face that day in the morgue. I would have split it if you looked like my mother. But..."

She held her breath.

"But I am very, very glad that you don't look like my mother."

He grinned. A breathless laugh escaped her.

She was no good at this, she thought. She never had been. Not even before. She wanted to touch him now. She *ached* to do it. To get still closer. And she didn't know how. She knew that if she tried, the reflex would be wooden and clumsy.

"Angela," he said softly, and it was as though he had read her mind. "I don't know how to handle this, either. Damn it. I don't know what to *do*."

She knew he wasn't talking about their current problems now. He was talking about what Charlie had done before. Her heart thundered in a paroxysm of hope and dread.

"I know what I *want* to do," he murmured. His voice changed, and her heart thumped so hard against her chest that it stole what little breath she had left. "I want to touch you everywhere he did. The same places, the same skin. I want to somehow erase it for you...the evil, the pain, and lay down different memories in each place instead. Good ones. And I'm scared to death that if I try to do that, you'll run and I'll lose you."

His words were so perfect. They made everything inside her ache more.

She couldn't answer. Her eyes filled. She yearned all over again...and still, in that dark place inside, she feared. But she didn't fear him anymore. She feared herself.

"I need to ask you something," he said. "I need to know. In all this time...has there been anyone else?"

Angela flinched. "Yes." She shook her head nervously. "No."

He almost smiled. "Which is it?"

"It doesn't matter."

He thought about it.

Maybe it didn't. He admitted that he wanted her to say yes for selfish reasons. If she said yes, then that would take some of the pressure off him. There was a difference between holding a nice piece of china and an heirloom antique that could not possibly be replaced.

If the answer was no, if it turned out that he *was* holding an heirloom, then sheer panic could make him mishandle it, drop it. If he was faced with an heirloom, and he knew it, then he thought maybe he might never be able to bring himself to touch her at all.

He wanted to touch her. Desperately. And backing off from her now could quite possibly be as cruel as moving in too quickly—marking her as different, damaged, unworthy of the effort. He felt overwhelmed and inadequate. He almost groaned.

"Okay," he said, letting out his breath, taking his hands back deliberately. "Where's the television remote?"

She looked at him blankly for a moment. "The remote?"

"Angel, I badly need something to do with my hands, and the way my instincts are going would scare you to death."

She tried to laugh. It came out more like a gasp. "On the table there," she breathed.

He shifted his weight to one side to look.

"Jesse."

"What?"

"Thank you."

"We've got all the time in the world, angel."

He managed to smile. He wondered how pained it actually looked.

Angela hadn't expected him to stay the night under the circumstances. She ached, both with her own need and with a helplessness she hated. She couldn't give him anything, and acutely aware of that, she was ashamed. She was terrified to try. But his wanting was there in his eyes anyway, a certain banked heat each time he glanced at her.

He was frustrated, she saw. He had to be. And frustration would inevitably lead to anger and disgust. She'd seen it happen before.

At midnight, he ordered a bottle of brandy from room service. "Want some?" he asked, pouring.

"It's a safe bet that I'm not going to be driving anywhere tonight. Yes. Thanks." She sipped nervously and settled on the sofa again.

Jesse sat down, as well. His eyes fell on the jacket and cap again. He grimaced. "I must have looked like an overgrown adolescent dressed up like that."

In spite of everything, she actually felt herself grin. "If you lose the election, I don't think you should go into private investigation."

"This sort of thing has never been required of me before."

"Good thing," she murmured.

He looked at her. "Are you laughing at me?"

She hesitated, then chuckled. "Yes." She sobered. "I don't think you should try to repeat the process."

"Why, Angela. Are you suggesting that I stay here tonight?"

Her face colored. She made herself look at him. He watched her chin come up.

Good enough, he thought. Plenty good enough. He nodded. "I'm staying."

He took up the remote again and flipped channels. He finally settled on an old movie from the fifties. A young Hepburn was doing a credible job of holding Spencer Tracy at arm's length, given the fact that they were probably all over each other off screen, Angela supposed.

"Are you relaxed now?" he asked.

Her head jerked in surprise. "Yes. I am."

"Then can I point out that six feet between us on this sofa is not really necessary?"

She felt foolish. She felt relieved. She slid closer. She simply hadn't known how to close the distance herself, hadn't dared to.

He shifted his weight to put his feet up on the table. He lifted his arm and drew her beneath it. And it was like it had been on her own sofa before he had known the truth, his heart thudding softly beneath her ear, his warmth good and strong against her. Angela closed her eyes and just let it be. If every once in a while the tempo of his breathing changed and he moved his weight again infinitesimally, almost uncomfortably, she chose to ignore any hidden meaning there.

She thought, impossibly, that she was as happy as she had ever been, and Charlie Price could be damned.

When she woke hours later, it was dark and Jesse was gone.

She sat up stiffly and half-unconsciously reached a hand across the sofa. No one was there, and she realized that she heard water running. She got to her feet, moving uncertainly toward the bedroom. The glowing green numbers on the bedside clock read 4:42. He probably hadn't slept at all.

She felt a guilty flush creep over her. How could she have been so naive, so *selfish* as to have wanted him to stay? Ah, the guilt. She thought of all the incredible things he had done for her over the past few days and she hugged herself, fighting another urge to cry.

Before she'd made a conscious decision to do so, she found herself inching her way toward the bathroom. He was in the shower. She stopped outside the door. It was not quite closed. A crack of light escaped.

She put her hand on the knob, then pulled it back again.

I can't.

In all this time, has there been anyone else?

There had been, and, if she was going to be honest with herself, that was what terrified her now. She wasn't afraid of *him*. She wasn't the least bit concerned that he would hurt her. She trusted him. It wasn't that.

It was her.

On the only occasion when she had gotten...physical with someone in fifteen years, she had forced herself. She had gritted her teeth and had closed her eyes and had *made* herself go through the motions. It had happened not long after the trial. She'd been angry, and it was the only way left to her in which to fight back. It had been a desperate attempt to prove that what Charlie had done would have no lasting effect on her.

She'd been wrong. It had been a painful, humiliating experience. It had been as bad as what Charlie had done to her, because she had, in effect, raped herself.

Since then, she'd learned to listen to her body. She'd tried for a while, now and again, just to see what would happen. But the jail doors had always slammed shut. Everything inside her had gone cold, rigid, even cringing, as soon as any man touched her. And when it happened, when she had stiffened and wanted desperately to pull away, then she had learned how to do it. She left men confused and angry, but since that first time she had been true to herself. And finally, she had simply stopped trying.

She was terrified to listen to her body now, because everything inside her wanted to open those doors.

She hugged herself, shivering. She couldn't bear to do the same thing to Jesse. To start, to try...and have those doors slam down. Jesse deserved more than that. *She* deserved more. Because she knew that with him, she would force herself again. She would make herself finish what she had allowed to start. This time, she would not do it to prove something to herself, but because she would feel she owed it to him. But that wouldn't really matter. It would still be ugly, awkward, and it would ruin a relationship that had become precious to her.

Still, in fifteen long years, she had never felt like this inside before. Maybe that was enough. Maybe she ought to trust it. Nothing had happened when he had kissed her, nothing but good.

I don't know how to handle this, either. I don't know what to do. She heard his voice again and knew that the admission was amazing in itself. Most men wouldn't have made it.

Ah, he was so different. So good, so strong and confident within himself. A Hadley. There were, she decided, some good aspects to such inborn arrogance.

She wondered, almost abstractly, if she was falling in love with him. The word reverberated in her head and terrified her. She pushed it away. She didn't dare love him...not if she couldn't give him anything.

But she could try. She could try to see if she could.

She didn't touch the doorknob this time. She laid her palm flush upon the door and gently eased it open.

How could he know she was there? That amazed her, frightened her. Because somehow he knew. Though the door hadn't made a sound, she heard the rattle of the little rings at the top of the shower curtain, and it parted. She thought wildly that every one of her senses, every sound, now seemed so magnified and intense. The steam from the shower wafted out to her, clinging to her hair, dewing on her skin.

She took a few hesitant steps into the bathroom, then she stood rooted.

His face went through a thousand transformations in the space of a heartbeat. There was surprise, concern and something that looked almost like panic. Then his eyes heated, and she melted at his look.

"Come on in."

"I..." It was useless. Her voice was gone, trapped somewhere beneath her heart. And her heart was filling her throat now, beating wildly. Her hands fumbled clumsily for the hem of her T-shirt.

What if she couldn't? What if she was awful? What if—

She gasped and jumped when his hand flashed out and caught hers. "Leave it," he said hoarsely.

"But—"

"Come on in," he repeated, then he pulled on her hand.

Angela stumbled the remaining distance to the shower enclosure. And then he smiled. It was a grin that made his dimples come out—the dimples that should have made him look angelic, but now he had the devil's own glow in his eyes. Her pulse went wild.

When she didn't step into the shower, he reached out with both arms and lifted her. She cried out again and expected him to freeze when she did, wishing desperately that she could somehow choke the sound back again. But he didn't freeze. Somehow, incredibly, he recognized the sound as one of pure surprise this time, nothing more troubling than that.

The water pelted down on them. It made it almost impossible for her to remain tense. The heat of it melted her. It drenched her shorts, her T-shirt, made them cling to her skin as she stared up into his face.

"If I can't—" she began.

His hands left her waist and tunneled into her hair on either side of her head. He held her, watching her eyes. She was acutely, agonizingly aware of his nakedness. Her pulse slammed, but she was afraid to look down.

"Then just tell me," he said quietly. "We'll stop." It would probably kill him, he figured, but he would. Somehow he would.

"You asked...about before," she croaked. "I've tried. Something always dies inside."

"We'll find out."

He lowered his mouth very slowly to hers, keeping his eyes open, watching her. And it was the way it had been in the parking lot, but his lips were wet and warm. And somehow she relaxed even more, her spine easing back to meet the tiles. Her arms went around him briefly, her hands sliding over his back, skittishly, experimentally. Then she brought a palm back to rest it flush against his chest. Not to push him away, to stay there, just in case.

She *could* push him away if she wanted to. She knew that, and so did he, and it made her feel safe. But she didn't want to, because she didn't want to hurt him. And that made everything tangle up inside her all over again.

His mouth was doing incredible things to hers. His tongue coaxed and teased. She thought she felt him tremble beneath her hand. With restraint.

What was she doing to him? This was just as bad as asking him to stay the night. It was worse. He could have any woman he wanted, one who was warm, giving, practiced and generous. And she had so little to give.

She needed to stop this after all, but it was so hard to think. His tongue caught hers. It touched, slid away, found her teeth, came back again. She gave a little cry and moved her arms around his neck, holding on.

His mouth left hers. It slid over her cheek, to her temple, and she looked at him, surprised that he had stopped kissing her. His eyes were closed again. His teeth found her earlobe. She gasped again and she felt as light as air. His touch was easy, almost a whisper, but forceful enough to be a promise.

She held on to him, feeling something incredible in the pit of her stomach beginning to coil. But no doors. Nothing screamed, slamming closed, barring her heart and soul.

One of his hands left the side of her face to gather her hair together from behind. "There's something I want to do," he murmured. "I want to see you tilt your head back. I want your throat to arch. I want to see you yield."

A tremor rocked through her. Pure terror. And flash of fire.

"Do you remember what I told you earlier?"

She nodded convulsively. *I want to touch you everywhere he did. The same places, the same skin. I want to somehow erase it for you...the pain, the evil, and lay down different memories in each place instead.*

"That's the only reason," he said softly. "The only one at all."

He tugged gently on her hair. She let him. His mouth came back to hers, and this time his kiss was harder, hungrier, more demanding. His tongue swept rather than slid. She met it, feeling desperate, and then he groaned.

His mouth left hers again and moved to her exposed throat. And she tilted her head back even more, of her own accord this time, making it easy for him. Heat arced through her from the point of contact, from the easy slide of his lips over her skin.

He caught her around the waist again, holding her with both hands so she wouldn't slide into the tub. And his mouth moved lower, to her collarbone. He found the hem of her sodden T-shirt and pulled down on it, stretching it. Her pulse scrambled where the base of her throat was revealed. He kissed that spot, as well.

"Did he touch you there?"

She moaned something inarticulate. He hadn't. No one had ever touched her like this.

"One down," he murmured. "More to go."

He let go of the hem and slid his hands up beneath her shirt this time, over her skin, peeling the fabric slowly away where it clung to her. He moved his fingers over every rib in turn, tracing one, then another, until she shuddered.

"There, too?" he asked.

"Yes," she breathed.

"And here?"

His palm slid up to the side of her breast, barely grazing it. She couldn't answer. He felt her tremble. It was answer enough.

Cover me. Touch all of me. Please. What if she had driven him so far away that he didn't dare? She kept her eyes closed and *willed* his hand to move, to touch her fully, because she couldn't find the words to ask him aloud.

His palm kept sliding until her breast filled it. Then he waited, just cupping her, letting her feel it, get used to it, revel in it.

"And here?" he crooned. His thumb brushed gently across her nipple. It sprang up to greet him, then her knees buckled.

She drove her fingers into his hair, holding on. She was beyond thought, beyond caring. He moved, catching her weight, bending his head to touch his mouth to her breast. He did it through the clinging cotton of her shirt, his hand still underneath, and it wasn't enough. She wanted his tongue on her sensitive flesh, wanted nothing between her skin and his mouth.

"Please," she groaned. He seemed to understand. The pressure of his mouth changed, drawing her in, cotton and all, then he finally pushed her shirt up and away. "Oh, don't stop," she whispered.

His mouth trailed to her other breast. She gave herself up to sensation. His hands stroked, soothed, made everything inside her hum. She lost track of time, of everything but his mouth and the delicious, almost-rough texture of his tongue. He demanded nothing in return. And some part of her felt that that was wrong, but she was beyond doing anything about it.

His mouth left her breasts and roamed lower. The water began to cool, but inside she was heated. She moaned and dug her fingers into his shoulders.

His tongue dipped into her navel. Again, and again. She felt his fingers at her waist, sliding over her skin beneath her shorts. He pulled at the drawstring. His mouth moved along the loosened fabric. And that was the only time she really thought of Charlie, because nothing inside her had shut down and she knew then that it wasn't going to.

She needed to touch Jesse, as well, but it was impossible now. All she could do was grope for him. He reached up and caught her wrists, holding her hands still when she tried. His mouth closed over her through her shorts, through her panties, and she cried out again, her back arching through no conscious will of her own. Her head hit the shower wall. She didn't feel it. Her knees bent.

"And here?" he whispered.

"Yes," she pleaded. "More."

The request almost killed him. He let her wrist go to find her shorts again, easing them down.

She would have fallen if his weight hadn't been bracing her. He moved cotton and lace, but slowly, so slowly that it was both agony and hope. And because she could still stop him, she didn't want to.

"Okay?" she heard him ask.

"O...kay," she thought she answered.

And then his mouth was back with no clothing barring its touch, and incredibly it was almost a comfort at first, just pressure and warmth. The intense intimacy of it was more sweet than thunderous and needy until his hands slid up her thighs, parting them, touching her, and then everything changed inside her.

She had thought she was melting, but she was burning, on fire. She was not the candle, but the flame. Something inside her was becoming almost violent. It swirled and tightened, and when she felt his tongue again, a voice that she couldn't even recognize as her own burst from her throat.

It was his name, and Jesse realized that that was really all he needed.

Everything ached inside her, but it was a new pain, a delicious one of wanting. She didn't know what she was doing or where she was. There was only this amazing sensation growing stronger and bigger inside her until she did not think she could stand it and would die if it stopped. His tongue left and she felt his fingers slide inside her, stroking, drawing the heat inside down toward them. Then it erupted, rocking through her.

This time he didn't hold her up. He caught her as her back slid down the shower wall, easing his weight on top of her as her legs folded. His mouth caught hers again, cleaving there, his tongue sweeping deep as the last of the tremors spasmed through her.

"I really wanted to hate you," she confessed shakily. "But you turned out to be so perfect."

Jesse grinned over her shoulder where she couldn't see it. "Hey, I'm a Hadley."

What he didn't tell her was that for a while there, he'd been even more terrified than she was.

Chapter 17

A pounding on the hall door finally roused them.

Angela was startled and she slipped and slid as she tried to get to her feet again too fast. Jesse slid an arm around her waist to help her. He reached to turn the shower off.

It took her a long moment to realize that although he seemed outwardly calm, he wasn't. His movements were tense. As he helped her from the tub, she brought her hand to his chest, and his flesh was as hard and solid as rock beneath her touch.

Her head cleared. "It's Melanie! We locked her out all night!"

"No," he said tensely, "it's not Melanie. She doesn't have a fist like a jackhammer."

He grabbed a thick terry robe from a hanger on the back of the bathroom door. There was no time to appreciate his body now, either. Much too late, she remembered his nakedness, and her pulse skittered and her breath caught all over again, but then he shrugged into the robe.

"Stay here," he said shortly.

Angela tugged her sodden clothing back into place and raced after him. She reached the living room just as he wrenched open the door.

Gunner. Angela gave a glad cry and ran to him.

Jesse moved aside. Something unseen and unexpected grabbed his throat. In a moment, he felt supplanted. Unwanted, unneeded. The invisible fingers at his throat grew hot. It took him another heartbeat, another breath, to realize that what he was feeling was jealousy.

It was another emotion he had never experienced before in his life. He had never lacked for anything. He had never been unable to achieve anything—female or otherwise—that he had set his sights upon having. But now Angela had her arms wrapped tightly enough around John Gunner's neck to cut off his breath. There was not a sign of her reluctance to be touched, of the trembling fear and awe he had felt in her just moments ago. The man—his *brother-in-law,* for God's sake!—actually lifted her off her feet in a bear hug. And Jesse had the most incredible, unbelievable urge to plant his fist in Gunner's jaw, for both his own sake and his sister's.

Tessa came in behind Gunner. Her face showed no appreciable change when she saw their embrace. Jesse felt as though the whole world had suddenly gone mad.

"What the hell are you two doing here?" Jesse growled.

Gunner looked at him over Angela's shoulder. "It's good to see you, too," he said dryly. And then, by degrees, his jaw fell slowly open.

He set Angela carefully away from him. He really looked at her. He took in her dripping hair, her sodden clothing, and his gaze went back to Jesse. Who was wearing a bathrobe. He gave a disbelieving, unintelligible sound of rage.

Tessa's expression still hadn't changed, but she took a hasty step backward. "John," she said a little breathlessly, "perhaps we should go back downstairs for a cup of coffee."

"What the hell is going on here?" Gunner snarled.

Tessa's voice took on a little more spunk. "John, let's *go.*"

"Perhaps we should go downstairs for a cup of coffee," Angela echoed. She looked at Gunner and his new wife, then she looked at Jesse. And suddenly, with all the stress of the past several days, it was just too much. She laughed. Hard. She went back to the sofa and flopped down. "When the rest of us were getting flash cards with our ABCs, were you two being flashed with awkward situations?" She hooted. "Now, Jesse, what would a Hadley do if..." She was laughing too much to continue.

Jesse managed a faint smile. Tessa actually grinned. "Oh, it was worse than that," she said.

Only Gunner wasn't smiling. "You're getting the sofa wet."

Angela laughed harder. She couldn't get her breath.

"You're hysterical," Gunner accused. "What's happened to you? You're out of your mind."

Trying for control, Angela shook her head. "No. *Yesterday* I was hysterical—or on the verge of hysteria anyway. Today I am very, very fine."

Jesse acted suddenly, with no conscious deliberation whatsoever. He went to the sofa and sat beside her. He slung an arm over the cushions at her back, not quite touching her, ready to do so if the situation warranted it.

Staking his claim.

Only after he was sitting did he stop to consider that male animals the world over probably did the same thing day in and day out. Marking their territory, keeping their female in and the other guy out. It made him feel foolish, especially given that the other guy was supposed to be newly married to his sister, but he didn't stand again. He glared at Gunner, steady and coldly.

"Let's start with the obvious," he said challengingly. "You're not in Australia."

Tessa moved to the phone. "It was a killer flight. I really do want coffee. How about if we order some up here?"

Angela's laughter had subsided to hiccups. She looked at Jesse, then back at Gunner, and tried to understand the tension she suddenly felt in the room. Gunner's reaction, at least, made some sense. He was no doubt stunned to find her like this. She looked down at herself. It was definitely a precedent.

"I...uh, I'll go change."

"Great idea," Gunner snapped. But Angela felt Jesse's hand touch her shoulder briefly, as though to hold her. Then it fell away reluctantly.

"We came back early," Gunner said, after she'd left the room.

"Obviously," Jesse said with mild aggression. "What I'm having a problem with is the fact that you're in this particular room. How did you know where to find us?"

"Four cups?" Tessa asked brightly from the phone. "No, no, we'll need more than that."

"Roger called us," Gunner answered.

Anger tightened Jesse's stomach. In retrospect, he realized that Kennery had acquiesced too easily yesterday.

"This was supposed to be kept under wraps," he retorted.

"It is. Except six people know now instead of four."

"Between Homicide and my investigators, we have everything under control."

Gunner gave a sound of disgust. "With all due respect, your investigators couldn't find a gift under a Christmas tree if their names were on it."

Jesse shot to his feet again. "They're working on it," he snapped. "They're leaning on Carper to try to find out who paid him to write that slanted piece about the rape. And they've turned copies of everything they've got over to Homicide—"

"Oh, now, *there's* progress," Gunner interrupted harshly.

Tessa hung up and moved quickly between them. "Come on, both of you. Jesse, you know he's right. Your investigators are out of their depth on something like this. Lisette was killed. We owe it to her to find her killer in the most expeditious way possible."

Gunner went on angrily as though she hadn't spoken. "Homicide does the dirty work! Your guys fill in the cracks. That's all they're *trained* to do! They're *lawyers,* for God's sake. They're not cops!"

"Hey, watch yourself there," Angela said mildly.

Gunner blinked and looked around as though coming out of a bad dream. She had returned to stand in the bedroom doorway. "I guess I put my foot in my mouth, huh?"

"You might say that," his wife agreed. She, too, had gone to law school.

"Well, at least you have the good sense to realize it." But Angela's voice was strained now. Reality was crashing back in. The tension in the room was beginning to get to her, to erase her lingering euphoria.

There was another knock at the door. Angela jumped, but Tessa went to collect the coffee. Jesse took a cup from his sister and raked his free hand through his wet, disheveled hair.

"Roger wanted us to come home," Tessa explained. "He thought we could talk some sense into you."

"It was your *honeymoon,*" Jesse responded disbelievingly.

"Since we're here," Gunner said, "I want it all, every minuscule detail from start to finish.'' He glanced at his wife again. *''Homesick?''*

''Roger was vague,'' Tessa said, ignoring him. ''I get the feeling that that's because you haven't told him everything?''

Jesse was grimly silent. Angela looked at Tessa. ''Better order more coffee,'' she suggested.

Tessa blinked. *''More?* We've got a whole pot.''

Angela sighed. ''I think this is going to take awhile.''

It was nearly nine o'clock before they finished filling Gunner and Tessa in. Gunner dragged them through each incident over and over again, until he was satisfied he had all the details in place. Tessa took notes, asking a question or two of her own.

''All right,'' Gunner said finally. ''Laying low here is good. It's a start. But it's not enough.''

''No,'' Tessa agreed. ''All it does is get Angela off the hook, and that's only if Charlie does something else, if he doesn't know she's covered.''

''I should have killed the bastard when I had the chance,'' Gunner growled suddenly.

Jesse felt a quick, sharp pain in his chest again. For the first time, he wondered just *why* Price had stopped harassing Angela all those years ago. He had just assumed it ended when his uncle had let the man off the judicial hook. Apparently not. But that was something he would deal with later.

''I don't want Homicide running this,'' he said flatly.

''I thought we'd settled that,'' Gunner snapped.

''Not to my satisfaction.''

''What the hell *would* satisfy you?''

Angela saw Jesse's eyes shutter. ''A quiet resolution that won't affect my candidacy,'' he answered flatly. ''I won't be caught in a firestorm of accusations here. I can't afford it. We need to quietly and emphatically get our hands on one unequivocal shred of *proof.*''

Gunner stared at him. ''What's important here?'' he demanded. ''A psycho rapist and killer on the loose, or a goddamned election?''

''Both. And you'd realize it, too, if you'd calm down and think about it.'' Jesse paused pointedly. Gunner waited. ''Price is clever," he went on. "If I let this investigation get beyond my control, out of my office, then there's no telling how it might be handled. Do you have any idea how it will look for me if something goes wrong and the guy *walks* again?"

Gunner opened his mouth to answer, then changed his mind.

"You're afraid," Angela said, touched, watching Jesse, her voice soft, disbelieving.

Jesse glanced at her. "Damned right I am." His voice lowered with intensity. "Oh, I want him. But I want to make damned sure that he's taken the right way, with our *t*s crossed and all our *i*s dotted. I don't want him out on the streets again in two weeks, running against me and telling everyone how I tried to put him out of the race. I want to make sure *nothing goes wrong*. I want to err on the side of caution."

"I'm not a cautious man," Gunner retorted.

"Well, you'd better learn," Jesse said shortly. "Let me illustrate what will happen here if he gets off. He'll play the press like a finely attuned fiddle. He'll turn this entire situation around to favor himself, just as he did to Angela. And I'll come off looking like the dirty player. *My* name will be associated with sneaky underhandedness and lousy campaign tactics. And the worst-case scenario is that I'll lose the election because of it. And if I lose the election, guess who's your next D.A. And possibly *mayor*."

"Mayor?" Angela squeaked.

Jesse's gaze softened as he glanced her way. He told them what he'd learned from his father. "I found out late yesterday afternoon," he explained. "You were right. He wants the whole enchilada—he *needs* it because his family's all over him—and this is his only chance to save his sinking ship. He can't wait for another, later election, for some other post, because he'll probably have gotten the boot from the ACLU by then, ruining his chances. It's got to be now, this D.A. campaign. But Angela turned up, back in town, in a position of some prominence. He must have seen his life pass before his eyes. Not only did he have to worry about somehow unseating me, but he had to worry about Angela opening her mouth again. And people would believe her this time. At least a handful would, and that would be enough."

Angela sat back weakly. "Setting it up to look like I'm framing you undercuts both of us."

"Exactly." Jesse looked at Gunner. "Now are you willing to do this my way?"

"With your investigators? No way." Gunner held up a hand when the others were about to argue with him. "It could take months for them to get to the bottom of this. They're *lawyers,* not a one of them went to the Police Academy. They know the law, but they don't know squat about investigation. Damn it, if evidence can't be found through records, through computer sources, your people are at a loss!"

Jesse was quiet for a long time before he finally nodded. It was true enough, and he was honest enough to admit that Gunner's argument had merit. For the most part his team *organized* evidence. The police department compiled it.

"So we'll compromise," Gunner went on. "We've got four of the sharpest minds in Philadelphia right here in this room. We'll take care of this ourselves."

"We have another whole week of vacation," Tessa added. "We don't even have to technically report in with what we learn until then."

"And there won't be any leaks," Gunner affirmed. "Nothing will get out before you're ready to point your finger."

Jesse nodded, then he had to smile. It was a tight reflex. "I was laboring under that assumption yesterday—that Kennery was going to keep this business quiet. Next thing I know, you're banging our door down."

Our door. Angela's heart lurched then swelled.

Tessa looked at her husband again. "So where do we start?"

It was Jesse who answered. "Here's a kick in the right direction. I think someone in Angela's department might have recognized Price when he went to collect Lisette."

"But your people interviewed everyone there already," Angela argued.

"They asked about a suspicious-looking funeral-home employee," Jesse countered. "Not about Charlie Price."

"I rest my case," Gunner said dryly. "They don't know what the hell they're doing."

Jesse ignored that. "It's possible it's another dead end," he agreed. "Maybe he got out of there before this person actually saw him. But he was worried enough to try to set up an alibi. He turned up at my office immediately afterward. I literally bumped into him on my way to the morgue.''

They were all quiet at that. Finally, Gunner blew out his breath. "Okay. Let's get started." He veered in his pacing to head for the door. Then he stopped by the chair and stared down at it in dismay. "That's my hat." He looked at Jesse. "You took my hat."

"Live with it," Tessa suggested.

"And my jacket. You took my *jacket*? That's my favorite jacket!"

"Actually, I hate it." Tessa wrinkled her nose. "It's old and it's ragged."

Angela got up and grabbed the hat. She plunked it on Gunner's head. "Satisfied? Come on, I'll walk you as far as the elevator."

Jesse watched them go through narrowed eyes. It took him more than a moment to realize that his sister was watching him with a similar look. "What?" he asked warily.

Her voice crackled with anger. "Damn it, Jesse, *you* should have called us!"

"Actually, I probably would have, but Kennery beat me to it. It took me until last night to swallow that it really *is* Price, and that we've got bigger problems here than even a homicide investigation."

She stopped in her tracks and looked at him, surprised by the admission. "You never reach out. You always think no one can do anything better than you can do it."

"They generally can't."

She smiled, then sobered. "You're different. You've... changed."

"Maybe I'm mellowing."

She looked at his robe. "I'd say so." Her eyes narrowed again. "Don't hurt her, Jesse. She's not like...well you know," she finished lamely.

Jesse's grin came slowly. "She's a lot tougher than she looks."

Tessa watched his eyes. Her own widened at what she saw there. "Oh, boy. Mom and Dad are going to keel over in a faint when they get wind of this."

"I think they already have."

"What have you done?" she gasped, but it was partly a laugh.

"For starters. I escorted Angela to Monday's fund-raiser. Isobel just loved the idea that she was so close to Gunner. They might as well get used to it. She'll be by my side for a while.''

"Does Angela know this?"

"Not yet."

Tessa gave another delighted burst of laughter as she stepped into the hallway. "You know, I'm really glad I came home. I wouldn't miss any of this for the world."

Jesse was dressed—minus the jacket and the hat—when Angela came back. She stopped just inside the door and leaned her back against it, watching him. The invasion of Tessa and Gunner had kept her preoccupied, off balance. Now she realized this was the first they'd been alone since they left the shower. Suddenly, she felt shy.

But Jesse's gaze was shuttered when he looked at her. "Was it him?" he asked bluntly.

Angela blinked. "Who? What?"

"You said you tried, but couldn't. Did you try with Gunner?"

Her jaw dropped. "With *Gunner?*"

Jesse felt something overpowering move inside him. Relief. But he *was* a very good judge of character, and he thought that just as she had been stunned when he suggested that the hair in Lisette Chauncy's hand was his, now she was equally taken aback.

"Never mind," he said hoarsely.

"No." She shook her head and pushed away from the door. "I want to settle this."

"You don't owe me anything."

"I owe you *everything,*" she said simply.

"I don't want to know who it was," he admitted, and that shook him up, too. Because such information had never bothered him about any lover before.

"I doubt if you know him anyway."

"Oh. Well, good," he said stiffly.

She stopped in front of him and took a deep breath. "My mother drank a lot. My father was in and out. I saw my share of foster homes. Gunner's was one of them."

His heart kicked.

"We dated, briefly, when we were teenagers. Nothing came of

it because we were *too* close. We were—are—like brother and sister. The first time I lived with his family, I was eight.''

''The first time,'' he repeated carefully.

''I ended up going back when I was eleven, and again when I was fourteen. While my mother was away drying out. Gunner's been the only real friend I've ever had. Until you.''

''He did something to Charlie.'' He wasn't sure he really wanted to hear this, either, but the words were out. When you were the district attorney, sometimes it was wise to be ignorant of certain goings-on.

But Angela didn't even hesitate, and that was when he understood just how much she had come to trust him. It had been a hell of a morning, he thought, shaken.

''The last time Charlie came to...to harass me, Gunner was waiting for him outside,'' she said, and her voice had taken on a toneless quality. ''John had been waiting for him every night, until he showed up again. I didn't go out when I heard the ruckus. I didn't call the cops that time. I don't know *what* happened. I really couldn't say with any certainty in a court of law, and it occurred *after* the trial. But...'' Her face took on a pained expression. ''I ran into Charlie not long afterward. Downtown. He was on crutches and he had a broken arm.'' She smiled thinly. ''I think they call it street justice. I imagine it's worlds away from the kind you Hadleys swear by.''

''Thank God for that.''

She looked up at him quickly. She wanted to hope that he understood it had been the only way to stop Charlie, but didn't quite dare to.

''By any name, it finally put an end to things,'' he avowed.

She should have known that he would always say just the right thing. She just barely managed to nod before he drew her into his arms. She relaxed against him with a deep, shuddering breath. ''I thought so,'' she whispered. ''I thought it was ended—until a few weeks ago.''

Jesse closed his eyes and rested his cheek on the top of her head. She didn't know it, but she had just answered yet another question he'd had. She *had* been duking it out on her own for a very long time. And not once, not ever, had she broken all the way through. It wasn't going to happen this time, either. This time *he* wouldn't let it.

"We'll get him," he said quietly. "We'll get the bastard. And he's going to weep with regret. For all of it."

Chapter 18

In spite of everything, Angela floated through the day. She knew it was crazy, even ill-advised, to let herself become so preoccupied with thoughts of Jesse. Besides all her other responsibilities, Charlie was still roaming the city somewhere. Who knew what the next trick up his sleeve might be? She had to be ready, on her guard...and the only thing she could think about was what Jesse had done to her, for her, how he had set at least part of her free.

No one had ever cared so much for her, she thought, trembling a little. No one had ever been strong enough to be so kind.

She forced herself to wonder what was in this for him. It had always been her experience that no one ever committed any act without hoping to gain something by it. But with Jesse, she just couldn't be sure. She found herself praying that she was capable of giving whatever it might turn out to be.

She didn't hear from him all day. Nor did she hear from Tessa or Gunner. But she knew they were all out there, doing their part. It gave her a strong sense of comfort, even as it frustrated her. All she could do was appear to go about business as usual...and wait for Charlie to play another card.

While she worked, she wondered how and if her relationship

with Jesse might continue when this nightmare with Charlie was over. Once circumstances stopped throwing them together, would he just...drift away? Something in the area of her heart spasmed at the prospect. If it happened, that part of herself he had returned to her would die again.

As the day wore on, she wondered, too, if he would stay at the hotel with her again tonight, and something in her stomach curled. She promised herself that if he did, this time she would find a way to give something back.

And by five o'clock, she realized that she had barely thought of Charlie all day at all.

It was half past five when Gunner burst into Jesse's office. Libby trailed after him, angry and rattled.

"I asked him to wait!" she cried.

"It's all right," Jesse said neutrally. This was his turf. And it was a visit he had been expecting. He did *not* expect what Gunner said first.

"We've got him."

Jesse stared at him. "Who?" he asked blankly, waving Libby out. The woman closed the door behind her.

"Price."

"You *got* him? Just like that?" He was incredulous.

"We've got *something*," Gunner clarified. He began to pace. "A couple of somethings, actually. Tessa is picking Angela up right about now." He glanced at his watch. "They're on their way here. I'll fill you in when we're all together."

Jesse didn't like it. Waiting gave Gunner a subtle edge; he knew something that Jesse did not. He forced himself to sit back and crossed his arms over his chest as he watched the other man.

Gunner moved to the window and stared out at the street below. "Look, I wanted to beat them here because I owe you an apology," Gunner said at last. "I was...rough on you this morning."

"You were," Jesse agreed.

Gunner looked back at him sharply. "Do you have any idea what she's *giving* you? Hell, I'm the first to admit that she comes off a little prickly at times, but—"

"I know," Jesse interrupted calmly.

Gunner went on as though he hadn't spoken. "Inside, she's vulnerable."

"I'm aware of that."

"Damn it, if you're just playing with her, it'll kill her. Then I'll have to kill you. And I just married your sister. Ugly."

Under any other circumstances, Jesse might have laughed. "Give me some credit," he said shortly.

"I don't know if you deserve it," Gunner replied bluntly. "That model you've been running around with...well, let's just say neither one of you was the picture of commitment."

There'd been a time, Jesse reflected, not too long ago, when he would have wondered if Gunner even knew the meaning of the word. But that had been before Tessa.

"Angela's not like that," Gunner declared. "I mean, there are women, and then there are women." He paused again, looking miserable. "I'm not good at this."

Jesse didn't let him off the hook. Now he was *enjoying* waiting. He did it silently.

"Sometimes you get into it with someone, and she gives you something so...so profound, so special, it changes your life," Gunner said, struggling. "What I'm trying to say is that it's a *responsibility* to take something like that from her. You can't just play around with it, man. It'd be like juggling with Fabergé eggs. How's that for terms you understand?"

Jesse's mouth quirked. "It'll do."

"You look at a woman," Gunner went on, "at the way she's watching you, and the trees are whispering, and it's so damned cold, but there's this incredible warmth in her eyes. And then everything changes. You're not the same. You can't ever settle for less again. Everything that ever went before is...hollow."

Jesse finally let loose a big grin. "John?"

Gunner looked at him again, confused. "What?"

"What the *hell* are you talking about?"

"I'm—" Then he smiled, as well, looking almost abashed. "I'm remembering. I was...uh, talking about Tessa, anyway. Did I get my point across?"

"Yes." Jesse waited a beat. "Are you asking me my intentions?"

Gunner let out a breath. "Yeah."

"I don't suppose it would help to point out that Angela is well past the age of consent?"

"Nope."

"Or that this is really none of your damned business?"

"Doesn't matter."

"Well, then, all I can tell you is that I haven't yet been able to give it a lot of thought—"

Gunner's face hardened. He advanced on him from the window. Jesse thought he was actually going to hit him.

"Well, you'd better damned well start thinking, because this morning it looked to me like you'd found plenty of time for everything else."

"Either mind your own business, John, or let me finish," Jesse said mildly. But Gunner was heating up again.

"When I left for Australia, she was dancing with you—and that alone blew my mind! Then I come home and find her standing there sopping wet and you're half-naked."

"I believe I was wearing a robe."

Gunner scrubbed a hand over his jaw again. "Showers are wicked places," he muttered to himself.

"I haven't had time to think about where I want this to go or how I'm going to get it there," Jesse admitted. "There's been this little matter of Price hanging over our heads. But I'm not treating it casually."

"Well, good," Gunner answered, slightly mollified.

Then the door swung open and Tessa and Angela came inside. Angela's cheeks were flushed. No doubt Tessa had told her a little bit, as well—not everything that was going on, but enough to pique her curiosity and raise her hopes. Her eyes were golden today, clear and bright. Her hair was caught back in a thong again, and she wore the short black skirt. The bright yellow blouse caught the golden tones in her eyes, and it shouted at a man to notice. It was silk and clung to her.

She was incredibly beautiful, yet she had just spent a day doing things he couldn't even imagine, couldn't bring himself to do if he tried. Her world was coming apart at the seams with an old nightmare exploding again, and she looked around at them all expectantly, clearly ready to fight back.

"What?" she demanded. "What did you find out?" Her gaze swung to Jesse. "Do *you* know?"

"No. *I* wouldn't be so cruel as to keep you guessing."

"Okay, okay," Gunner said. "Everybody sit down."

Tessa dropped into the nearest chair. Gunner leaned back against the windowsill, and Angela hovered. Jesse looked at her questioningly, then his heart slammed again.

Her eyes said that she wanted to come close, maybe to touch him, at least to be near him. They said that she had been thinking of him all day, as well. But there was Gunner, and Tessa, and a lot of problems and unanswered questions, and for a moment she waged a war with herself.

Jesse held a hand out to her. He thought he heard a soft sound as she breathed. He was eminently aware of his sister and brother-in-law watching them, and he actually wished for a moment that they would take their news about Price and go. Then Angela took a deliberate step toward him and slid a hip onto the edge of his desk beside him. Her back was half-turned to him, and he knew that that, too, was a small measure of trust.

Jesse put his palm to the place where her spine curved, then a moment later, he tugged impatiently but gently on the back of her blouse. He slid his hand beneath the little gap he created and rested his hand against her skin, out of sight of the others.

He felt her breath catch, then felt something jerk to attention inside himself. It was good—in fact, he thought, it was pretty damned terrific.

Tessa cleared her throat and he had to forcibly drag his attention back to her.

"Ed Thackery recognized Charlie Price the other day in the morgue."

There was a stunned silence. "Then why didn't he say so?" Angela demanded.

"No one asked him that," Gunner said pointedly. "And he wants your job. He sure as hell wasn't going to pipe up and bring a lot of controversial attention to himself. I twisted his arm today. It sort of changed the complexion of things in his mind."

Jesse's face hardened. "So we've got Price in the right place at the right time trying to lift a corpse. It's not enough."

Tessa glanced at Angela. "Your night watchman also says Price was masquerading as a cop the night the note was left on Lisette. We talked to him, too."

Angela shuddered.

"Better," Jesse allowed. "But we need something more definitive than that to pin him to Lisette's murder."

"I haven't found that yet," Gunner answered. "But how about another rape? That ought to at least keep him out of the election."

Angela's heart stalled. She could almost feel her blood drain to her toes. Jesse's touch became firmer as though to give comfort. But no one, none of them, could possibly understand.

"Oh, God," she breathed. "He did it *again?* To someone else? How do you know?"

Gunner's expression softened considerably. "Angie, I've always told you that he wasn't going to stop. Not given that he got away with it the first time."

"How did you find out about her?" Jesse snapped.

"I pulled open files from the rape and sexual assault unit. And I found one that sort of fits. At least, there are a lot of similarities. The problem is that we can't locate the victim. Either she's left the city, or she's changed her address, or is making herself scarce. I haven't had a chance to dig deep enough yet to be sure which way it is."

Tessa tugged the file out of her briefcase and slid it onto Jesse's desk. "The woman met her rapist at a bar in city center repeatedly over a three-week period," she began, taking over. "She said she thought it was all harmless flirting. This guy bought her drinks and paid her compliments, but she swears she didn't want anything more than that."

"That happens all over the city all the time," Jesse argued.

Tessa held up a hand. "One afternoon, this guy came directly to her house. She had never told him where she lived, or her last name, and she says it would have taken a good bit of determined effort for him to find out. But she opened the door, and there he was, uninvited and without warning."

Angela made a strangled sound.

Jesse could feel her start to tremble under his touch. He stroked his fingers down her spine, trying to calm her, but he knew he couldn't. No one could. His stomach was beginning to feel sour again.

Tessa flashed an apologetic look at her. "I'm sorry to bring this all up again, but his method almost exactly matched your old complaint. We pulled that, too, just to be sure."

"No weapon?" Angela whispered.

"No. Just physical force and battery. He restrained her by tying her with her own clothing. And the woman's description of her assailant fits our Charlie to a T."

Jesse clenched his jaw and something red touched his vision.

Tessa cleared her throat. "He beat her up, and some of the things he said to her, some of the phrases and words she claims he used, were exactly what you said Charlie said to you during your own attack."

Angela was fairly vibrating under his touch now. Jesse stood abruptly and wrapped his arms around her from behind, as much for his own comfort as for hers.

Gunner picked up the tale. "She called the cops and filed a complaint as soon as he left. She was all fired up. But less than three weeks later, she tried to withdraw it."

"Yes," Tessa agreed quietly. "There's more. She said she couldn't go through with it because the guy would kill her if she did. He kept turning up in her home, even in the lavatory at her office, warning her to shut up, and she told RSA that she was going to do just that. She said she was scared."

Angela stiffened beneath his arms.

"Except you can't really back off from charges of rape," Tessa continued. "Like any violent crime, it's something the state is compelled to at least investigate. Rape is a crime against the people, and she had been visibly harmed. She had bruises, abrasions, so it wasn't as if she could say she'd made it up. It was too late for that. All she could do was back off."

"So the RSA unit went on with the investigation," Jesse guessed.

"Sort of," Tessa returned. "What could they do? The woman swore the act was consensual, and she was uncooperative through every other interview. So the case has just been sitting open on the books."

"He got to her," Angela breathed.

"Yeah," Gunner agreed. "And now she's gone."

"So she doesn't do us any good," Jesse said angrily. "Then what's the point?"

"We need her to come forward," Tessa said. "Wherever she is. We need to reach out to her."

There was something about her tone that Jesse didn't like.

"What I'm thinking is this," Gunner proposed. "Who knows

what Charlie has been up to in the years between what he did to
Angela and what he did to this woman? Maybe he kept his nose
clean. Or maybe he mastered the art of coercing his victims into
silence. I've got to think it was the latter. I mean, rape isn't about
sex. It's about *power*. And no way is this guy going to get a taste
of it, then say, 'Oooh, I was bad, better knock it off now.' It
would have been too heady for him. He would have to have kept
going back for more. Carefully. Covering his tracks and bullying
the women to keep their mouths shut. Anyway, if I'm right, then
there are still *more* women out there who've fallen victim to this
predator.''

Angela felt her heart sink. She understood what he was saying.
''I need to talk now,'' she whispered. ''I need to go public. Again.
If I do, maybe this other woman, maybe *more* than one woman,
will be encouraged to come forward, as well.''

''And press charges,'' Gunner added. ''With a sympathetic,
successful and respected D.A. who will then go for Price's throat.
I grant you that it won't tie him to Lisette's murder, but it'll get
him the hell out of the D.A. race, and then Homicide can go after
him full throttle without tiptoeing around your campaign.'' He
glared at Jesse.

Angela felt Jesse's arms tighten almost spasmodically around
her. ''No,'' he said hoarsely.

''Speaking as a Hadley for a moment,'' Tessa said quietly, ''it
will garner you the female vote for certain.''

''This isn't about politics,'' he grated. ''This guy *killed* Lisette
Chauncy in order to set this all up.''

''But why *Lisette?*'' Tessa asked, still troubled by that, glancing at Gunner. ''It's what just won't click for me. Why poor
Lisette? Price had to know that no one would readily believe Jesse
was involved with her.''

''Let's just say that that model he was seeing ought to be
damned glad she and Jesse broke up,'' Gunner answered.

''Lisette was simply available,'' Tessa realized slowly. ''She
was there.''

''And she was easy,'' Gunner stated rigidly. ''Think about it.
She would have opened her door to Price, would have let him
into her bedroom with no fuss. She was desperate for attention.''

''I want him,'' Angela said suddenly, fervently, her voice trembling. "I want to see him stopped. I want to fight back. I want to destroy him and have some closure here."

"You're not—" Jesse began.

"I've been waiting fifteen years for something like this!" she argued, her voice stronger.

"Has anybody ever told you that revenge is a dish best served cold?" he snapped.

"It's cold," she answered. "So's Lisette." She jerked away, wheeling around to face him. "Don't you see?" she cried. "He's challenged me! He thought he could do it to me all over again! The...the *fear*. And the powerlessness. But I'm not powerless anymore! If I call a press conference, I call his bluff! What's he going to do?"

"Kill you." Jesse's voice was strangled. He couldn't get past that.

"Why? What purpose would it serve then?" she demanded.

"You said he was crazy! Does he need a purpose? Okay, let's find one for him. How about he just gets ticked off and he wants revenge?"

The truth of that finally struck her into miserable silence.

"We'll cover her," Gunner said. "We'll put the whole damned police department on her until this is over. Hell, she's Code One."

"I want to do it." Angela was trembling. Hard. If she could only find the courage to do this, it would really, finally, be over. And then, maybe then, she would have something to give to another man.

What Jesse saw in her face in that moment brought Gunner's earlier words to mind. *She gives you something so...so profound, so special, it changes your life.* He felt humbled, small. And terrified.

"No," he countered, shaking his head. "It's not necessary. We'll work around what happened to you. We'll work around *this*. You don't have to do it."

"He's already dragged you into this, Jesse," she whispered. "He's been after me—I'm his worst threat—but he's dragged your name down into the mire with mine."

"Because he's got to run against me!" He was shouting without realizing it. "It's not your fault!"

"I want to do this," she repeated stubbornly.

"Not for me. Not because of me! Damn it, *no!*"

"For me, then. For both of us."

He didn't mean to, but he caught her shoulders and shook her anyway. "Listen to me. If what...if the way you're looking at me right now is true, then don't do this. I can't live with it, Angela. It's like waving a red flag in front of a bull who's already incensed to begin with."

Her eyes widened. Her breath caught. It was as much of a promise as he had ever given her. She touched a hand to his cheek. "Then I'll be careful."

Gunner cleared his throat. Angela turned around again. She found his eyes fast on Jesse.

"I know you can't believe that I'm any more wild about sending her into this than you are," Gunner began.

"You're willing to serve her up like some kind of sacrificial lamb!" Jesse shouted.

"It's a damned press conference! It's not a sting operation, for God's sake! We'll have cops all over the place, and we'll keep a team on her afterward."

"He'll come apart! He *shot* Lisette!"

"We'd be on our guard, expecting it," Gunner argued.

"No," Jesse replied with deadly calm.

"It's no one's choice but mine."

They all turned to Angela. Tessa reached out and clasped her hand. Angela looked straight at Gunner and Jesse.

"What you two big, protective guys are missing here," she protested, "is that in the beginning, Charlie did this to *me*. I'm the one with the score to settle. I can fight back with or without your approval. I know he'll panic, and yes, he might even do something drastic. So I think it would be much better if I had the police department and the D.A.'s office behind me."

"I don't like it," Jesse reaffirmed obstinately, angrily. "I'd rather kill him with my bare hands and spend the rest of my life in prison."

A single tear spilled over. Angela swiped at it. In that moment, she finally believed that, too.

But there was no way she was going to let him.

Chapter 19

Angela took a cab and returned to the hotel alone with the issue unsettled between them. She thought of brass rings, of reaching for a dream, of trying to have it all. She thought of being *happy*, just...happy, all the way through.

It made her ache in a strange new way, because she had never dared to dream of it before.

Tessa and John had gone home. They hadn't said so, but it was obvious that they felt the rest was up to her. And they were right, she realized, kicking off her shoes and pouring herself some brandy. Jesse's approval—or lack of it—shouldn't matter. But it did, and she nearly groaned aloud.

She paused with her glass halfway to her lips. Melanie was watching her closely.

"Why do I feel like there's a whole lot more going on here than I know about?" the detective wondered.

Angela surprised herself with a tired half smile. "Because there is." Oh, so much more. Personal fears. Professional horrors.

"What can I do?" Melanie asked.

Angela was overwhelmed all over again by how many times people had said that to her in the past weeks. Now it was time for *her* to do something.

The other woman sighed when she didn't answer. "Guaca-mole?"

Angela grimaced. "My stomach's a knot. Go ahead, though, if you like. I'm going to drink this and take a shower."

No sooner were the words out of her mouth than she felt memories flash through her of everything that had happened in there this morning. She flushed with the sudden heat of them.

She turned her attention doggedly to the television, pacing, sipping. There was no mention of her name on the news. It worried her that another day had gone by, and Charlie hadn't done anything else. She wondered if he knew where she was after all and refused to fall into their trap.

This time she did groan aloud. She finished her brandy and went into the bathroom. A shower didn't help. It didn't revive her and it didn't calm her. She touched her fingertips to the tiles, almost as though she expected to still find them warm and pulsing with the memories that lingered.

She had taken a cab from Jesse's office to the hotel. He hadn't mentioned that he would stop by tonight. He was upset.

She needed him.

She stood under the spray and hugged herself. "Please," she whispered aloud. "Please let me end this. Please let me be whole."

"You don't know what you're asking."

She gasped. For a moment, she looked around wildly, half-expecting to find him in the shower with her. Then she wrenched at the curtain.

Jesse was standing in the bathroom doorway, almost lazily, one shoulder braced against the frame. His arms were crossed over his chest, but there was a palpable tension about him. His eyes weren't on her face.

His gaze coasted over her breasts, down past her waist, her hips, along her legs. Angela fought the urge to cover herself. She realized that only half of her really wanted to.

"Melanie—" she began.

"Gone again," he said, his voice low. "You know, I think she loves this assignment. She's seen more of her kids in the past two days than she has in a month."

Angela opened her mouth and closed it again. He kept watching her. Everything inside her heated, and that was so incredible, so good.

He finally moved away from the door and came toward her. He cupped her face in his hands and looked down at her intently. "Maybe I haven't made myself clear. Maybe I haven't had the chance to tell you how I feel."

Her heart hurtled. She held her breath.

"If anything happens to you, *I'll* never be whole again."

He kissed her. He wasn't gentle this time. She could feel his anger, his frustration. Something quick and fleeting tried to spasm inside her. She lifted her hands as far as his chest with every intention of pushing him away, then slowly, languorously she relaxed again.

"You are so beautiful," he said against her mouth, nibbling a corner of it. "And you don't even seem to know it. I want you, and I want everything to be right, and I want this whole mess to go away and let us be." Then his lips covered hers again, and his tongue urged hers to play. It felt as though he plundered her very soul, and he was asking for something this time as he had not asked this morning. She would have given, would have tried, no matter how clumsy and inept she might seem, but she knew what he wanted most was impossible.

He pulled away from her.

"Your suit," she uttered dazedly. He was still holding her shoulders, and she was still standing in the shower, and his arms were drenched.

He finally stepped back. "I've got others. Finish up, angel," he said quietly. "We need to talk first."

She watched, her heart thudding, as he left the bathroom. One part of her wanted to hurry and go after him. The other part couldn't bear to argue with him again, to hurt him with the decision she had made.

She was going to give that press conference. She *had* to. But first she had to make Jesse understand.

If anything happens to you, I'll never be whole again. Was he saying what she thought he was?

She fumbled through the rest of her shower, quickly rinsing the shampoo out of her hair. When she was done, she bundled herself in the robe he'd worn that morning. It still smelled of him. She pressed her cheek to the terry cloth, then she went into the living room. She found him on the sofa. He'd taken his suit coat off. It was draped over a chair, drying.

For a single moment, she thought he was asleep. God knew, he had to be exhausted by now. He was sitting as he had last night, when she had been on his lap, with his head back against the cushions, his eyes closed. But when he heard her, he straightened and looked at her.

Angela cleared her throat. "This morning..."

Something about his eyes sharpened. "Regrets? It wasn't what you wanted after all?" He didn't think he could have read her that wrong. What had been in her eyes this afternoon had not been regret.

Angela shook her head. "No. But when you were...touching me, I kept thinking that you could have any woman you wanted. That you could have someone who was generous, giving...and that I had nothing to give."

He opened his mouth to argue, his eyes suddenly angry. She held up a hand to stop him.

"Please, Jesse. Let me finish. I *know* I was wrong. I *can* give you something. Maybe. If I can get free. All the way free of him."

"It's not necessary," he said harshly.

She gave him a pained smile. "Of course it is. Sooner or later, you'll chafe over what I can't give you. You'll want more. You'll resent me for not finding a way to please you."

"Have I complained? I just want you alive. We'll take it slow—"

"No!" she erupted. "I don't want to *wait* anymore, Jesse! I've been this way for *fifteen years!* It's a prison! It's hell!" She took a deep breath, but her voice broke anyway. "You don't know what it's like. It's like being a ghost, and everybody else is real. People can see me, they can touch me and find substance, and they think I'm normal. But it's like there's nothing inside. I watch movies, I read books, and everyone else is part of this wonderful, exclusive club, doing this amazing act with each other and *enjoying* it. And until this morning, I could only yearn to have what they have, to...to connect with another human being that way. *He stole that from me.* Can't you see? If I fight back, if I finally talk loud and clear and refuse to let him cow me, it might make me normal. It could give me back my self-respect, maybe give me

some kind of substance *inside*. I could be part of that club, Jesse, and I want that. I want it so badly.''

He felt something almost unbearably painful fill his chest. He realized in that moment that she'd been a virgin when Charlie had raped her. He'd come here to talk her out of this crazy idea. And in that moment, he knew he couldn't. He couldn't condemn her to the life she had just spoken of, never knowing, never once being free enough to fly.

''Angela—''

''*Please,* Jesse,'' she interrupted. ''Please. Now that I know there's a way of settling this, I don't even want to try to be with you until I do it. Do you know why I came back here, why I took this job?''

He kept silent, knowing she had to let the hurt out.

''Maybe I always thought that if I was important enough, maybe, *maybe,* I would find the courage to shout. Maybe people would hear me. Maybe I came back to Philly to give myself that chance. But I was still scared. I thought I was still the same person inside, not particularly worth listening to. Then I met you. There must be something there within me, because you like me anyway. Even though I kept trying to push you away, you wouldn't go.''

He gave her a tight smile. ''I think this is coercion, angel.''

''I don't need your approval, your go-ahead,'' she replied shakily. ''But I want it, Jesse. I want it badly. I need you to stand beside me on this.''

He watched her tremble. He saw the desperation in her eyes and remembered Gunner's words. *It's a responsibility to take something like that from her. You can't just play around with it, man. It'd be like juggling with Fabergé eggs.* Not so different, he thought, from his own ideas about priceless heirlooms. And damned if he didn't have one in his hands.

Jesse got to his feet. ''I'll call Gunner.''

Tessa and John arrived half an hour later. Angela realized that they had been ready to move, that they had only been waiting for her—or Jesse—to give the nod.

Tessa had stopped by Angela's house and picked up a royal blue, almost-professional-looking suit. It was a classic, even as it demanded attention.

Jesse had reluctantly called all three television networks and both daily newspapers. The word would spread like fire through the media community, and the weeklies and radio affiliates would no doubt be out in force, as well.

The press conference was slated for nine o'clock. None of them—certainly not Angela—could bear waiting until morning now that she had made up her mind. And they wanted to do it fast anyway. They couldn't allow word of their plan to leak and give Charlie ample time to lash out and stop her.

They would hold the conference in Jesse's office. It was a subtle slap in Charlie's face, and besides, there was no telling what might move by within camera range at Angela's place of business. They had vetoed the Four Seasons suite because they didn't want to give up her location and either of their homes for similar security reasons. Charlie might know where they both lived, but the remainder of Philadelphia's loonies did not.

Melanie checked in with them at eight. This time, Jesse asked her to stay. "We'll still need more backup," he said tersely, looking at Gunner.

"We've got it," he answered. "Thirty-two cops in and around your building. Not counting the two who will flank her at the podium."

"They don't know exactly whom they're watching for."

Gunner gave him a withering look. "Neither do the president's bodyguards." Then he let out a heavy breath. "I can't tell you to chill out. But I can say that I'm pretty damned sure this is going to go off without a hitch."

It should have been enough. The truth was that Jesse didn't feel comforted.

Angela was almost beyond hearing them, she was so wrapped up in her own tension. Her own fear. *No more.* Tonight she would banish it. Tonight she would stand up for herself. And maybe, in the process, she would finally find the confidence and the strength to be whole.

At eight-forty, Gunner looked at her. "Ready?"

"Yes," she breathed. "Oh, yes."

Jesse thought she looked ready to push her sleeves up and do actual physical labor. Her expression was set and grim. There was something too bright about her eyes. It scared him a little. Her color was high. Excited? he wondered. Or terrified? He hoped for the latter. It only made sense, and it would keep her cautious.

They went down the hall to the elevator. Tessa kept Angela's hand firmly in hers. Jesse's was at the small of her back. Gunner went ahead, his shoulders rigid with tension, as though to beat back all the demons in their path. Melanie brought up the rear, as though guarding them from behind.

Angela felt bolstered, protected, and doubted if she'd have been able to do this without all of them. Unfortunately, they weren't gong to be able to speak into that microphone for her, and she still had no clear idea what she would say when the time came. She was riding on nerves, and they were electric, sizzling.

Gunner had left nothing to chance. An unmarked car waited at the curb to take them to Jesse's office. An armed detective drove.

"Word's all over the city by now," Jesse muttered worriedly. No matter how tightly they'd tried to plan it, they'd been forced to give the media more than an hour's notice. "He knows. He's got to know."

"Good," Gunner grated. "I hope he's sweating."

"I'd say he's frantic," Tessa contributed. "You know, I never particularly liked that guy. Just like Christian Benami, there was always something about him. His eyes were always too cold."

"Who?" Melanie demanded. *"Who?"* They hadn't told her yet. It was just another security measure, hopefully unnecessary. No one really believed for a minute that she'd go running to Charlie, but stranger things had happened before.

"Roger is going to drop flat when he hears about this," Tessa guessed, and earned a hoarse chuckle from her husband.

The thirty-two cops at Jesse's office did not include the uniformed officers at the door, working crowd control. The moment they pulled up, the reporters and cameramen swarmed. It was apparent with one glance that more than just the Philadelphia media had come out for this. The whole thing smacked of scandal, and that had brought out news hounds from New York to New Jersey to Delaware—all of those who'd had time to get here.

"Oh, my God," Angela whispered, feeling something quake inside. *What was she going to say to them?*

Then the answer came, and it bolstered her like all the well-meaning touches and encouragement of the others couldn't. She was going to tell them the truth.

The uniformed cops had cleared a path from the curb to the door, keeping the media back with crime-scene tape—the best they could do on such short notice. They dashed from the car. Only Gunner held back a moment.

"Give us ten minutes," he told one of the cops, "then let them in."

Ten minutes. But she was ready.

Angela began feeling something else under her nervousness. It was anger, she realized. But no, that was too mild. She was *infuriated.* She'd had enough, and she was going to end it.

A few cameramen—those from the major networks—had been permitted to come inside and set up. They were watched critically by more police officers. The podium was placed in Jesse's anteroom. His office per se was not large enough to accommodate the crowd. Angela saw Roger Kennery push through the bodies, and she winced a little.

"Hope this is all right with you guys," Kennery said sarcastically, looking from Gunner to Jesse. "Given that I have no damned idea what's going on, given that I'm judging crowd control solely on the basis of all those bodies downstairs, I thought this would be the best place."

"Yep," Gunner said mildly.

"What, I've got to hear it with the rest of the nobodies?" Kennery demanded. "I'd like to remind you that I'm still your boss."

"Not mine," Jesse returned.

"Not mine, either," Angela echoed.

Gunner looked at his watch. "We're still on vacation," he reminded him, slinging an arm over Tessa's shoulder.

"You're going to have to report back in to me eventually," Kennery warned.

Gunner looked thoughtful. "You've got a point there. What do you say?" He glanced around at the others.

"Now's a good time as any to see him drop," Jesse said. "Better now, in fact, than with a camera on him." He was only half joking.

"Charlie Price," Gunner said easily.

"Huh?" Kennery stared at him.

"Killed Lisette Chauncy. Is trying to frame Angie and our D.A. here, and he thinks that's going to get him into the mayor's office.

Charles Price III. And no, we don't have a lot of proof, but we're hoping like hell this will keep him out of the D.A. race. Then you can give the Chauncy case to me, and I'll find a way to hang it on the bastard.''

Kennery's jaw dropped slowly.

''You ready, Angie?'' Gunner asked. ''It's nine o'clock. Let's do it.''

She managed to nod. She and Jesse moved to the podium, flanked by two officers.

''Charlie *Price?*'' Kennery bleated. ''*Charlie Price?* Oh, man. Oh, damn it. *Damn* it.''

Gunner actually grinned at him. ''Don't worry about a thing,'' he assured him. ''We've got it all under control.''

''That's what you told me in January before your wife took out half the Walt Whitman bridge!''

''Yeah, but we got our bad guy, didn't we?''

The lights blinded her. Angela felt a trickle of perspiration run down between her shoulder blades and could only be thankful that it was where no one could see it.

She had spoken to the media before in her role as medical examiner. There had been a few hot cases in her tenure where she'd announced her findings publicly at the request of the P.D. public relations department or Jesse's people. She had never done it in front of cameras. Besides, this was *her*. This was personal.

Jesse stepped up beside her and nudged her gently aside. He didn't displace her. For the moment, if only for a moment, he would share the spotlight with her.

''We've called you here to release a few facts pertaining indirectly to the murder of Lisette Chauncy,'' he began, '''indirectly' being the key word. While we have no new information regarding that case per se, we hope to dispel some of the many rumors you've heard regarding it.''

There was a murmur of intrigued speculation from the press. The only rumors circulating had been about him and the medical examiner.

Angela clenched her hands in front of her, out of camera range, she hoped. Most likely all the lenses were zoomed in on Jesse's handsome, arrogant, Hadley face anyway.

God bless him.

"Please bear in mind that we are making no accusations. We're stating facts. We'll offer no speculation." He paused and stepped back a little again. "I'll let Dr. Byerly continue."

She panicked. Briefly. A wild fluttering filled her chest. Then she was alone in front of the microphone. Cameras flashed. And words came to her.

"Fifteen years ago, I was very much like the rest of you. A student with goals, aspirations, dreams. We've all got those things we work toward. We've all got long-range plans. Fifteen years ago, I wanted to be a doctor.

"I was attending Princeton University on a scholarship when a man changed those goals. In all honesty, though it was a painful lesson, he changed them for the better. Being a doctor was no longer enough for me. I wanted to become a doctor in the field of law enforcement. And therefore, I also got my law degree. As most of you know, I worked several years for the federal government, with the FBI, before I returned to Philadelphia as your chief medical examiner." She stopped for breath. She was damned well going to get her credentials out there, she determined. They were one of the few weapons she had.

She was no longer shaking.

"The man who changed my plans is one well-known to all of you. He's a man currently running for public office. And he's a man with secrets." She paused and looked around the sea of faces. "I know some of you personally," she said. "And I know that there's a strong possibility that sometime during the course of this political year, you might well have ferreted out this information on your own. In fact, that's already begun this week with a piece that appeared in the *Inquirer* mentioning that I once pressed charges of date rape in Philadelphia's courts. However, that short article cleverly omitted the name of the man I pressed charges against. I'm here now to tell you my side of the story, to tell you who he was. My case was thrown out of court fifteen years ago. Nonetheless, I stood by my allegations then, and I will continue to do so now."

She let that hang for a moment. She took a deep, steadying breath. She let it out on a slight shudder.

"The man who raped me was Charles Price III."

The crowd exploded. It took everything she had not to step

back, away from them, as the sound rolled toward her. More lights flashed. It took several minutes for things to calm down again, though various reporters still shouted questions.

"Do you have proof?"

"Are you planning to reopen the case?"

Angela held up a hand. "Let me finish. I approached the district attorney's office with this information once I learned that Mr. Price plans to run for public office." A small lie there, she realized, but she went with it. "I cannot in good conscience stand by and allow this man to be elected knowing what I know about him. So I'm making a public plea." She found a camera and looked directly into it. "If there are any other women out there who have been a victim of this man, please, *please* come forward. I know it's intimidating. I know you're terrified." Her voice caught. "But you're not alone. Please contact either my office, or that of the D.A."

"What *about* the D.A.?" someone shouted. "What about your personal relationship with Mr. Hadley? Are you doing this now to facilitate his campaign against Mr. Price?"

She'd known that was coming. She swallowed carefully, and for a moment, she floundered. *What* personal relationship? Oh, God, what *was* it between them?

Trust, she thought. Trust and need and caring. She'd take the first step. She would protect him as best as she was able.

"Our personal relationship is, at present, one entirely brought about by the rumors and allegations against us. Against *me*. Our offices are working in tandem. I felt it was crucial for me to share with him what I know about Mr. Price. This has nothing to do with Mr. Hadley's campaign at all, although I obviously would not want to see a rapist take over the district attorney's office."

"Are you concerned Mr. Price might charge you with slander?"

Angela's smile was slow and full. "I would like nothing better. I've waited fifteen years to have another day in court with this man."

"Mr. Hadley said this ties in to the rumors circulating about your involvement in the murder. Now you tell us that Mr. Price raped you. What's the connection?" someone challenged.

"Are you saying that Mr. Price is framing you in this matter?"

"Someone is framing me," she said sharply. "I haven't killed anyone. I did the autopsy and turned the results over to the proper authorities. I found a tape splicer in my home subsequent to a break-in. I discovered this myself and turned that over to the authorities, as well. And we have proof that Mr. Price is involved at least on the periphery of this case.''

''What proof?''

''I'm sure the police and the D.A.'s office will give you all the details at a time when it won't jeopardize the remainder of their investigation.''

More shouts, more questions, loud and demanding and intimidating. Angela had to shout over the noise.

''I'll release a written statement in the morning,'' she called out, ''detailing the fine points of my accusation. I have not decided at this time whether or not I want to reopen the case.'' That ought to worry him, she reflected with a quick little thrill of victory. Then again, as far as the media and his reputation were concerned, the damage was already done.

''If what you're saying is true, then why *wouldn't* you want to reopen the case?'' someone demanded.

''Because evidence disappeared at the time. I no longer have access to it. Witnesses declined to testify. Unless they—and others—come forward now, I have little recourse. They know who they are.'' And so, she prayed, would at least the one other woman who in all probability had also been Charlie's victim.

''Mr. Hadley, how exactly are you involved in this?'' someone pressed.

For a moment, Jesse couldn't speak. There was something hot, large and painful lodged at the back of his throat. He wasn't at all sure he could get words around it.

He looked at her, her golden hair shimmering in the harsh lighting. She was pale, but her chin was high. Something rolled over inside him, something unnameable, a tangle of pride and awe, need...and love. He'd thought once that she was smarter than he was. Now he knew that she was stronger, as well. The only person she'd needed to prove it to was herself.

He stepped up beside her.

''My office is open to any and all citizens who feel any crime has been committed against them. In this case, as in every case, I will do whatever I have to do to get a conviction if the charges are substantiated, regardless of who the perpetrator might be. I feel great regret that in this case, allegations have been made against my opponent in the current election. Obviously, it puts me in an awkward position, one I'd really rather not be in. Mr. Price is a personal acquaintance, as well. However, I will not shy away. If witnesses come forward and evidence is accumulated, I will nonetheless prosecute him to the fullest extent of the law." He allowed a crooked grin. "For the next several months, at least, that's still my job."

Someone laughed. It was a faint sound, almost a cough. Then one of the female reporters clapped. It was buried beneath another rush of voices, of questions.

Jesse took her elbow. "Come on, let's go."

Angela wanted to sag against him. But not yet. Not now. She turned her back on the podium.

Before they even got into Jesse's inner office, telephones were trilling.

desk, where she had moved when the window had become too uncomfortable. "Let's make a run for it."

But Jesse caught her elbow. She looked up into his eyes, startled. They were dark with terror. For her.

"We have no choice," Tessa said quietly, reading his expression, as well. "We've got to leave sooner or later."

"I hate it," Jesse said tightly. "I still hate this whole thing."

"Of course you do," Tessa soothed. "But it really went well. And it's over. Now there's nothing we can do but let the dust settle."

"And watch our backs," Jesse corrected. But he was still watching Angela, and his face softened. "*You* were incredible. Have I told you that?"

A thousand times so far, she returned silently. But it still made pleasure wash through her like warm rain.

"Let me call John first," Tessa interrupted. "I want to make sure there are still cops on the premises."

"Good idea. I feel a little vulnerable," Angela admitted. Even Melanie had left, first to help beat back the hordes, then to assist John with the phones over at the homicide office. She'd still been muttering and shaking her head in shock when she'd left.

Tessa went back to the desk. Jesse said nothing more. He paced. Angela realized, pained, that he wouldn't look at her now. He'd been avoiding her eyes intermittently all night.

Her heart felt as though it was tearing, not only with fear, but also with pride that she'd come this far, had done as much as she had. And with exhaustion, because it wasn't finished yet. And she knew Jesse was feeling most of those things, as well, and that she was the one dragging him through it.

No, she denied immediately. *No.* She was done with that. Charlie was dragging both of them through this. She refused to take the shame and the blame upon herself ever again. Unconsciously, she squared her shoulders as she had been doing all night.

Tessa finally hung up. "We're all set. Roger has sent six new guys to hang around downstairs on the street, on the corners. And there are still four on every floor of this building."

Jesse nodded. This was the hardest part of the night now. Things had gone beyond his office, were out of his control. He hated depending on others. His nerves felt like live wires.

He had an inkling, in that moment, of how Angela must have

suffered all those years ago. And the *fear,* he thought. He shared her helpless terror, knowing all the while that there was little he could do to stop anything that might happen now.

"All right," he said finally. "Let's get out of here."

Tessa went outside first. Kennery had officially put both her and Gunner back on active duty, and she was armed.

Angela was trembling badly. It was a deep, subconscious re-action. She didn't want Jesse to see it and couldn't control it. She felt irrationally certain that a bullet was going to come for her from one of the windows across the street or from a passing car.

As they went out onto the street, Jesse caught her arm. He drew her close and kissed her hard despite what she had said in the press conference. The remaining cameras caught it and bulbs flashed crazily. She knew what he was thinking, and it chilled her. *Just in case. The hell with all of them.*

But there were cops all over the place. Nothing would happen, she told herself. Nothing could.

"You're making a liar out of me." She tried to laugh. It didn't work.

"No. Everything you said was true. As far as it went. Angela, when this is over..." He didn't finish. He realized he didn't know what he wanted to say.

"Come on!" Tessa urged from the unmarked car waiting for them.

Jesse turned away with something that sounded like a groan. He let go of her hand to get into the car. Then his heart started thrumming so painfully, so fast, he felt physically ill. This was all wrong. He knew it instinctively with his heart. He turned in the seat and started to get out again.

"What is it?" Tessa asked.

Then they both heard Angela scream.

She'd forgotten that on at least one occasion, Charlie had mas-queraded as a cop. They'd all forgotten. She wasn't expecting the cab that pulled up to the curb, either. The block had been closed off earlier, but now it was apparently open again.

She hesitated on the sidewalk for one lethal moment, and some-thing slammed into her from behind. She half jerked around as she fell, screaming. She saw a blur of blue. Charlie was one of the cops on the door. Seven cops, not six. Not just the six new guys Kennery had sent.

He hit her again with nearly enough force to make her neck snap. She hurtled forward again, expecting to fall this time, crying out and throwing her arms up to brace herself. Someone shouted in surprise. She heard Jesse's voice, raging. And she heard at least one gunshot before pandemonium set in.

At the last moment, Charlie caught her from behind, his arm around her waist as he pushed her into the cab. She had a startling moment of revelation, razor sharp in intensity. Now she knew why the taxi was here. Charlie had arranged it.

No one could get a clear shot at him without hitting her. He held her close to prevent it. The entire police department was on her side, but she realized it wouldn't make a bit of difference this time, either. Because Charlie had struck quickly and cleverly enough that none of them could help her after all.

Terror filled her, and something else. Revulsion, horror. A deep, crawly feeling spread from her waist into her limbs because he was touching her again,.

She screamed once more and prayed wildly that Jesse—that anyone—would get to her in time. She couldn't see anything, anyone. Charlie had pushed her head down. He held it.

"Shut up," he hissed in her ear.

"Don't touch me. I'll go with you. *Get your hands off me!*"

He laughed cruelly. "Right."

She'd landed hard on the seat on her hands and knees. She scrambled to the far door. He caught her arm in a painful grip and hauled her back to his side of the seat. His breath was in her face. A scream began inside her, an endless wail in her head, a cry that had gone beyond reason.

The driver watched them in the mirror, bug-eyed. "Hey, man, you didn't say nothing about cops and a gun! You just said come around the corner when she came out!"

A gun? Her heart stalled. Then she saw it, in Charlie's hand. Jesse was right. He'd kill her this time.

Maybe that was better than the alternative.

"Drive," Charlie said to the man. He was grinning. "Drive, or I'll use it on you, too."

The driver's throat worked. Angela could see it in the mirror.

The cops were all around the car now, and she laughed shrilly at their helplessness as they shouted for Charlie and the driver to get out of the car. Their weapons were drawn. But what could they do? They couldn't storm the vehicle without risking her getting hurt. She wanted to scream at them to do it anyway. They wouldn't hear her. The windows were up and Charlie had slammed the door shut behind him.

A cop was holding Jesse back. He was fighting viciously to get free and she changed her prayer. *Let's go, let's go, before he gets loose and comes to get me and Charlie shoots him, please, please, please!* The driver was too terrified to move. She whimpered aloud. "Drive," she begged.

"Where do you want me to go?" the driver bleated.

"Penn's Landing. The north side." Charlie looked at Angela and leered cruelly. "That ought to give us some privacy."

Angela stared back at him. She realized that she couldn't even cry. She was so cold inside. Finally, in the oddest of circumstances, the jail doors were slamming shut again, locking her in.

She had to think. It was her only salvation. But she felt as though someone had stuffed cotton into her head. Fear and revulsion...and the doors, always the doors...had dulled her senses.

The cabby finally gunned the engine. There was a horrible thud and a distant-sounding scream beyond the glass as he hit one of the cops. Rubber shrieked as the tires gained purchase on asphalt. But there was nothing else the poor driver could do.

Charlie had the gun pressed to the back of the man's neck.

Jesse managed to wrench away from the cop who was holding him. He drove his elbow back into the man's gut. He was running after the cab before the sound of the wounded cop's voice died in the air. Almost unconsciously, he saw a man on the far corner also move, his weapon drawn. One of the plainclothes cops.

There hadn't been enough. The entire police department wouldn't have been enough. The bastard had been dressed like one of them. Why the hell hadn't he counted when they'd gone outside?

Another cab rounded the corner just as he reached it. He lunged for it, still roaring senseless words like a madman. He caught the door handle and it would have pulled his fingers clear off if the driver hadn't slammed on the brakes. "What the hell do you think you're doing, buddy?" the man shouted when Jesse wrested open the door. "Are you nuts?"

His sister was half a step behind him. She'd left the unmarked, as well. Something told him that she hadn't been planning to give chase on foot. She'd been coming after him.

Jesse turned and picked her up almost bodily, pushing her into the car ahead of him. He had one last rational thought—that he needed her because she had the gun and the badge.

"Follow that other cab!" Jesse shouted.

"Hey, man, I ain't making a U-turn and getting no ticket!"

"Do it!" Tessa shouted. She dug frantically in her pocket for her ID. "Police. Now *go!*"

The driver hit the accelerator.

Jesse knew that of all the new emotions Angela had made him feel in the past weeks—jealousy then relief—none was as strong, as clawing as this fear. None was as debilitating as the persistent worry over losing her. He realized why he hadn't easily been able to look at her upstairs. He'd been trying to pull away from her, had been trying to prevent feeling like this when everything went wrong.

He'd known, damn it, he'd *known* that something was going to go wrong. And it was too late. There was no pulling away from her. There was only this agony in his chest.

"Get out of my way." Tessa pushed at him. When he moved aside on the rear seat to give her room, she scrambled over into the front. She grabbed the radio microphone. "How do you work this thing?" she demanded.

The driver told her.

"What are you doing?" Jesse asked hoarsely.

"I'm going to have their dispatch put me through to John," Tessa said.

Jesse didn't answer. He couldn't. His heart was in his throat.

"At least Price incriminated himself," she said after a moment. "Loud and clear. Everyone saw him this time."

Jesse could barely nod. He didn't care. He just wanted her back alive.

* * *

Charlie's gaze was on the window, but every once in a while, it flicked back to her. "You're too quiet," he said finally. "You used to scream. Cry."

"No," she said flatly.

"Sure you did."

"I won't let you get to me this time." Even her shuddering had finally stopped. She was numb.

Something like surprise flitted across his face, almost too quick to be noticed. "We'll see. I think I can get some reaction out of you when we get to the Landing."

He really didn't know her determination, she realized. If it was going to happen again, she did not *dare* feel. He was right. The first time she had been crazed and wild, and emotion had scoured through her blood, making every moment excruciating, clear in her memory for an eternity. But she had learned her lesson. Now she could shut down.

Then she thought of Jesse. And for a brief, deadly moment, emotion did flare in her. It was a longing, a terrible, agonizing regret. *I'm so sorry.* He hadn't wanted her to do this. *If the way you're looking at me right now is true, then don't do this. I can't live with it, Angela.*

If only she had listened to his fear. If only, if only...

Angela finally let out a quiet moan. Charlie looked over at her sharply, and something in his eyes brightened.

"That's good. That's better."

"*Damn* you!" she spat.

He laughed quietly, then looked out the window again. "Right here," he said to the driver. "This will be fine. Get lost now." He pushed a wad of bills at him—incredible, Angela marveled. The man actually thought he could buy anything. He had forced the driver at gunpoint! What did he think he was buying? His silence?

He opened the door. He dragged painfully on her arm, pulling her out of the car. "Perfect, Angela, wouldn't you say? Not a soul in sight. We'll be alone. For old times' sake." Then he hit her.

The blow sent her reeling backward against the car. She almost fell inside again, but Charlie still had her arm. He twisted it hard behind her, and she bit back another cry of pain. Tires screamed and the cab took off.

Surely Jesse and the cops were following by now. Charlie couldn't get away with this. He couldn't. Except they had driven several miles. And she hadn't seen any particular vehicle tailing them. Did anyone know where they'd gone?

Charlie still had her arm behind her back. He wrenched it higher until the pain was unbearable. She saw stars exploding in her vision.

"Goddamn you," he grated, breathing hard, tearing at the hem of her dress. "What did you do? I warned you to keep your mouth shut! Did you think I was going to let you get away with it?"

"If you kill me," she gasped, "they'll know it was you! It serves no purpose!" But she remembered what Jesse had said about revenge.

He backhanded her even as he held her arm. Her head whipped with the force of the blow, but her body couldn't go with it. "I'm going to make you pay for this, that's what I'm going to do. *Nobody's going to get me for this. You owe me.*"

He was crazy. He was out of his mind.

He had her skirt up to her hips. She didn't care if her arm came out of its socket. She couldn't help feeling now. All her protective defenses were gone. His hands were on her thighs, then all over, grabbing, groping, all the places that Jesse had made her feel clean again. She couldn't stand it. She would die before she allowed it.

She screamed and heaved all her weight backward. The pressure on her arm became excruciating. The stars at the edge of her vision turned into white streaks. But her weight took him down.

They fell together onto the gravel at the edge of the parking lot. She felt his hand in her hair. He grabbed handfuls of it, enraged. He had gone over the edge. He slammed her head against the asphalt. The stars streaked whitely across her vision and pain exploded behind her eyes.

Jesse, John, please, somebody. And then she heard a voice roar out of the night. Jesse. An answer to her prayers. Again.

That was when she finally began to sob. The jail doors were gone and too much emotion came rushing through for her to bear.

There was the simultaneous sound of tires squealing. She tried to look up and Charlie got his hands in her hair again. Then there were pounding footsteps, and his weight miraculously lifted off her before the next blow came. She thought she heard a woman shouting. It was Tessa's voice. Angela managed to get up as far as her knees.

Jesse had Charlie by the front of his shirt. His right fist slammed into the man's face. Again. And again. Charlie's nose broke, and blood sprayed.

"He has a gun," Angela gasped just as Charlie managed to bring it up.

No more. He would not take anything more from her. He'd had her life, her soul, her world, for fifteen years. Everything she had done, every move she had made, had been prompted in some measure by this man.

No more. She had never known hatred could feel like this. So blazing. So white-hot that it had an odd purity. He had nearly destroyed her. He had committed murder. He would not kill Jesse, too.

She was on her feet before she realized it. She wobbled a moment, dizzy, and then she realized, incredibly, that she still held her purse. Her fingernails had dug so deeply into it that they had punctured the fabric.

She let it fly.

She was afraid it was going to hit Jesse. But it sailed over his left shoulder as he was shifting his weight to punch Charlie again. It caught Charlie in the face, just enough to startle him. Just enough to keep him from shooting right away.

"*He has a gun!*" She screamed the warning as the weapon went off.

The bullet was wild, digging up the gravel near her feet, making her cry out. She staggered back and fell again. Jesse chopped the weapon out of the man's hand and drove him down, falling on top of him, still pummeling him.

The gun skittered to the edge of the parking lot before coming to rest. Angela crawled over to it and cradled it on her lap.

"Don't kill him, Jesse," she sobbed. "Please don't kill him. Don't do it to yourself." Not for me, she thought helplessly. Oh, God, not for me. She wasn't worth it.

Or maybe she was. They had caught him. She had stopped him. As long as they all came out of this alive.

Jesse wasn't punching him anymore. Tessa had finally reached him. She was pulling at the back of her brother's shirt with one hand, but with her right hand she trained her own gun on Charlie.

"Don't move," she gasped. "Just...don't move."

Angela heard sirens. The adrenaline rushed out of her. Her vision blurred. She dropped the gun and covered her face. A moment later, she felt Jesse's strong arms come around her as he knelt beside her.

"Stop," he said hoarsely. "Don't cry. I didn't kill him."

But he would have, she realized. Oh, God, he would have. She looked up at him, and only hoped the feelings in her heart were reflected in her eyes. She couldn't speak.

Squad cars were spilling into the lot now. Gunner jumped out of one of them and raced toward them. His face was white. He came to a stop over Charlie's prone form. Slowly, dazedly, his eyes moved over all of them.

He looked at his wife, standing over the man, holding a gun on him.

He looked at Angela's tear-streaked face, her eyes wild and too dark, her face pale. But her spine was straight.

And then he looked at Jesse. The man was staring back at him levelly, almost expressionlessly, but fury crackled in his eyes.

Gunner grinned and gave Angela, then him, a hand up. "Well, hell, you weren't supposed to start without me."

Chapter 21

It was dawn before they left the hospital. Jesse had broken a finger. Angela's arm was sprained and she had a mild concussion. But she'd refused to stay overnight for observation, not with Charlie right upstairs, under police watch in a room on the sixth floor. And Jesse hadn't argued with her.

He didn't speak as they waited for a cab, and Angela didn't breathe until he gave the driver her own address. Not the hotel. Her breath caught in her throat. She wondered if he was simply going to drop her off. There was nothing to protect her against any longer. It was over.

Say something, she pleaded silently, glancing at him out of the corner of her eye. When he didn't, she cleared her throat. "You're angry."

His gaze moved away from the window, toward her, and she was relieved to see that he looked genuinely surprised. "I don't know what I am. There's too much inside me to name."

The cab stopped at her house. She waited, her pulse thrumming. "Well, it's been quite a night."

"Can I come in?" he asked almost neutrally. "Or would you rather be alone?"

"No," she blurted, relieved. "Oh, no."

But when he followed her up the steps and inside, he still felt like a stranger to her. Distant. Stiff. She almost convinced herself that she knew what had happened—the whole attraction between them really *had* been a matter of circumstances throwing them together. And without all those circumstances, he felt awkward.

She just hadn't expected the change to come quite so soon.

Then he made a growling sound deep in his throat and paced to the window. In the light spilling in from outside, she was finally, clearly able to see his face. It was haggard, tortured.

"I have never in my life done that to another human being," he said finally, hoarsely. "I never thought I was capable of it."

Her heart kicked. "Is that what has you so upset? That you punched him?"

He looked back at her. "*Punched* him?" He held up his hand. The skin over his knuckles was cracked, torn. "I damned near *killed* him."

"If you hadn't pulled him off me, *he* would have killed *me*."

"Which is why I did it."

She hugged herself, her eyes tearing. "Your actions were justified. Haven't you ever declined to try a case because of mitigating circumstances?"

"Often enough. I just never knew I had those mitigating circumstances in me."

He went wearily to the sofa. She followed him cautiously and he reached for her, pulling her into his lap the way he had that night in the hotel. He grimaced, and she remembered the injury to his hand.

She touched a finger to it. "Oh, Jesse."

"Look at me," he said, his voice raw.

She did, meeting his eyes. Something was beginning to tremble inside her.

"I was an animal. If I had been alone with him, if Tessa hadn't somehow pulled me off—and I don't know how she did it—then I *would* have killed him. And knowing that is something I'm going to have to live with for the rest of my life. I'm not civilized. I've always thought I was civilized. But I was...wild."

"Jesse—"

He put a finger to her lips. "And I was wild because he had harmed *you*. It was as much what he did all those years ago as what he was threatening to do right then. I was thinking about *you*. And I saw nothing but red.

"At some point while my fist was connecting, it occurred to me that I've never felt anything like that—good, bad, or otherwise—before in my life. I've always been in this damned cocoon. A Hadley. A *male* Hadley, required to walk the line on the perfect side of normal." He laughed, the sound raw. "Always wondering what people could do for my career, always thinking about image, or gratuitous satisfaction, but not *feeling*. Until Gunner made me jealous. Until you trusted me and made me feel awe and relief. Until someone hurt you and made me feel rage." He almost smiled. "I don't know what it is about you. I don't know how you do it. But from the start, you've opened up the floodgates, angel."

"I'm not all that complicated," she managed to respond.

"Oh, yes," Jesse said, "you are."

"Maybe I'm just normal, and you've spent your whole life with dull people," she ventured.

He made a snort of laughter. "Could be." He thought of the hat he still had. "I doubt it."

"Does it matter?" she asked cautiously.

He thought about it. He nodded. "Because I need to know where to go from here." He made another hoarse, almost disbelieving sound. "I promised John."

"To hell with John." Angela took a deep breath. "Upstairs comes to mind."

His brows rose. "You're hurt."

"My body's a little broken. I don't feel it. My heart's back and willing."

His hands caught hers. "Just like that," he said a little harshly.

"No. It's all going to take some getting used to, I think. That you believed me about him. And that together, we did something to stop him."

"Angela," he said roughly. "I didn't do anything. I didn't even want you to do the press conference."

Her mouth curved. "I know. And that was why I could—because you were scared of him, too. Jesse, no one ever believed me about him before, that he was so dangerous." She had trouble with her next words. Her throat was tightening. "Stay with me tonight. Let me start over."

Compromising Positions

Start, he thought. *Start.* He liked the sound of that word.

Angela protested. It took almost more than he had in him to hold his ground. But in the end, they only slept in her big, brass bed as the sun came up vividly over the Delaware River. Angela realized that she was too exhausted now to argue, and Jesse told himself that it would be the last time he'd have to exercise such painful control.

When Angela woke shortly after noon, she was alone again. The shower wasn't running this time. Her heart slammed and she scrambled from the bed—and almost fell over the suitcase sitting on the floor beside it. She circled it warily, as though it might bite her, and went downstairs.

She found Jesse in the kitchen, his jaw shadowed by the day-old beard she was really starting to think looked incredible on him.

"What's going on?" she asked, puzzled.

"I figured if I let you pack, we wouldn't leave until Sunday." He watched her over the rim of a coffee mug. "So I did it for you."

"Leave?" she echoed blankly.

"Go take a shower. Get dressed. I'm going home for a bit, but even you should be ready by the time I get back here. Do you realize you were an entire hour late for my sister's wedding?"

"You didn't even see me come in." She knew. Her eyes had found him the moment she'd stepped into the church.

"Tessa noticed."

She wondered what Tessa had been doing watching the crowd. Then her brain cleared.

"Ready for *what?*" she demanded. "What am I getting ready for?"

His eyes found hers. "To do this right. I've thought about it. All morning. And I know what it is about all this that's been bothering me."

Bothering him. Her heart clenched again. She stared at him mutely.

"I want to do this the way I would have if you had stormed into my office that day for any other reason than that release form. I want to do this as though I had met you for the first time at my sister's wedding...and no one was killing people and trying to ruin us.''

Her heart was beating so hard she could scarcely speak. "Oh."

"Call your office," he said. "Tell them you won't be in today. Or Monday, either, for that matter."

"You're giving orders again," she chided. "You're sounding like a Hadley."

He smiled, and it stole her breath away. "I know. Sometimes it has its advantages." He held up the mug. "I'll return this."

She laughed. Actually laughed. "I won't hold my breath. You still have the last one."

"I know that, too, it was a keepsake. Like your hat." And a single golden hair that he'd tucked safely away.

She sobered quickly, bemused. He always managed to surprise her.

It took her a long moment after he had gone to look down at the open newspaper on the breakfast bar. The story about Charlie Price was front-page news. The Republicans were scrambling, bloodied, probably beaten, although it was still early enough for them to nominate someone else.

Then another, smaller headline underneath that coverage caught her eye. Hadley Clan Closes Ranks Around Medical Examiner. Angela read the piece fast, then again aloud in a disbelieving whisper.

"'In an interview given prior to the explosive conclusion of the evidence piling up against Dr. Angela Byerly, Ryan Hadley made it clear Wednesday that his law firm stood ready to represent Dr. Byerly in any proceedings brought against her.'"

Angela put the paper down and gaped at it. Then she saw Jesse's handwriting in the margin. "Don't let it go to your head," he'd written. "They just want to keep me happy so I'll run for mayor. Here's your first lesson in Hadleyese. They—not me— always have an ulterior motive." There was a little cartoon figure next to the words, with lecherously lowered brows.

She laughed aloud. And for the first time in her life, she knew what it was to feel lighthearted.

When Jesse came back later, she was ready.

They caught a flight to Martha's Vineyard. Angela settled back in her first-class seat with a glass of champagne. "Actually, you've disappointed me," she said with deliberate reserve.

One of his brows shot up. She couldn't believe it, but she thought she actually saw panic in his eyes. "How so?" he asked.

"This isn't that Cristal stuff."

"There's some on ice at the cottage."

She pretended to think about that. "Still, I would have taken you for the Monte Carlo type, or—what was that place—the Îles d'Hyères?"

"I'll have the pilot turn the plane around."

"It's not a private plane. The pilot won't listen to you."

"Sure he will. I'm a Hadley."

She laughed happily. And it felt good.

By nightfall, they were in a cabin he had rented, the sea rushing outside, low clouds coming in and turning the twilight purple. Angela watched the sun fall through the living-room window, and she felt him come up behind her.

"It's perfect." She hesitated. "You didn't have to do this."

"And you didn't have to stand up to Charlie Price. Obligation has very little to do with some matters. Thank God."

He turned her to look at him. She expected him to kiss her. And he did, but not on the mouth. His lips roamed, over each of her eyes, to her ear, to her jaw. And that easily, that simply, she began trembling, and this time it was with everything good.

"This morning," he said, "in Philadelphia, it would have been part of the nightmare. I needed to draw a line."

"Yes," she whispered. And she knew then that she had needed it desperately, as well.

"Even that morning in the shower was part of the nightmare. A way to push him away. This is for us."

His hands were in her hair. She reached for his wrists and held on to them. "You're so perfect."

His mouth crooked into half a grin. "And I keep telling you why."

"I couldn't have fallen in love with anyone less kind, less patient, less *wise*." She thought about it. "Less arrogant and determined."

His hands went still. *Love.* "Is that what this is?" But of course it was, he realized. It was what had been in her eyes in his office yesterday afternoon. It was what had been in his own heart when he had turned back out of that unmarked car, unable to lose her and unable to save her, and unable not to die inside. "Yes," he said quietly. "It is. I love you, angel."

"I just couldn't quite admit it before now. Even to myself. It was too scary." But she wasn't scared anymore. She wasn't scared at all.

He'd meant to do everything right this time. He'd meant to take her into the bedroom, where there was a fire in the hearth and the windows were open to the cooling sea air. The breeze just made the fire plausible, and he'd counted on that.

But there *was* something different about her, and he felt it as soon as he kissed her mouth. It was something both daring and tremulous. He thought she might be holding her breath. And this time, for the first time, she really kissed him back. He knew then that he was lost, that there was no way he was going to make it into the bedroom.

Her hand found his jaw and rested there as he lowered his mouth to hers, again and again. Kissing him, she discovered, was like no other experience she had ever known. It was safe, even as it made everything inside her tremble on the brink. And this time she knew that touching him was going to be richer, fuller, better than it had ever been before.

She *was* free. Her heart soared.

Still, his mouth played over hers cautiously. He touched his tongue to the corner of her lips and traced them as though not quite sure what he would find. And that gave her still another kind of freedom. She held herself very still for a moment, scarcely breathing, giving *him* a chance to pull away if he was not entirely sure about what he wanted.

He didn't. The experience they'd shared had taught him something, he found. The best-laid plans, the most certain goals, could so easily go awry. Even the bedroom waiting for them was proof of that. No, they wouldn't get there. He had learned that, in the blink of an eye, it could be too late for second chances.

Maybe, he decided, maybe it was best to grab what you could when it was offered. To revel in it, to feel it as she had finally taught him to feel.

His kiss hardened. Angela wrapped her arms around his neck, held him, held on. She groaned, and with the sound of her voice, everything changed.

A dam burst inside her. She'd thought she had healed, that she'd achieved some kind of closure at last. But she knew then that she hadn't, not entirely. There was too much inside that still needed to get out. There were feelings and emotions and needs that had been held in check forever, waiting...for this moment, this man.

Need and hunger became paramount. Suddenly, only sensations existed, smells and tastes, a fleeting touch here, a skimming of his hard hand there. And then he was pulling her down to the carpet.

"Here," he said. "Now." And this time he didn't ask her if it was okay, and that alone was exhilarating.

His weight came down on top of her and his teeth closed, not gently, over her collarbone. *She was alive.* She had lived past Charlie, and now she would celebrate. She moved her hips against him, hesitantly at first, then with more confidence. She took his mouth again and felt more than she heard the guttural sound in his throat.

He found the hem of her sweater and dragged it up over her head, growling again when he met with her bra. It had a center clasp, and he thrust a thumb beneath it, popping it, spreading the lace wide of her breasts. His hands covered her greedily, without hesitation.

He was different, too, she realized wildly. He was a man on the brink, with emotions raging, and no, he was not entirely civilized. It didn't frighten her. It inflamed her. She felt the wet heat of his mouth tugging on her nipples, making something pull tight inside her. Touching him, being with him now, was as natural and elemental as breathing. She reached for a handful of his hair and dragged his mouth up to hers again, wondering how he could make her feel so brave.

He dragged her jeans down her hips, and she wriggled to help him. When he revealed bare skin, she was unabashed, unafraid.

Her breasts were the way he hadn't allowed himself to remember, for fear it would drive him crazy. They were satin and smooth and full. Her nipples hardened, responding to his touch. So much of him wanted to take her now, fast and hard, right here, because he had held back for too long, with more willpower than he had ever known he possessed. It was almost an overpowering need, but he took his time instead, sliding a hand over her breasts one more time, then again. He traced his fingers down her ribs, to the hollow inside her hip, then lower. He took the time to watch her shudder with anticipation—and she didn't even really know what lay in store.

She'd said she had tried once, after Charlie, and couldn't feel. In spite of himself, he thought of that again, and suddenly, fear that he, too, would fail her took his breath away.

She seemed to feel his hesitation. She began touching him frantically as though to memorize everything about him before she lost it. Her palms skimmed over his chest, the hair there so soft it startled her. She felt the hardness of him and closed her hand over him through his jeans.

She gave back everything he had given her. Her own skin felt flushed and warm with the heat that was growing inside her. She dragged at his shirt and at his jeans. She could not remember what she had ever been afraid of.

She swept a hand through his dark hair again, met the deep green of his eyes. "Please," she whispered. "Please. Show me. I want to feel this."

His eyes darkened. He kissed her again, as though to protract the pleasure, but something inside him threatened to explode. Restraint was gone.

She was tangled around him now, her arms and legs holding him, skin to heated skin, but he eased back from her a little so he could watch her face. He slid into her more gently than he needed to, and watched her body spasm. He watched pleasure melt through her. Then she moved to meet him, moved in perfect counterpoint against him, and he saw climax slam into her first. Even as she reeled from it, he kept on.

It was everything she had dreamed of, and nothing she could have anticipated. She'd fully believed there would be pain, in some measure. That he, too, would have to force his way inside, no matter how her heart yearned for him. But he filled her easily, and she felt more than his flesh inside her. She felt the essence of him.

He rolled, changing position, bringing her on top of him. She gasped and cried out, but this time it was a sound of need, still not thoroughly quenched. He caught her hips and held her as he pumped, craved, let himself go. And something shattered inside him.

He made a hoarse sound as he lost control, and the last thing he remembered thinking was that he was still feeling, truly feeling, and it was the most incredible experience of his life.

Sometime later, they roused and moved into the bedroom. The fire had died.

"The best-laid plans," he murmured, kneeling to agitate it into embers again and to lay some new wood.

Angela watched him, her gaze moving over the lean, strong lines of his body. Something quickened inside her again. She felt she had a lot of time to make up for and she was going to enjoy every moment of doing so.

"We don't really need it," she murmured.

"Which is all the more reason to do it." He looked over his shoulder at her. "I'm sick to death of doing things because I have to, angel."

She sat down carefully on the edge of the bed. "Does that mean you're not going to run for mayor?"

He straightened, then looked thoughtfully out the window. "No," he said firmly. "I'm not. I'm going to remain as D.A., and when that Shokonnet character hurts his child again, or his wife, I'm going to nail him."

"What about Charlie?" She hesitated. "Are you going to ask for the death penalty?"

Something inside him tightened, then relaxed, because she understood. She was close enough to his world to understand. It was just one more thing he loved about her.

She had sensed all day that it had been bothering him, more and more as the evidence began pouring in. Gunner had caught up with them before they'd left for the airport. A total of seven women—including the one who had backed off after pressing charges—had claimed that Charlie Price had raped them. Those were just the ones whose stories seemed especially credible. Faced with the mounting evidence against him, Charlie had confessed, in a weak, rattled moment, to trying to frame Angela, and in a roundabout way, to killing Lisette Chauncy. But he had finished with a sneer and the vow that he would have the best attorney money could buy.

That attorney would not best Jesse Hadley. Angela had no doubts on that score.

She watched Jesse's jaw harden.

"I'm going to give the death-penalty option to a jury and let them decide," he told her flatly. "I'm going to let justice work the way it was designed to. It's all I can do."

"Yes," she agreed. She nodded slowly, then closed her eyes. "It really is over."

"Almost."

Her eyes flew open again. "What's left?"

"Us." He crossed to the bed where she was sitting. "I'm going to marry you."

He heard her gasp. He thought she recoiled. Pain clenched deeply inside him. "What? Too soon? I know a hell of a lot of craziness has been going on, but it doesn't change the way I feel. You've opened everything up for me and I can't let go of that again. I can't go back to the way I was, without you."

Angela shook her head fretfully.

"You said you loved me." His voice was becoming strangled.

"Are you asking me or telling me?" she whispered.

He thought about it. And, as always, he told her the truth. "If you say no, I'll keep trying to change your mind. So no, I'm not technically asking."

She smiled slowly, shakily. "Well, at least your heart's always been in the right place."

"So?"

"I can't be a Hadley," she said quietly, looking sober.

"Why not?"

"I hate those stuffy, preppy clothes you guys always wear."

He startled himself by laughing. "Try again."

She looked up helplessly into his eyes. "I don't know *how* to be a Hadley."

He sighed and caught handfuls of her spilling, golden curls. Then he sat beside her and took her in his arms. "Don't you get it yet, angel? I want you, just the way you are, crazy bright shoes and all."

"I want my hat back."

"Not a chance."

She laughed. Then another shiver worked through her. "Can I think about it?"

He moved against the headboard and pulled her with him. "I keep telling you that, too. We've got all the time in the world." His words were easy, but she felt his arm tense.

I took her only two short moments—one to think about losing him, the only man she'd ever felt connected to, and another to think of his family, the skinny woman who was his mother and all the other people he associated with.

"Let's elope," she suggested, and was rewarded with his laughter again.

"What, and miss you squirreling away hors d'oeuvres for the honeymoon?"

"I doubt if I'll be hungry for hors d'oeuvres."

He was quiet for a moment, then he found her mouth. "You're on."

*   *   *   *   *

SILHOUETTE

Sensation ®

COMING NEXT MONTH

THE ONE WORTH WAITING FOR Alicia Scott

The Guiness Family

Suzanne Montgomery had always known that one day Garret Guiness would walk back into her life. Now he'd come home, but he had a multitude of injuries and no idea how he'd got them. He'd come back to her, but would he go away again?

FOREVER BLUE Suzanne Brockmann

Tall, Dark & Dangerous

Blue McCoy was Lucy Tait's hero and even now, when he was suspected of his brother's murder, she felt something special for this dangerous, irresistible warrior. But she was keeping her feelings under control because...she was the investigating police officer!

BRIDE OF THE SHEIKH Alexandra Sellers

She'd been kidnapped from her wedding by her husband! Swept away in the arms of Crown Prince Kavian Durran, Alinor was powerless against her former husband's will. No man could ever love her as he once had... Was it fear that made her heart pound—or longing?

NIGHTHAWK Rachel Lee

Under Blue Wyoming Skies

Esther Jackson welcomed the darkly handsome Craig Nighthawk into her home, hoping he could protect her. Nighthawk understood how Esther was feeling; most people in Conard County considered him guilty of a crime he hadn't committed. Esther's loving arms were a haven of peace that he would safeguard at any cost!

COMING NEXT MONTH FROM

 **SILHOUETTE**®

Intrigue
Danger, deception and desire

MIDNIGHT WISHES Carla Cassidy
MAN OF THE MIDNIGHT SUN Jean Barrett
LOVER UNKNOWN Shawna Delacorte
BAYOU MOON Rebecca York

Special Edition
Satisfying romances packed with emotion

A LAWMAN FOR KELLY Myrna Temte
TEXAS DAWN Joan Elliott Pickart
MOTHER TO BE Cheryl Reavis
THE LADY AND THE SHERIFF Sharon De Vita
THE WRONG MAN...THE RIGHT TIME
Carole Halston
MATCHMAKING BABY Cathy Gillen Thacker

Desire
*Provocative, sensual love stories for the
woman of today*

LUCY AND THE LONER Elizabeth Bevarly
THE NANNY AND THE RELUCTANT RANCHER
Barbara McCauley
THE TROUBLEMAKER BRIDE Leanne Banks
ONE TICKET TO TEXAS Jan Hudson
WRONG BRIDE, RIGHT GROOM Merline Lovelace
DADDY BY ACCIDENT Paula Detmer Riggs

LAST NIGHT
IN
RIO

◆

JANICE
KAISER

Michael Hamline could never resist his ex-wife. This
time she'd conned him to help clear her brother,
languishing in a Brazilian jail. But they got more
than they bargained for in sultry, dangerous Rio.
This time, it could cost them their lives.

"...this one has big screen written all over it"
— Publishers Weekly

**AVAILABLE IN PAPERBACK
FROM OCTOBER 1997**

Elizabeth Lowell

Tell me no Lies

An international crisis is about to explode unless a desperate trap to catch a thief succeeds. Lindsay Danner is the perfect pawn in a deadly game. Now it's up to ex-CIA agent Jacob MacArthur Catlin to make sure Lindsay succeeds—and survives.

"For smouldering sensuality and exceptional storytelling, Elizabeth Lowell is incomparable."
—Romantic Times

FREE!

FOUR FREE
specially selected
Sensation™ novels
PLUS a Mystery Gift
when you return this page...

Return this coupon and we'll send you 4 Silhouette Sensation® novels and a mystery gift absolutely FREE! We'll even pay the postage and packing for you.

We're making you this offer to introduce you to the benefits of the Reader Service™– FREE home delivery of brand-new Silhouette novels, at least a month before they are available in the shops, FREE gifts and a monthly Newsletter packed with information, competitions, author pages and lots more...

Accepting these FREE books and gift places you under no obligation to buy, you may cancel at any time, even after receiving just your free shipment. Simply complete the coupon below and send it to:

THE READER SERVICE, FREEPOST, CROYDON, SURREY, CR9 3WZ.

EIRE READERS PLEASE SEND COUPON TO: P.O. BOX 4546, DUBLIN 24.

NO STAMP NEEDED

Yes, please send me 4 free Sensation novels and a mystery gift. I understand that unless you hear from me, I will receive 4 superb new titles every month for just £2.40* each, postage and packing free. I am under no obligation to purchase any books and I may cancel or suspend my subscription at any time, but the free books and gift will be mine to keep in any case. (I am over 18 years of age)

S7YE

Ms/Mrs/Miss/Mr _____
BLOCK CAPS PLEASE

Address _____

_____

_____ Postcode _____

RISING *Tides*

EMILIE RICHARDS

The reading of a woman's will threatens to destroy her family

As a hurricane gathers strength, the reading of Aurore Gerritsen's will threatens to expose dark secrets and destroy her family. Emilie Richards continues the saga of a troubled family with *Rising Tides*, the explosive sequel to the critically acclaimed *Iron Lace*.

AVAILABLE IN PAPERBACK FROM OCTOBER 1997